FLASHES OF FIRE

FLASHES OF FIRE

Flynn's Crossing Romantic Suspense Series
Book 2

Yvonne Kohano

K
E

Nanokas Press

A Division of Kochanowski Enterprises

FLASHES OF FIRE
FLYNN'S CROSSING ROMANTIC SUSPENSE SERIES BOOK 2

Nanokas Press/KE Press books may be ordered through booksellers or by contacting:

Kochanowski Enterprises/Nanokas Press
PO Box 1274
Clackamas, OR 97015-9594
www.yvonnekohano.com
yvonne@yvonnekohano.com

Flashes of Fire is a work of fiction. People, places, events, and situations are the product of the author's imagination. Any resemblance to actual persons, living or dead, or historical events, is purely coincidental.

This book contains an excerpt from the forthcoming book *Naked Intolerances* by Yvonne Kohano. This excerpt may not reflect the final content of the forthcoming edition.

Any people depicted in stock imagery provided by Thinkstock are models, and such images are being used for illustrative purposes only.

Certain stock imagery ©Thinkstock
Cover design: John Kochanowski

ISBN: 978-1-940738-32-1 (sc)
ISBN: 978-0-989330-56-5 (e)

Original Publication: 10/15/2012
Nanokas Press re-release date: 6/16/2015

Also by Yvonne Kohano

FLYNN'S CROSSING ROMANTIC SUSPENSE SERIES

Pictures of Redemption, Book 1
(Serena & Dane)

Flashes of Fire, Book 2
(DK & Vince)

Naked Intolerances, Book 3
(Gabby & Rick)

Tastes and Consequences, Book 4
(Mac & Roxy)

Blooms on the Bones, Book 5
(Tess & Powers)

Wine Into Water, Book 6
(Marguerite & Deke)

Love and the Christmas Tree Nymph, A Flynn's
Crossing Seasonal Novella

Love's Touch of Justice, Book 7
(Jake & Marlee)

This Proposal Between Us, A Flynn's Crossing
Seasonal Novella

Measure Twice, Love Once, Book 8
(Geno and Agnes)

And more to come!
Learn about upcoming releases at
www.YvonneKohano.com.

Subscribe to Yvonne Kohano's enewsletter to be among the first to learn about new releases and special offers. Visit www.yvonnekohano.com for more information.

Follow Yvonne at www.yvonnekohano.com, on Facebook as Yvonne Kohano, and on Twitter @yvonnekohano to learn what tickles her about being a writer, and at www.GooseYourMuse.com for creativity tips.

FLASHES OF FIRE

Prologue – Chicago Over Twenty Years Ago

"Patrick, settle down and eat your dinner. Your father will drive you to practice as soon as you're done, and you're already late, so hurry up!"

"Ma, I don't want to…"

"Quiet! You'll do as you're told! Elisabeth, that science project won't build itself! Mary Margaret, the piano is waiting – at least 45 minutes now, mind, or you won't be ready for your lesson with Miss Christine. Michael, have you finished your confirmation assignment for Father Esposa?"

The chorus of voices continued throughout dinner, Ma and Dad directing and demanding, her siblings complaining because they didn't want to do what they were told. She could sit among the confusion and be completely overlooked. Her brothers and sisters were always busy doing something, practice for sports or music, their catechism lessons, studying for school. If she stayed quiet, Ma would pass right by her since she didn't seem to take to anything. It helped to be the middle child too, and with an older sister and brother and a set younger, there were few expectations put on her.

They thought she was shy and afraid of the world, so she was regarded with something akin to pity when she wasn't being teased by her brothers. Her sisters liked to boss her around, even the younger one, but they were all protective too.

She played with the stew in her bowl. If she turned the chunks of beef just so, she could create a pattern with the potatoes and carrots, making a nice design.

"Diane! Diane Kathryn! Stop playing with your food and eat it. There are children starving in Africa who would appreciate that fine stew. And don't forget to study your spelling tonight! You got a C on your last quiz, and you need to do better than that."

She cringed to hear her full name, which meant she was in trouble again. Shoveling in a spoonful of dinner, she sighed. She hated spelling, math too. She was completely lost in science class and was sure she only passed because her teachers felt sorry for her. They knew that her brothers and sisters got the brains in the family.

School was a painful chore, except when she got to art class. She loved art! From the time she could hold a crayon, she knew inside that this is what she was meant to do. She could draw well even before she could recite the alphabet. Give her clay or paints, and she was in heaven, producing fanciful things that her teachers loved.

But her parents, they were another story. They didn't believe that art was a real skill, something that could earn her a living when she grew up. And that was their focus, hoping that each of their children would go to college and be successful in some field that didn't involve manual labor. To them, playing with clay and drawing had no future.

"Diane Kathryn! That's it, you obviously aren't hungry. Up to your room. I will come up in one hour and we will see if you're ready for that spelling test tomorrow. And stop chewing on your nails."

Her mother was staring at her, expecting compliance. Then her mother's expression softened. "You want to go to college, have a good job, don't you? Just like your brothers and sisters? You need to study, my girl, so that you can have a profession when you get older."

She didn't want to go to college, but she would do as she was told. She'd end up going wherever everyone else wanted her to go, and she'd muddle through as she always did. A career, a profession? She had no clue what that would possibly be. The only thing she was any good at or interested in was art, and her parents had already been clear that they didn't consider that a way to make a decent living.

Diane picked up her bowl and took it to the sink, rinsing it out before placing it in the stack. It wasn't her turn to wash up tonight, but she liked doing that sometimes. The bubbles could make some pretty colors if the lights hit them just right.

She took a moment to look at her nails, chewed to the quick when she was nervous. Hanging her head, she shuffled to the doorway that led to the front hall and the stairs. Conversation resumed behind her, her father prompting her brother to get a move on it and her mother now intent on her other brother's religious studies.

No one noticed her as she paused and looked back at them. She was, again, forgotten and invisible.

Chapter 1

The water was balmy, but in the late afternoon heat, even the warmth brought relief to her overheated skin. DK McGiven pushed more effort into her crawl and let the rhythm of the stroke empty her mind and stretch out her body. The water caressed her like melted chocolate or heated satin, more appropriate to thoughts of winter than the high point of summer. The sun would kiss her, leaving behind raw pink on her fair skin and darker freckles, but sunscreen took too much time.

It had been a taxing day. Her art was her passion, but she also needed it to pay the bills. Her success over the last few years allowed her some luxuries, like this pool and the open space around it. But to keep them, to keep her independence, she needed to fulfill the contracts she had. And she needed to produce wonders.

Walking up the pool's steps after twenty minutes, she felt loose even if the heat and exercise hadn't melted the tension between her shoulder blades. Toweling off wasn't necessary in the late August afternoon. The dry air wicked off what little moisture remained on her skin, and she rubbed at her short red hair, knowing it would turn into a halo of frizz around her head no matter what she did. That was why she kept it short. The return of sizzling heat on her body did nothing to improve her mood.

The art event in Flynn's Crossing was two weekends away, and her display area at Sierra Shining, the gallery where she showed her work, was looking a little bare since so many of her pieces had sold. Those events meant a lot to the economy of the rural town, bringing in tourists from Sacramento, the Bay Area and beyond to enjoy everything the foothills region offered. DK's creations were a big draw and she had work to do.

Standing at a central point on Main Street, the gallery reflected the mixture of quaint and chic found along the rest of those blocks and filled a niche for locally inspired art. Some of the adjacent shops were dedicated to a particular medium, like watercolors or weaving, and others, like the cooperative gallery DK belonged to, encompassed any technique. It made for interesting offerings combining bright and nuanced, large and small, modern and traditional, and the tasteful alongside the whimsical. Her unique style was a favorite of gallery customers and fellow artists alike.

That place had added so much to her life. She'd met her best friends through it. When she was relatively new to the area, she'd been behind the counter at a Saturday night art walk when two women came in to examine the featured work in the window more closely.

"Excuse me, what can you tell me about this piece?" A stately Native American woman, her good looks emphasized by straight raven black hair with a white streak framing one side of her face, had been intrigued by the distinctive metalwork that was DK's signature. She had been fascinated in particular by an intricate vase of flowers welded out of different types of copper placed in the gallery's window.

DK explained the steps in the design process and the methods she used to weld and finish it. She'd stuttered out the price, embarrassed at how high it seemed. A curse of her Irish heritage probably had her face glowing bright red. Her fellow gallery artists were constantly reminding her that her work was unique and valuable, but she wasn't as convinced about its worth.

"I don't care how much it is – I have to have it." And Tess Willowspring bought it on the spot for her flower shop at the end of Main, Buds and Blooms.

While DK was wrapping the piece, the other woman quizzed her about her background, where she learned her welding techniques, and what brought her to Flynn's Crossing.

"I'd heard so much about the thriving art community in the area. It's a huge draw. And I wanted to move as far away from my over-protective parents as I could," DK replied with a self-conscious laugh.

"That took a lot of nerve and gumption. You go girl!" The woman's chestnut ponytail bobbed enthusiastically as she congratulated her.

The sentiment warmed DK. She had never been credited with having gumption before. In fact, just the opposite.

DK spilled so much about herself in that first conversation, which was not surprising since Serena Williamson ran the counseling nonprofit in town, Balance. She learned all about the people she was talking with before they even realized how much they were sharing.

It didn't take long for the three of them to forge a hard and fast friendship. DK appreciated the unquestioning acceptance, trust and respect they had for one another. Their group had grown with the addition of other close friends, and pretty soon, the girl tribe was the kind of supportive network she'd always hoped her family would be. They'd helped her branch out and take risks that she'd been hesitant to try by herself without the comfort of a safety net.

She smiled at the memories. So much had happened since then. Her work had been featured in a regional lifestyle magazine, and that brought an agent to her door. He'd gotten her spreads in major publications and juried show placements where she brought home awards, and before she knew it, she was creating art under contract, elaborate pieces that brought her thousands of dollars for just one piece.

She'd finished creating four new additions today to fill the holes in the gallery's display, happy to have distractions she could complete. The final touches were necessary on a handful more. With those done, though, she could not longer avoid her bigger predicament.

It was incredibly complex, her current major work, the tale of wine from vine to glass for a winery that was opening up in a few short weeks. The Dawsons, the new owners of what had once been an abandoned vineyard, had approved the conceptual drawings of her design, but still, was it good enough to be the centerpiece of the tasting room's elegant courtyard?

*****

"Come see the latest piece, the one I'm doing for the new winery owners at Witch Hill. They want to unveil it at their first crush event next month." DK grabbed Serena's arm, careful to avoid spilling their wine, and headed for the old barn. Tess linked arms with Roxy and they strolled more slowly behind.

Roxy LaFollette was another wonderful girl tribe friend. She owned a fabulous restaurant named Roxy's south of town, and she'd expanded her empire with a grocery store next door providing gourmet prepared foods as well as people's every day needs. She loved to feed everyone. Dressed in her chef whites, blond hair in a bun and face intense as she concentrated on her cooking, Roxy guaranteed the girl tribe a wonderful eating adventure whenever she was in the kitchen.

"I'm a little nervous about this one," DK shared with Serena as they moved towards her studio and workroom. "I'm not sure I'm doing justice to the concept. Davinia and Marcus have high expectations for this installation."

They pushed through the door into the old barn. She'd kept the original structure, making few changes to the hay storage bays and stalls that dated back almost a hundred years. She loved the sound of the door as it creaked, the way the place still smelled a little like hay and horses, and the open space it offered for her welding work.

"I'm sure it will be incredible. All of your work is amazing, you know. You really need to stop worrying about being worthy." Serena gave her arm a squeeze before she turned towards the major work area. Then she stopped and gasp.

"Wow, DK, this is beyond anything you've done before! Look at the complexity! How does this all go together?"

Serena circled the four segments of metalwork, each on its own stone pedestal to raise the piece off the packed dirt floor. Occasionally she touched a shape or curve.

"It's, ah, it's not done yet. I still have a few finishing touches on each of these parts of it. It would be too heavy to move all in one, so I designed the four parts to fit together like a puzzle. I'll lift each one on to my truck using the winch and boom, then assemble it on site and do the final welding in place. What do you think?" The sip of wine rolled over her tongue, untasted.

Roxy and Tess joined Serena in their examination of the pieces, each one exclaiming over the intricate details depicted in the grapes, the wines, and the barrels. They loved it, that was clear.

But they had to, right? They were her best friends.

"I'm thinking it's all, well, too much. And the top, ah, that top section has major work left. It's... intimate I guess would be the right word." She bit her thumbnail, then forced herself to put her free hand in a pocket of her shorts and clutched her glass stem more tightly.

Her friends turned to stare at the top piece that currently resembled nothing so much as a mass of metal plates and rods. The final design, whatever it was going to end up being, was waiting in there somewhere.

"Intimate? How intimate?" Roxy quizzed her.

DK shifted uncomfortably.

"Well it's not porn, but it's not G-rated either. Parts of a couple entwined, wine being poured. I'm worried about it – it might be a little… sexy." Her voice trailed off as she looked at the piece in front of them, uncertainty written all over her face.

"The Dawsons, did they like the idea?" Tess as usual cut to the bottom line on things. DK always appreciated how her friend held her accountable and didn't let her wallow.

"They loved it, but I'm not sure. They're not prim and proper, but they are refined. Classy people making great wine, and their place is stylish too. Will this send the right message?"

"Well I think it will be fine," Roxy chimed in. "What you do is always tasteful and appropriate, so I'm sure you'll hit the right balance of sex and sophistication."

DK realized that she was nibbling on her thumbnail again and forced her hand back into her pocket. "You're probably right."

Her friends waited, watching her carefully.

"There's more, isn't there?" Serena posed the question while the others nodded their heads in agreement.

"I'm just, I don't know, lacking in inspiration I guess." DK flushed, glad for once that the darkened barn space might hide her flashing discomfort.

Roxy gave a bark of laughter, and Tess and Serena joined in. "And that's probably," Roxy said, emphasizing the last word, "because it's been a long dry spell! Think back to your last sizzling relationship for inspiration, my dear!"

DK smiled at the gentle teasing. "It has been a while…"

Her friends threw arms around her shoulders and clinked glasses with her.

Tess started pulling them to the door. "Too true for all of us! Let's go find some more wine, kick our sandals off, and diss on guys for a while. If we can't have 'em, at least we can talk about 'em!"

Chapter 2

"Ladies and gentlemen, we're on our final descent into San Francisco. Please make sure your seat belts are fastened and your tray tables and seat backs are in their upright and locked positions. Thanks for your cooperation on this very long flight. We'll be on the ground shortly."

He could recite the words along with the flight attendant, could even recognize them in a few different languages. He'd lost count of how many tens of thousands of miles he'd traveled in the past year alone. It all blended together until he needed to look at the calendar in his smartphone to determine where he was now and where he was going next.

Vincent Michael Cassidy was bored.

"Sir, can I get you any last little thing before we land?"

The female flight attendant had been very attentive on the trip across the Pacific. Flirty, actually, sitting on the arm of his first class seat, asking him about his work and what had brought him to Hong Kong. Groupies, he knew from long experience, were attracted to his bad boy image and his wild reputation. He cultivated the first and wasn't sure where the second came from. He was never in any city long enough, it seemed, to do more than sample a lot of dishes, take in a minimal amount of the art and history, talk to a few people, get a little drunk, and head to the airport.

Soon that would stop for a while, thank god. In addition to being bored, Cassidy was tired, dead fucking tired of coming up with something to say about the latest internationally acclaimed chef or renowned interior designer or up-and-coming artist. There was nothing left to say about any of them, even anything superfluous.

"Ah, no thanks, don't need anything else. You've been very… helpful."

She looked disappointed. He was sure she'd been hoping for a request for her phone number, or maybe an invitation to keep him company when they landed. She'd already shared that she had a three-day layover, angling for some additional quality time with him, going out, or more probably staying in.

He bit off a sigh and shifted uncomfortably in his well-cushioned seat. The first thing he wanted to do when he got to his hotel was sleep, welcoming the darkness and uninterrupted oblivion that didn't require him to talk with anyone or comment on anything.

Or maybe he'd eat. Eat and drink. He didn't even want to go out to any restaurant, just have room service deliver what he wanted. He liked hotels. They were impersonal and anonymous and a hell of an excellent place to hide.

The jumbo jet taxied to the terminal and Cassidy turned on his cell phone. He wanted to clear any calls and e-mails before he got to the hotel. Then he could order some food and booze and crash into blissful unconsciousness once he'd finished it all.

And do it all alone, totally and completely alone.

"Have a wonderful day, Mr. Cassidy. It's been a real pleasure talking with you during the trip. If there's ever anything…"

The flight attendant, brilliant smile in place, was trying one last ditch effort to capture his attention. He didn't snarl at her, though he was tempted. He gave a grimace that might have passed for a smile and headed into the jet way.

His cell phone beeped, notifying him of downloaded e-mails for his review. He hated being this connected. It was hard to ignore the various ringtones that signaled a message left in his voicemail or a text or yet another e-mail. But leaving the phone off for longer than a flight never seemed to be an option.

It continued to beep, an indication that someone had set a high priority on something they'd sent him. Waiting at the baggage turnstile, he scanned the messages to see what was so damned important. His agent – great. The guy was diligent, detail-oriented and determined – determined, that is, to use every minute of Cassidy's time to the advantage.

Light flashing and klaxon blaring in warning, bags started sliding out on to the rotating carousel, handles crammed against the railing where they were impossible to reach. People crowded in close as usual, as if standing right next to the slowly advancing line of luggage would make their own appear more quickly. Excusing himself and elbowing a guy who didn't move fast enough, Cassidy grabbed his bag and mumbled under his breath about goddamned amateur hour, heading for the customs line for returning Americans.

He didn't want to read his agent's message because he knew it would mean he's supposed to be someplace on some particular date, or he needed to write up some adventure – though he'd never call any of them that himself – for a new audience. Randy had good ideas, but he could have fewer ideas and Cassidy would be just as satisfied with him.

He moved through the customs line slowly, mind numb in the endless sea of humanity, queued like cattle awaiting branding and braying with just as much concern. He answered the stock questions as the agent flipped through his well-worn passport, examining the picture closely. Cassidy tried a smile, almost a mirror image of the mug shot that appeared inside the cover.

"Welcome home, Mr. Cassidy." The agent was already frowning at the family of five that waited to pounce on the station next.

He joined yet another line for the taxi queue at the curb. It wound back and forth through three sets of pylons. By the time he reached the front of that line, his snarl barely conveyed any thanks to the attendant.

"Mark Hopkins," he said to the cab driver.

"Please, sir, put on your seat belt." The driver waited, ignoring the blare of horns behind them as he stared back in the rear view mirror.

"What the...?" Cassidy barely bit off the expletive as he stared back. "Why?"

"Please sir, it is the rules, you know?" The driver's accent was pronounced though his English was perfect. He pointed to the sign hanging in the center of the cab.

'Passengers are required to wear their safety belts to prevent injuries during their ride. Please have a nice day.'

So fucking polite. He wondered how long the cabby would wait, the attendants now adding to the noise by yelling at the driver to move on. He was tempted, sorely tempted, to see how long the guy would hold out.

Exhaustion and hunger won instead. Grimacing and keeping his string of curses to himself, Cassidy reached for the belt. He hated wearing them, ever since he'd almost been robbed on a trip a year ago. Someone reached through an open window and grabbed his briefcase. The seat belt he was told he had to wear kept him from grabbing the guy by his shirt and banging the idiot's head into the cab's frame like he wanted to. But at least the guy hadn't gotten the briefcase. Probably in league with the driver, he'd thought at the time. What a goddamn scam.

The belt smelled, as they did in so many cabs, of clashing perfumes and stale cigarettes and something else sour that he didn't want to think about. Buckled in with difficulty over his tall frame, he looked up at the driver who was now wearing a big smile and pulling out into the press of traffic in the arrivals area.

He sat back for the dash north from the outer reaches of the city to its center and Nob Hill. The historic hotel he would lose himself in for the short duration had been renovated, and it now sported all of the modern conveniences while retaining an old world charm and grandeur. It reeked of comfort. It didn't hurt to have a fine drinking establishment at its pinnacle and good food available round the clock.

Yes, a few days in this outrageous city and then he could head home. He needed to visit a couple of places to complete a story he was writing for one of the premier international wine publications. It wouldn't take him long, and if he felt like it after staying unconscious for at least a day he might also be willing to try a couple of the new restaurants everyone was raving about. Maybe there were some emerging gems to share with his readers. He was ahead on his syndicated lifestyle column, but he'd need some fresh material within the next month to plow forward again.

But at least he'd be home by then, New York City. And he didn't plan on leaving again anytime soon.

Traffic was a snarled mess, the air coming in the open window unusually warm for San Francisco in the summer months. Sun reflecting off water pierced and throbbed despite his shades. He thought about dropping his head back and closing his eyes, but based on the smell of the seat belt, he wasn't sure what he'd be setting his head on.

He sighed deeply before looking back to his cell phone and the e-mails. He couldn't avoid it any longer. The persistent beep was annoying him. Scrolling down the screen to the offending message, he opened it and scanned it quickly.

"What the fuck?"

His outburst earned him a hard stare in the rearview mirror from the foreign-born cabby. He glared back at the man, curbing his desire to continue the rant.

Staring back at the screen, he strung together another long list of silent fucks in more than one language.

Chapter 3

"Diane Kathryn, I want to know when you're arriving for Thanksgiving. Your brothers and sisters are all coming, and they're bringing their families. Everyone else will be here. I know you think it's too early to plan anything but really, prices on the airline tickets will just keep going up. When are you going to do something about your arrangements?"

DK sighed. Her mother's insistent voice coming through the phone set her nerves on edge. Even two thousand miles away in Chicago, she felt those tendrils of control oozing through the phone line, sapping her will. She didn't want to travel that week, hated the packed airports, and got lost in the endless noise of her parents' overcrowded house.

And she hated even more the constant reminders that she, alone of all of the kids, was still not married and producing the next generation.

At her age, she really should be able to stand up to her mother. She should be able to state her own personal wishes and act on them. She should, she should, she should…

"Diane Kathryn, are you still there? When do you plan to arrive?" Her mother was not letting up. And she only used DK's middle name when she was in trouble.

She cleared her throat. "I don't know, Ma. I have plans already here. An art installation." Okay, not really, but it was only a little fib. "And the man that I'm seeing, he was hoping we could have his family over for the holiday." A much bigger fib, but one that was sure to throw her mother off the travel track.

"You're seeing someone? Who is he? What does he do? How did you meet him? How serious are you?" Her mother peppered her with questions.

DK gave herself a mental kick. Now she had to come up with a bigger fable.

"He's, ah, he's a writer. I met him at an art show. And we're still figuring out how serious we are." She hoped the big lie would be enough. Fighting the urge to nibble on a fingernail, she took a deep breath and waited for the next line of interrogation to come through the receiver.

"A writer? Does he make decent money? Never mind. You tell him that we expect you both for Thanksgiving. His people can have you for Christmas. He is Catholic, I assume. You know how important that is to your father and me."

She was going to have to create a better story, DK realized. But first she needed to buy herself a little time. "I'll tell him, Ma. Listen, I have a client coming in a few minutes, so I need to go. Give my love to Dad, okay? I love you Ma."

"Your father and I love you too, dear. We only have your best interests at heart, you know. I hope your young man is nice and respects you. That is so important. Make us proud."

The line went dead and DK put down the cordless phone on her dining room table, the call alone exhausting her. Her parents would never give up. They hated the fact that she alone of all of their children lived so far away, but she needed the distance to claim any sort of life for herself. In Chicago, they pestered her to find what they would consider a real job, which art to them definitely was not. They constantly introduced her to single sons of their friends in the hope that she'd marry and give them more grandkids. She wasn't sure she even wanted kids. And she definitely didn't want to marry the nice guys with boring jobs that they kept parading in front of her.

She circled the table and headed for the living room. It was all one big open space separated by seating areas and rugs on the plank wood floors. She loved this house and had made it her own over the four years she had lived here. It made her feel strong and independent.

Constructed to look like the old barn next door but with all of the modern conveniences, the house had been in sad disrepair when she first saw it. She hadn't planned to buy anything by herself, thinking instead that renting a small place to live in and finding workspace to lease would be enough. Lisa and Dannie, the landladies for her little rental condo, had told her about some studio space that might be available.

"The thing is, DK, the old guy with the space, Thomas Brunner, has a tendency to be, well, critical, constantly. He's kind of difficult to live with, by all accounts." Dannie wasn't warning her off exactly.

Constant criticism she had been used to. Her parents were specialists at it.

But she'd fallen in love right away with Thomas, a gnarly old potter who lived off his land and shared the bounty he raised as freely as he shared his many strong opinions. He was always gruff, full of harrumphs that could pass for approvals, and if he didn't like something, you knew it.

"So you're a welder, eh? Ya don't look like ya got enough meat on your little bones to pick up a pin." He'd coughed, scratched himself, and continued to stare at her.

DK smiled, recognizing already that the gruff exterior was a sham. The way the man handled clay as he turned it into his magnificent creations told her that somewhere, he hid a gentle and tender nature. Artist to artist, she knew the signs.

Over time, DK realized that his opinions about her work were helping her to clarify and improve in ways that she hadn't seen before. He even got her into Sierra Shining, an amazing feat since artists were always clamoring to have their work accepted in the gallery. She felt like she had a second father in Thomas, the kind who would honestly praise as well as critique her work and her life, even if he didn't sugar coat the delivery.

On a late afternoon drive to clear her mind after a long day of welding, she'd stumbled on the barns by accident. Her pick-up bounced in the potholes on the paved road, passing a worn for-sale sign that announced a bank repo. The recent collapse of the housing market had forced many people to walk away from these places, upside down on mortgages and lacking buyers. It was overgrown and evidently the bank hadn't thought to have anyone check on the buildings for a while.

But when DK first laid eyes on it, she knew it was a place she would love. The people who had built the barn-styled house had big ideas about what they wanted. The details were incredible, big beams in the two-story ceiling of the great room with its huge fireplace, a master bedroom loft that felt like a cozy aerie, hand carved features and rough hewn lumber everywhere. The fact that it had been a home to various critters who had come in through broken windows didn't detract from its beauty.

She hadn't planned on moving. The old shed on Thomas's property suited her work needs, and the condo was only a half hour drive away. True, he didn't like her to be there working late, and since she was a night owl and had a day job as a grocery checker to pay the rent, that didn't work as well for her, but she'd learned to adapt. DK was well-trained in being adaptable to other people's needs over her own.

She ran her hand over the granite counter in the big kitchen, cool and soothing to the touch. Roxy told her it was designed for professional entertaining, something that DK didn't worry about since her skills ran more towards pasta and grilled cheese. But it served as a great platform for

Roxy's creations, and the girl tribe spent many happy hours here enjoying the results. When DK put in the pool two years ago, that sealed the deal. Summer get-togethers were most often spent here, with her friends happily bringing food and flowers, wine and lots of laughter into her home.

Her home, one that she bought on her own and without the help of any man, despite what her mother might think she needed. Her success had grown over the past few years. She was now nationally known, and if her agent Randy had anything to say about it, soon that would become international acclaim.

The call from her mother unsettled her. Old habits were difficult to cut away, and her mother's insistence on her sharing the upcoming holidays with them made her stomach clench. She'd been on her own for over a decade now, but the influence of a lifetime of family pressure still weighed on her.

Work, that was what she needed. She opened her back door and smiled as she took in the pool and its surrounding concrete patio. She wasn't much for gardening any more than she was for cooking, but luckily, again her friends had come to her rescue. Tess and her marvelous skills with anything that grew had planned her flower beds, full of things that added structure and color year round with minimal effort.

Every other month, Tess arrived, pruners in hand, and between the two of them, they cleaned up whatever needed it.

"I did remind you to deadhead these roses, right? At least you remembered to spray them so the deer stayed away."

She hadn't, but since the deer had kept her secret, who needed to know?

"The daylilies are really coming on strong this year. It's too bad that they don't last longer. Of course, you probably won't notice until the snow flies that they're done too." Her friend shook her head in disbelief and snipped, pointing out DK's next task with her pruners.

DK took Tess's directions with good humor, and she'd even learned a little bit about how to take care of her plants by herself. It wasn't her first love as it was for Tess, but the artist in her appreciated the simple beauty that growing things offered.

And beyond the garden areas close to the house, she'd let the rest go wild. During the heavy grass growing season in the spring, girl tribe member Gabriella Cooley-Burke brought her son Jeremy over to mow fire breaks into the meadows. From the boy's perspective, it was perfect – money in his pocket that he earned himself and time to play with DK's big black lab, Fusion. DK was simply grateful not to have to do the work.

An added benefit was the quality one-on-one time DK then got to spend with Gabby while they watched her son toil away. Working in the economic development department at the county, Gabby always had great gossip about the new businesses coming into town.

And despite losing her cherished husband two years before, Gabby was a diehard romantic too. Flipping her wavy brown hair over her shoulder and settling her tall frame into a chair by the pool, she'd fill DK in on the buzz about new cute guys in town and the latest love stories.

"And you know, even if he's a good foot shorter than her and twice as wide, they make a cute couple," she'd exclaim. "Holding hands and walking down Main Street, with over a hundred and sixty years of life between them. He can't see, and she can't hear, but they seem to get along just fine."

Yes, it always made for an entertaining afternoon when they got together.

DK smiled as she looked out over the open areas. California gold was the color of summer, when the grasses dried up and trees took on muted tones, their leaves covered with ever-present dust. Even in the dry conditions, she loved the land, a far cry from the heavily weighted greens and layers of humidity in the Chicago summers of her youth.

What she loved most, though, was the structure in front of her. The big old barn had been part of an original homestead in the area. She'd researched it thoroughly, and the people who had built it almost a hundred years ago had owned a big parcel, a few thousand acres that had been divided up over time. The last in that family line had been an old woman who had sold this 10-acre plot and a larger one next door before moving away. DK's neighbors grew grapes, a common crop in this agricultural area. DK loved keeping her land open, though. It reminded her of what it must have looked like when Native Americans or settlers first laid eyes on it.

The door creaked, as it always did. She could have greased the hinges, but she loved the sound. The barn was huge, spacious and airy. In the summer, it baked as the sun beat down on the hottest summer days, and in the winter, the chinks between boards let wind come in. She'd installed a potbelly stove in the center, the only place where the barn's floor had been covered in concrete. Her office was in back in what had been a stall at one time. She'd added insulation and covered the walls to give that space some protection, but for the rest, she'd left as she'd first found it.

The packed dirt was so well-trampled that very little dust rose from it anymore. A few dust motes danced in narrow shafts of sun that found their way between the warped boards. The contrast of light and dark corners was comforting. As it always did, the space gave her a feeling of peace, something that was only broken by her concern over this current work.

She crossed the open space to the stone pedestals for her creations. The base of the sculpture for Witch Hill Winery was done and she would install that next week, but the top, well, what could she do there? Roxy had suggested she think back to her last big romance for inspiration.

Easy enough for her friends, she thought. But for her? Sex she'd had, but passion and romance?

That was the trouble. She'd never had that kind of relationship.

Chapter 4

"What the hell do you mean I have to spend the fall in California? I just got back from a month in Asia, I have deadlines for pieces already in progress, and I hate that state!"

Okay, so he was an East Coast snob, even if he did travel the world. So sue him.

"What the fuck are you thinking, Randy?"

The view from his agent's big corner office did little to ease Cassidy's rant. It was, as always, spectacular and ever-changing, construction cranes still visible where the Twin Towers once stood and on a myriad of other urban in-fill projects to clean up blocks that were less attractive. Usually he found the sights mildly interesting if not fascinating, but today he was on a tear. His mood about his upcoming assignment hadn't improved over the last few days.

"Damn it, Randy, I told you I wanted some down time. I told you I wanted to concentrate on what I had in the pipeline already. I'm tired and I need a break. And I told you that next time, I wanted to spend my time on something deeper, get into the history, man!"

He realized he was shouting, but if he couldn't shout at his best friend – though why he ever liked the guy he didn't understand at this particular moment – then when could he shout?

"Vinnie, really, calm down. It's no big deal. You want to dig deeper, I got you a place to dig deeper. Besides, the exposure on this work is incredible! It's for Lifestyle Worldwide, the European magazine that's dying for all things American. It feeds hundreds of thousands of

European tourists into the U.S. each year, the best of all the rags in the EU countries. Really, Vinnie, you know it's a good gig!"

Vinnie, no one called him Vinnie except Randy. They'd met as college roommates a couple of decades ago. Cassidy was intent on earning high honors, even if it was in history. His Virginia matron of a mother demanded nothing but perfection. He loved history, but never did have an idea what he wanted to do with that degree. She never had an idea why he wanted it either, as she always said with a faintly disapproving air. She'd be much happier if Vincent would be ready to take over the family businesses when she was willing to retire.

Cassidy felt like he was always bucking the family's expectations. He was a natural student, which made goofing off and getting in trouble easier since he could always pull down good grades.

"Your wild streak, Vincent, must come from your father's side of the gene pool," Mother sniffed in displeasure. "People in my family are much more... refined."

He wasn't sure if that was completely true, since he rarely saw his father growing up except when he blew through town from one adventure to another. And his mother was cold enough to freeze a blazing fire.

His parents didn't have what could be termed as a close marriage by any stretch of the imagination. Hell, it wasn't even friendly at a distance. Then just as Cassidy was finishing his sophomore year of high school, Father indulged his wild side once too often and excited the wrong people in a third world country on the other side of the planet. Cassidy had to spin the globe in the library a few times to figure out where the place even was.

There was a kidnapping and the murder of a young woman that his father was evidently traveling with. His mother remained tight-lipped about what else might have been going on. A ransom was demanded and paid, but his father still came home in a box.

His mother became quite strict about his bad boy side after that. Wildness, even with good grades, was no longer going to be tolerated.

And so Cassidy had been forced to buckle down. It was easier to comply with his stern and less-than-loving remaining parent than tolerate the loss of car privileges and his motorcycle, curfews and an empty wallet. Mother controlled the purse strings, and as long as she did, he needed to toe the line.

It made it easier to maintain distance from everyone too. He'd never been close to either Mother or Father, though he expected that he loved them both in his way. They'd been isolated, so he learned to be the same. He had wanted to be the kind of buddy his father seemed to want, but that hadn't worked out. He'd craved affection from his mother, but she didn't seem capable or interested in giving it.

It was better to avoid disappointments by not having any close relationships, that's what he took away from his childhood. Satisfy expectations, but keep his heart to himself. It was better to study the stories of others in the past, their commitments and passionate zeal, than try to live with that level of personal risk himself. When he got to college, even his directive mother couldn't turn him away from the one subject where he could delve into tales deeply, history, without getting his heart involved.

There was one blessing in college, though. He was far enough away from Mother to let the wild out. His bad boy persona left a string of young ladies with happy smiles on their faces, even if they were more than a little disappointed that they weren't going to become part of the Virginia Cassidy dynasty. Study history by day, and anatomy, female anatomy to be precise, by night. And other times of the day. As time passed, he wasn't sure what he was going to do with the degree, but he enjoyed the knowledge he was accumulating in the other subject just fine.

His buddy Randy, on the other hand, always knew he wanted to make money, lots of money, and he went for passable grades in his business major and spent all of his free time creating little schemes to make some cash.

"Look, I got a great deal on some tapes, just need a VCR and you're golden. Your house'll love you, I promise." Randy would hand over a stack of bootlegged movie recordings and the frat brothers would have a fun evening watching god only knows what. He was good at finding out what people needed and hooking them up with someone who could provide it. It's how he'd gotten through college.

Graduation meant cleaning up their acts some. Cassidy didn't want to go back to Virginia, back to his parent's pressure to get a real job, namely in some part of the family empire. He stuck it out in New York, lucked into one writing gig and then another, and finally became popular enough to find he needed an agent. Randy'd continued his matchmaking into his job for the last fifteen plus years, managing talent in all sorts of artistic realms. And he'd been Cassidy's agent since the beginning.

Cassidy's degree? It hadn't gotten him much. He'd thought about teaching history, but hated the idea of leading bright, or not so bright, young minds. Besides, he really didn't like people all that much. Funny how life plays tricks on you. He hated interacting with people and needed to interview them at every turn to make his living. But at least he could maintain his personal distance from them. History, it was only old or new history. The idea rarely caused him a pang anymore.

"Randy, first, you're an SOB. Second, I hate even the idea of spending months on that coast of the country. And third, I'm wiped out, man, completely wiped out." Cassidy stopped his pacing to drop onto the couch and stretch his long legs. A headache that had nothing to do with last night's whiskey rapped at his skull. Cab horns and pounding steel outside added to the impact.

"I understand buddy, I really do." Randy came around his desk to perch his paunch on a corner, looking down at him. "Listen, it won't be so bad. Remember at the beginning, when you were unknown and Lifestyle took a risk on you? You owe 'em, man."

Yeah, Cassidy remembered. That feeling stayed with him after all these years, a sure guarantee that he'd always take the next assignment because he never wanted to be beholding to his mother for a job. He never felt he could say no to Lifestyle's contracts.

He owed Randy for sticking with him too. The guy was the closest thing he had to a brother. Someday, maybe he'd find something else to write about that brought in the same steady stream of regular income. But until then…

Randy's tone was now just shy of pleading. "Look, I'll find you a good place to stay, someplace quiet without being in the wilderness. A place with cable and lots of good restaurants, I promise. You can write, hang out, learn more about the area and then create some of your usual Lifestyle International masterpieces that will engage and intrigue tens of thousands to follow in your footsteps!" He beamed down at Cassidy, though he was wringing his hands.

Crap, was all Cassidy could think, rubbing his temples. Crap, fuck and crap again.

Chapter 5

DK loved the long driveway that led up the hill to the spectacular vineyards with Witch Hill Winery at its crest. Legend had it that a witch had lived here for decades. In reality, the woman was the product of an Indian raid on a wagon train, left to her own devices after the subsequent death of both of her parents. She was strange and unique and some said capable of cursing the unlucky and bringing unlikely fortunes to others. Some swore she still haunted the hilltop.

The previous vineyard owners obviously fell in the cursed category, and they'd lost their property to bad fortune years ago. Nevertheless, the vines they'd planted continued to thrive, the product of the witch's care, the superstitious claimed. The current owners were proving to be much luckier, though since the winery was only opening officially with this autumn's crush, the jury was still out.

Davinia and Marcus Dawson had selected the perfect location for the winery and tasting room, the top of the hill where the witch had reportedly made her home, and had copied the design of a modern Tuscan villa for its style. While it seemed odd initially since the area around the vineyards was so rugged, it fit somehow. Clearly they had a great vision for what they wanted to achieve here.

Her truck took the steep grade easily despite the weight of metal tied down in the back. The base was always the most cumbersome to move. DK had coordinated her visit with the winemaker, Marguerite Devereaux, asking for help muscling the big piece into its final resting place in the center of the circular drive. She could do it alone, but with help, it would go much faster and there were fewer opportunities to damage the piece.

The concrete pedestal that was the base for the work had been poured early in the summer, with screws protruding up to anchor the metal in place. Above that, all of the other components would be welded together, but the base would require the heavy duty bolts. DK had mapped the bolts precisely, so the base should theoretically slip right into alignment. A few turns of a wrench and this part of the work would be set in its new home.

Construction workers were still putting the finishing touches on the exterior of the tasting room. Fine stonework covered the face of the building with flagstone walkways leading to the tasting room door and the surrounding patios. Another path of bark led out to an area in the vineyard where guests could sit at tables and enjoy their wine right next to the vines that had produced it.

Or visitors could take their wine glasses to the museum the Dawsons were building next to the tasting room, featuring the rich wine history of the region. The vision for Witch Hill had been both a high-end wine experience and an educational opportunity. DK grinned, because she knew that her piece resting here would be seen by thousands of people over the coming years.

"Hello DK!" The melodious voice with its marked French accent made DK turn around. Marguerite was walking towards her from the winery's barrel room entrance. Even without make-up and with her long black hair pulled back in a messy bun, she looked gorgeous. If she wasn't such a nice person, friendly and always handy with an encouraging word, DK would be incredibly jealous. As it was, she had to fight down the envy she had for her new friend's easy confidence and eye-stopping striking looks.

"Hi Marguerite. I have that base piece in the back of my truck, ready to lift out. Do you still have those strong extra hands to help me get it into place?"

Marguerite gave her a quick hug, then moved to the back of the truck to examine the sculpture's base.

"How did you get it in here by yourself? What are you, Superwoman?" The exclamation was accompanied by teasing laughter, but she was clearly curious.

"I back my truck up into my barn, attach the hook to the bracket on the piece – cleverly disguised here as a grape vine – and I winch it in with the help of the boom. I tie it down, then bounce my way over here. Simple."

"Ah, you are clever, my friend, very clever. Let me call a couple of the guys to come help us. They're working in the barrel room moving things around. We've been bottling for the last week so things needed some reorganizing."

Marguerite moved away to call to her workers and DK took a moment to appreciate the compliments she'd received. She had devised her method of transportation when she realized that hiring someone to help her each time she wanted to move a heavier piece would get expensive, not to mention sometimes inconvenient. Clever, and something she'd designed and fabricated all by herself.

Two strapping young men followed Marguerite out to the truck, and between the four of them, they had the based aligned with the bolts and in place in no time. She'd been right to ask for help in this case. Getting the holes lined up would have been very difficult to do by herself while she ran the boom and controlled any swing of the metalwork.

"I must say, I am eager to see what you have created for Davinia and Marcus," Marguerite said when they were alone again. "Davinia has described it to me, and I am intrigued by the passionate couple, you know, at the top."

DK moved her slight weight from foot to foot. "Well I hope you won't be disappointed. I'm a little nervous about that part, frankly. I can't seem to make it work in metal."

"You are an artist. You can use your imagination to create anything you like." Marguerite paused in her inspection of the detailed welding in front of them and turned to DK. "You know, just tap into your passionate experiences."

DK felt she knew Marguerite well enough to be honest. The woman was already as close to being a girl tribe member without meeting the rest of the group as anyone could be.

"I can't seem to find that passion to inspire me." Damn that blush again.

"My dear, just imagine the most passionate encounter with a man that you've ever had in your life, and use that to inspire you." Marguerite's face looked wistful for a moment, and something akin to pain entered her expression before her ready smile moved to her mouth again.

Her mouth alone, DK realized, but not her eyes.

"I, ah, don't have a wealth of experience in that arena. What with building my business and the time it takes to create my art, I haven't had a lot of time for, ah, relationships." She shifted and scuffed the driveway, suddenly finding the toe of her worn leather work boots absolutely fascinating.

"Really? With your looks and your talent? An artist with all of that milky Irish skin and bright green eyes? I would think men would be hovering all around you! Tell me, have you ever been in love?"

DK kicked more gravel and felt her face turn redder. "Once, I think. But I wasn't sure. He was a guy my parents wanted me to date, from a good Irish Catholic family in Chicago, where I grew up. But in the end, he decided that he wanted someone more stable – that was how he put it – than an artist. And I think maybe another time too, but that didn't work out either."

How embarrassing to be telling this to a woman who, she was sure, could have her pick of men any day of the week.

"Ah, I understand." Marguerite's accent had become more pronounced. "I too was introduced to a man who my parents thought would be a good match. He was very charming, said all of the right things, behaved like an admirable gentleman. But I knew something wasn't right."

Intrigued enough to forget her own discomfort, DK asked, "So what happened?"

Marguerite looked out over the vines and her expression grew somber with the memory. "I married him, to the great joy of my parents. He was everything that they wanted in a son-in-law. I liked him. We were very compatible. But his lovemaking…" She stopped.

"Okay, you can't stop now, not just when the story gets good! It's a girl tribe rule!" DK put a hand on her friend's arm and shook it for emphasis.

Marguerite turned to her and a grin replaced the frown. "His lovemaking was very distant, like he was somewhere else. Very mechanical. Two years later I finally discovered why." There was mischief in her eyes now. "I caught him with his male lover. He was gay! The uproar when my parents learned of this was – as you can imagine – quite the noise. Oo-la-la!" She laughed, even as something sad crossed her face.

"Besides," she added, "I have yet to meet this girl tribe. When is the next – what would you call it – pow-wow?" Now her tone was teasing and she linked arms with DK, drawing her towards the unfinished tasting room.

"Come, my new best friend. We will taste some wine, discuss the difficulties of interacting with all things male, and talk about your problem."

Chapter 6

The Friday night crowd at Roxy's was boisterous, or at least what passed for loud at a foothills fine dining establishment. There was a lot of laughter, happy exclamations about the food, and a general buzz of energy that marked everyone's excitement about their experiences. Elaborate mouth-watering aromas came up from every artisan dish that passed by.

The girl tribe settled into their table on the lush patio expectantly. They usually didn't venture here on a weekend night because Roxy was too busy to join them past an occasional comment on a fly-by. But there was salmon on the menu, a special variety flown in from a river in British Columbia that was only available for a couple of weeks of the season. Roxy had insisted they find the time to enjoy it.

"I am so happy to finally meet you!" Marguerite sat on DK's right at the circular table and beamed at the other women. "I have heard so much about all of you and about this girl tribe that I feel welcomed and at home already."

Gabby jumped right in. "Well, we're dying to learn more about you. Like, for instance, that wonderful accent of yours. Are you originally from France or somewhere else? What brought you to the States? And what's it like to make something like this?" She held up her wine glass and gestured in Marguerite's direction.

"Ah, yes, the wine! Do you like it? It's part of our first release, so don't tell anyone you had it yet. It, like DK's gorgeous sculpture, will be unveiled at the crush party in a couple of weeks." Then she looked serious. "You do like it, don't you?"

"It's lovely, incredible." Serena raised her glass in a toast. "You've done an amazing job! Who knew that there was this kind of gold in the quartzite on that old property."

"Yes, it is surprising on so many levels. But no more so than DK's wonderful metal monument to wine! You will see it at the party. I am so impressed!"

All eyes turned to DK, who looked around, then dropped her eyes to the wine glass, turning it around in her fingers and leaving a series of circles denting the white tablecloth. The noises of the restaurant seemed to grow more pronounced.

"Yes, tell us about finishing it," Tess urged. "Did you finally come up with the vision that you needed to complete the top part?"

DK didn't know what to say. The third part was ready. They hadn't discussed the top fourth of the sculpture recently. And the reason was that despite coaching from her friends, she still didn't know how to finish that provocative segment.

In her continuing silence, Tess and Serena exchanged questioning glances. Gabby's smile was fading and Marguerite was eyeing her with sympathetic speculation.

Finally, the silence punched through her self-absorption. She looked around at the expectant faces and sighed. "The third component is done and I'll install that next week." She paused, then took a deep breath to continue. "But the top part? Truth is, I haven't finished it yet."

When voices started to quiz her, she raised a hand to stop them and added, "I just don't know how!"

"Who needs more wine?" Marguerite extended the bottle expectantly and all of the other women offered their glasses. DK used those seconds to gather her wits and come up with a better explanation of what was happening.

"Okay, it's like this. I don't think I've ever felt the kind of passion that I intended to include in the sculpture, not really." Before they could talk over her, she added, "Sure I've had good sex." At least she thought maybe it had been good, but who could judge? "But great passion? I don't think so."

The table was silent. All of the women stared at her with varying degrees of pity, memory or curiosity on their faces. They'd discussed many things as their friendship had cemented over the years, but never exactly this.

"I've had great relationships, but never one that was the kind of heart-wrenching passion that I think I need to go for on this piece." She waited as they all looked at one another.

Tess cleared her throat first. "It's been my experience that you know it when you feel it. If you'd have felt it, you'd know."

DK had to ask. "So you've felt it, that great passion." Tess sounded certain.

Her friend smiled sadly. "Great sex, yes. Great passion, the kind that rings all of your bells and sets your heart on fire? No, sorry to say."

Marguerite joined in. "It is easy to have great sex – that is mechanical. But that great passion, ah my friends, that is rare indeed."

They all pondered this as they sipped their wine. Gabby finally added. "I had great passion. With Doug. He was an incredible lover and a wonderful friend. Now, I have Jeremy as a memory of that." Serena rubbed her arm in sympathy.

"And what about you, Serena? Do you have great passion now with your mystery man?" Tess's tone was mildly teasing.

"Maybe, not sure yet. It's definitely great sex. But there's a connection there too, you know? It's too early yet, too early for me to tell."

The women toyed with their wine again and fell silent.

Finally, words needed to be said. "So, can you finish it? The sculpture?" This came from Marguerite.

DK answered honestly. "I'm not sure. I've built the third layer so that it doesn't look obvious that part is missing. I just can't finish that last piece. Who knows, I may never be able to get it right."

"I know what you need!" Gabby's exclamation startled them all. "You need a hot little affair! Maybe then you can create what you need out of that. You know, life gives you lemons?" She looked around the table for confirmation.

"Hey, that might do it!" Serena joined in. "Find yourself a sexy guy, heat up the sheets, and maybe you'll have enough of what you need to allow your imagination to do the rest."

*****

The night was quiet, or as quiet as the country ever got during the late summer's heat. It was easier to work at night when the pounding sun didn't bake the barn's interior like an oven. Frogs and crickets raised a loud racket and the owls hooted occasionally. A city person would probably complain about the noise, but it was a lullaby that rural folks were very accustomed to.

DK couldn't hear the creatures stirring, hidden as she was under her welding gear. The bright flame of hot metal and electrode filler illuminated the barn to its darkest corners. She only saw it as a point of heat, though, protected as she was by her helmet with its darkened face panel.

She worked steadily for a few minutes more, then set the arc welder aside and kicked up the helmet's face plate. The small piece sat in front of her, an attempt to capture the emotion and passion she wanted for the top of Witch Hill's sculpture. She hoped that creating something in a small version would serve two purposes. She could practice for the top and make a piece she could sell right now in the gallery.

Shedding her protective gear and stretching, she looked at the big clock on the wall. Past two in the morning. She had been at it for hours, and still she wasn't satisfied with the results. The small piece was pretty, a couple entwined in a dignified manner, a PG version that could be placed in public view in the gallery. But it lacked that spirit of passion.

She knew that sometimes, it helped if she changed artistic mediums, so she often took to drawing out her ideas in charcoal when she couldn't get them to materialize in metal. Stepping out of the work boots and overalls and hanging her gear on its pegs on the wall, DK unkinked her neck and back as she drifted to the large drafting desk that served as her drawing area. Papers were covered with different designs of what she thought she wanted on the top of the big sculpture, but none of them seemed right.

Sighing and stretching again, she grabbed a bottle of water and a piece of charcoal to keep things in her hands. She wanted to chew a fingernail out of habit, a bad habit she had when she felt her self-confidence waver. This had her wavering in a major way.

Her friends were right, she knew. It was hard to design something that she had no knowledge about. It would be like trying to depict a tree if she'd never seen a forest. Having never shared great passion with a man herself, she was hard pressed to understand how she could represent it in metal. It was something she needed to experience first.

And that was part of the problem too. She'd had some wonderful boyfriends, men who had rung her bell on the physical side but never truly touched her soul. She'd even thought she'd been in love a couple of times, but not enough in love to make a life commitment. No, she had never felt that driving passion engulfing her that Gabby described with Doug and Serena seemed to find these days in her new mysterious boyfriend.

Fusion stirred with a big doggy stretch where he lay sleeping, paws up in the air and flat on his back, opening one eye to see what she was doing. She rubbed his belly with her foot until he snored again. What a goof, but he was her goof, and she was glad for his company, even if he was sleeping.

Still too keyed up, she found a blank sheet of paper and started drawing a man's face. If she went looking for passion, what kind of man would she be looking for? He'd have a strong face, filled with both determination and spirit. Someone who was gracious and confident, comfortable with what he was doing in life and smooth when confronted with any of the challenges thrown at him. He'd also be happy and humorous, kind and gentle, and respectful of her personally.

She sketched more. If she was going to dream, she might as well dream big. This perfect man would be someone she could be herself with, the strong and confident parts of herself, not the wimpy part that she had been trying to bury for years. She wanted that weak-willed person, the one who her mother called Diane Kathryn and second-guessed at every turn, to be gone forever.

And in her place, confident and worldly DK would prevail.

Chapter 7

"Flynn's Crossing? What the hell kind of name is that? Should I expect banjos playing in the background?"

Cassidy paced the living room of his condo. It was bare, devoid of what many of the designers he'd written about over the last few years would call his personal style. But that's the way he preferred it. He didn't want a lot of clutter, and besides, he was rarely here anyway. He'd just have to pay someone to dust the damn stuff.

"Relax, man, really. It's a little town up in the foothills east of Sacramento in the area you need to write about. It's close to the wineries and restaurants. There's lots of art, plus great views and wide open spaces I'm told." Randy's voice was soothing over the phone, though Cassidy was sure that this friend and agent was multi-tasking across town even as he spoke.

"Yeah, just like I thought, the wild west!"

"Look, it's an up and coming area. Their wines are winning international awards. The food is supposed to be great, and some nationally experienced chefs have taken up residence. And the artists, well they're great too, international buzz and all. Your kind of place! Money's following the buzz, new mega-mansions on mega-properties, celebrities moving in. You'll be the first with boots on the ground. Just your type of assignment."

Cassidy moved the cell phone away from his ear, Randy still extolling the supposed pleasures of what he was sure was a backwoods disaster. How the agent thought he knew about the place, Cassidy wasn't sure, since he'd never known Randy to leave the confines of New York City. He cursed for a full minute, then put the phone back in place just in time to hear, "...and I've rented you a place, a house in town, for the next couple of months so that you can immerse yourself in the culture and the region. Someone will do grocery shopping for you if you like, clean the place, keep things up so you don't need to do anything but explore the area and write cutting edge but enticing descriptions that will tell your international readers all about it."

Randy finally fell silent. He was probably answering another e-mail, Cassidy thought with disgust. Couldn't the man just concentrate on what he was doing right now to Cassidy? He was ruining his life.

"I don't want to do it, Randy. Crap, I'll be bored to death! It's the middle of nowhere. Sure, I can write about all of the exciting places I've been – elsewhere. But I doubt I'm going to find anything worthy in a place with such a hick name."

His phone remained silent. Randy was his best friend as friends went, but sometimes despite their years together, he didn't understand him. It was like the man had an agenda. Here he was, sending him off into some crappy hole in the wall while expecting great stories to come out of it.

"Look, Vinnie, I'll lay it out for you plain and simple. You've been telling me for months that you're tired. You've been visiting some of the most interesting places on the planet and still you're saying you're bored. Have you ever considered that what's making you tired is the jet set lifestyle and the high end living that comes with it? I don't think you're bored – I think you've become jaded. The big experiences don't mean anything to you anymore, man."

Cassidy opened his mouth to protest but stopped. What Randy said was too close to being true. He had been bored for months, and the last few locations hadn't brought him any pleasure or inspiration. He missed being able to dig deeply into an area, learn its history and the tall tales that were the stories of its residents past and present. That's what made his work so appealing to his readers. Hell, it was what made it so interesting to him too.

And if he was honest with himself, which he tried not to be whenever possible because it usually brought on a wave of self-disgust, he'd lost interest in the stories of most of the well-known places because, after all, they were well-known and the tales had been told to death already. Living out of a suitcase and skipping across multiple time zones every week? That would make anyone tired.

Even the women were all the same. No one moved him. The sex was mechanical, like scratching an itch. Meet 'em, bed 'em, and move on, as quickly as possible.

Randy took up the conversation again. "Honestly, man, your writing recently? It's been kind of – how should I put this – cold. It lacks interest, it lacks passion, and it lacks reader appeal. Some of your long-time stalwarts in the papers and blogs that carry your column are saying that they might want to try someone new, something fresh. The articles you've been sending in? Those publishers have been cutting down your work to the key facts only, since the stories have been such downers. So head west, old man, head west and dig into the stories in this little town. You can feed the big pieces to the international mags and it could zing up your column too."

It was probably true, Cassidy knew. In fact, he'd felt a little uncomfortable with the last few articles. Truth was, he really didn't have any interest in the sites themselves, and when he couldn't find something to catch his interest, he wrote fluff. He couldn't find any good stories, or maybe he wasn't working very hard at finding them because he wasn't interested.

When exactly had things gone this sideways? Somewhere along the way, he'd turned his desire to write about people and places and their stories into just another money mill. The people and the places were written about to death. Maybe some time in a place that had yet to be discovered with a capital D would rev up his engines again.

He hated it when Randy was right. It was, after all, the wild west. Maybe he could find some good settler stories, something to add interest for the readers – and for him.

Maybe he could get some rest, recharge his batteries. He was sure he'd have plenty of down time. After all, how much could there be to do in the area? As to the claims of great food and wine and art, well, he'd just have to judge that for himself.

Cassidy cursed, more as a matter of form than with any real spite. He could hear Randy's smile across the phone connection. "That's my boy! I knew you'd see the good in all of this! Who knows what you'll learn, who you'll meet?"

"How long do I have before my frigging sentence begins?" At least he could enjoy his home, such as it was, for a while before heading out.

"Sentence, hey, that's funny! Actually, almost right away! Crush is starting up, harvesting the grapes to make wine you know. It's a great time to be in the area I'm told. So pack those country duds and head out, my friend!"

And Randy started to hang up, but not before Cassidy heard him twanging the scary banjo refrains from Deliverance.

Chapter 8

DK felt a mixture of relief and worry. The third part of the sculpture was in place, and altogether, it now told the story of wine from vine to bottle. The curve of the barrel's walls were perfect, and the tendrils of grapevine twining up and around looked like they could burst into new growth at any second. The bottles represented the various shapes typically used for the varieties at Witch Hill.

What it lacked, though, was its top. That last section, the one representing the passion wine could encourage, was still missing. DK couldn't wrap her brain around that part of the design. One by one, she'd interviewed her best friends in excruciating detail about what true love passion felt like. Gabby waxed poetic about her dead husband Doug, a conversation that ultimately led to tears. Serena was a bit more tentative about her new-found emotions. Roxy eluded to a great love in her past that was not returned, then clammed up.

But other than that, her friends had talked more about what they expected in that ultimate relationship, not what they'd yet experienced. Even the flamboyant Marguerite talked more in generalities than specifics. It was kind of sad, really. Here they were, a group of strong and accomplished kick-ass women, and so far they had missed out on life's greatest passion, or so it seemed.

A hand squeezed her shoulder and she turned to find Dr. Davinia Dawson, one of the winery's owners, gazing at the sculpture with a smile on her face.

"My dear, it's beautiful! Look at that detail work! You've even captured the different types of clusters on the grapes and the varying shapes of the leaves. It's truly inspiring!" Davinia moved forward to run fingers over some of the bottles.

DK so admired Davinia and her husband Marcus. Neither one had come from money, but they certainly had built up a wonderful lifestyle through their hard work over the years. Dr. Davinia Dawson was an internationally renowned university professor at the state university in Sacramento. Her studies of economic planning were must-reads at schools and businesses around the world. Dr. Marcus Dawson had earned his way through University of Southern California for pre-med on a football scholarship, but rather than going the pro team route, he'd continued on to become an emergency room physician. He'd founded one of the first staffing services to provide ER docs on demand in the busy Los Angeles market where he practiced.

And now the docs, as DK thought of them privately, had decided to get into the winemaking business. Actually, they'd visited this foothills region dozens of times in years past, attending the many wine events the area sponsored. They bought wine, talked with winemakers and grape growers, and explored properties.

Four years ago, they stumbled on this abandoned vineyard and quickly made it their own. Marguerite had been an early contact and they'd contracted with her to help them reinvigorate the neglected vines. The first three years of grapes had been processed at the winery where Marguerite used to work. Now, they had all of the latest and greatest high-end equipment in place, a barrel room full of nascent wines, and their first vintage bottled and ready to sell.

This would be their first event for the new tasting room, the first time the public had been invited to see all of their hard work on Witch Hill Winery. The tasting room was grand and they'd spared no expense in the specialty artisans they'd hired for stonework and hand-carved wood. And the unveiling of DK's large metal sculpture in the courtyard entrance at the top of the long driveway up the mountain was a big feature of the weekend.

Davinia had probably never felt a second of self-doubt in her life. DK shook her head to focus and felt that she had to say something about the missing part of the work. "Davinia, it's not exactly done yet." She hated to disappoint a client, particularly one she looked up to and liked so much.

"Not done yet? It looks complete to me. What's missing?" Davinia stepped back to consider the towering metal piece more critically. "Really, I don't see it."

"It's the top piece. I haven't found the right inspiration – yet."

Davinia focused on the top. "It doesn't look like anything's missing."

DK stepped forward and pointed. "I added more bottles and some grapes to the top of this third section so that it wasn't so obvious. I'm still going to finish it, Davinia, I promise. It's just that I'm, ah, having some trouble wrapping my inspiration around it."

Her client turned and considered her carefully. "What part is causing you difficulty? Maybe I can help."

DK shifted uncomfortably. It was one thing to quiz her best friends about great passion. It was another completely to discuss something so personal with this stylish and worldly older woman. True, she and her husband clearly were very close, and it wasn't uncommon to see the large form of the former linebacker and the petite professor walking hand in hand around the property. But that didn't mean that DK could discuss her lack of inspiration. It was too delicate a subject.

"I'm working on it, Davinia. And I hope to have that piece done soon. I'll install it as soon as I have it. Honestly, it shouldn't take me too much longer." She hoped.

"I'm not worried, DK. What you've given us is gorgeous, just the thing to intrigue and engage our visitors. And inspire them to spend lots of money on wine, I hope!" Davinia's expression was mischievous as she continued.

"Now, I'm expecting you and your friends to join us next Friday at the crush celebration, DK. No excuses! I want to introduce you as the talented artist that made us this wonderful piece."

Even after her commercial success on the national market, DK wasn't used to this side of being an artist. She didn't like to discuss her work, preferring to watch from the sidelines just in case someone didn't like the pieces she created. If they didn't like it, it was still a blow to her self-confidence. And when they liked it? It was embarrassing, like she didn't quite feel she deserved the praise.

But this work would draw that praise. She knew that she got the grapes just right, and the interlacing of vines and leaves with the bottles and barrels made for a wonderful representation of what wine was all about. DK straightened her shoulders and put some iron in her spine. She deserved the accolades on this one, damn it!

"This is a piece I'm very proud of, Davinia. Thank you to you and Marcus for giving me this opportunity. I'm just happy it will entertain people for what I sure will be decades of success to come!"

Chapter 9

He wasn't willing to concede anything, at least not yet. The nonstop flight to Sacramento was uneventful, which was the best thing you could say about air travel these days. His rental car, a sexy little red convertible, waited for him. The well-traveled suitcase and duffel barely fit in the trunk, but he'd needed a bit more than he usually traveled with since he'd be here for a while. His equally battered briefcase held his laptop and an e-book reader, along with a couple of old hard cover history books that discussed the region.

The small house on the hill overlooking Flynn's Crossing was picturesque, he'd grudgingly agreed with Randy when he'd called. Two women ran the rental agency where he'd picked up his key. He assumed they were a couple based on how they interacted with each other, which surprised him in this rural area. In his experience, people in these kinds of places were conservative and not necessarily that accepting of what they would call alternative lifestyles. While the women didn't look particularly prosperous, he was surprised to learn that they owned many of the houses they rented out. They were mostly full, so the area wasn't the poor economic wasteland he'd anticipated either.

He'd taken one short walk on the main street of the town, appropriately named Main Street, and was again surprised to find that the locals greeting everyone else represented a range of ethnic groups. It wasn't the redneck hick town he expected from the country-quaint name and foothills location.

More to the point, there were upscale restaurants with intimate courtyards next to trendy coffee counters and bakeries. Shops that catered to foodies lined the six blocks of what was called downtown. Someone could buy wine made from grapes grown in the region, artisanal cheese produced at a local farm, olive oil pressed just up the road, or charcuteries of meats cured in neighbors' cellars. The food options looked good, and the art wasn't bad either.

Maybe it wasn't going to be such a bad couple of months after all. He'd flipped through his books quickly on the plane and had been pleased to discover that there was interesting history about the founding of the area. Gold had been discovered a few short miles away, starting the famed California Gold Rush. The town sat on the Mormon Immigrant Trail where covered wagons brought people across the country when it was much younger. In more modern times, a winter Olympics games had taken advantage of Lake Tahoe's beauty, the state capitol of Sacramento stretched across the valley below, and San Francisco was only a couple of hours away.

There should be colorful stories to write about here, he knew. And there was a lot to appeal to his lifestyle readers. The dozens of wineries in the foothills should be a find, an area rarely written about in major wine magazines. Of course, that could be because the wines weren't necessarily that great, but since some were now winning national and international awards, he had hope.

The rental managers left a long list of local eating establishments, entertainment sites, and local events. The listings for restaurants offered cuisines reflective of the multicultural nature of the town. Some even listed their award-winning chefs, and more than one had been educated in a professional culinary academy and done time under a big star name or two. At least he wouldn't starve over the next couple of months.

His work would begin almost immediately. Local grapes had been delayed by bad weather in the early growing season and late-setting fruit. Picking those grapes usually began earlier in the year, but many of the wineries were just now having their big crush events. These marked the beginning of the long process of turning fruit into wine, and it wasn't uncommon to see trucks loaded with bins of grapes driving the local two lane roads.

And Cassidy had his first official invitation. Randy shared his arrival date with the local grape-growers and winemakers associations, and a stack of invitations to barrel tastings, blessings of the vintage, crush parties and other activities had been awaiting him. Witch Hill Winery wanted him to cover their first crush event, which included the public's first access to the fancy new tasting room and some kind of art unveiling too.

Cassidy didn't want to go to what he was sure would be a boring afternoon. He had little hope for the wine coming from such a new producer. He didn't want someone to ask him about how he liked their wine because he was sure he'd have to lie and say he liked it, even when he didn't. Or he'd tell the truth and word would get around pretty fast, branding him in this small town. He didn't expect to find anything here to intrigue him, and he didn't like to make nice, damn it.

And yet, in his heart of hearts he had a small flare of hope. He hadn't read the history of an area he needed to write about in a long time, relying instead on what the locals could tell him. True, in some of the international places he'd visited, the history stretched back for so long that it would be impossible to read enough for full comprehension and then write about it in a short article that would make sense to his readers. But this area was young enough, the history recent enough, and the stories and legends fresh enough that it might be fun.

And it might be at least interesting enough to help him shake this feeling of boredom. Maybe he would be surprised and the afternoon would be pleasant. If nothing else, he could make fun of the local folks in a piece for that international magazine, because by the time it came out, he'd be long gone, right?

*****

Cassidy drove the gravel road slowly, unwilling to have to explain to some car rental agent why there were pockmarks in the paint on the racy little convertible. He'd found already that the car marked him as an outsider, something that most expected a tourist to be driving along the winding country roads. Locals typically drove vehicles that would have more power and traction when the winter rains and snows came down.

But he would be long gone before anything like that occurred. Right now, the September days were still hot and the evenings carried welcomed cooling breezes. The air held a tangy scent that seemed to come from the wildflowers on the sides of the country roads. He was glad that he could leave the convertible's top down whenever he was buzzing around.

He had been told by his landladies that the typical attire for an event like this was rural business casual, so he'd selected tailored slacks, an open-necked shirt, and a sports jacket. He'd probably be over-dressed, but he wasn't here to win any awards for fashion or fitting in.

There was a significant crowd by the time he arrived, the ride taking him longer than expected on the unfamiliar roads. Parking the convertible, he walked up the drive and found himself staring at a large sculpture that dominated the center of an open courtyard. Set on a pedestal at the top of the hill, the metalwork itself was about ten feet tall, an intricate design of vines and grape clusters at the base. This supported large barrels and smaller casks topped by various styles of bottles, all in metal. It was strangely commanding and compelling, though he wasn't ready to admit that in public.

"Hello, and welcome to Witch Hill Winery! How are you today?"

He realized he must have been staring at the sculpture intently because he hadn't heard anyone approach him.

"My name is Davinia Dawson, and my husband and I are the owners."

The petite African-American woman, dressed to the nines in a cocktail length flare of bright burgundy silk and spiky heels, looked at him, obviously expecting him to answer with a name too. He wanted to stare at the art a while longer, but he realized he was being rude, and that didn't bode well for any future invitations in this small town.

"My name's Vince, Ms. Dawson. I'm sorry, I was just surprised by this art. I didn't expect to find something so elaborate in a winery up here."

His hostess chuckled and turned to stand next to him and examine the metal. "Yes, we're very lucky to have so many talented artists in our community. You'll see local work all around our property. We made keeping it local a priority when we furnished the tasting room and our events areas." She turned to him with a quizzical look on her face. "We get visitors from all over the world, Mr. Vince. Can I ask where you're from?"

Cassidy was still staring at the metal and appreciating the hundreds of hours that went into the work. And the thousands of dollars that the artist commanded for it. Or maybe it was a spec piece, something on loan until the artist could entice a nice fat check from someone for it. But it looked permanent, not like something that would be moved any time soon.

"Mr. Vince?" The owner was now looking at him with more open curiosity.

A mental head shake and he was focused again on the task at hand. "It's just Vince. I'm from New York, but I've traveled all over the world. I don't think I've ever seen a piece of metal sculpture this intricate and this large. It's distracting me."

He switched gears. Time to get to work. "I understand that you and your husband just opened this place. Please tell me all about it."

She patted Cassidy's arm with a laugh, and guided him towards an open door in a huge Italianate building. "First, please call me Davinia!"

Chapter 10

DK was glad that she had armed herself with a killer gem-green dress and heels that added a few inches to her short stature. Even for an agricultural activity in the foothills, people dressed up to celebrate. The girl tribe members were all in slinky bits of something, and other guests were wearing everything from tuxedos on some of the men to jeans on some of the women. It was, as usual, a little bit of everything here.

More than helping her to fit in, though, the dress gave her confidence. She smoothed the silky material with hands that were now only slightly damp. The jitters in her stomach were giving way to a feeling of satisfaction.

So many people she knew had come up to compliment her on the sculpture, and she'd eavesdropped on many others she did not know singing its praises. DK smiled when some asked for photos of themselves standing in front of it, and when they found out somehow that she was the artist, they pulled her into the shots too and then asked for her autograph. It was a kick! She was actually beginning to relax and enjoy it.

She'd asked Davinia and Marcus not to focus on her or point her out, despite the unveiling of the sculpture. In large crowds like this, she was always a little uncomfortable tooting her own horn about her work. Those who knew her could connect her right away with the name on the plaque next to the tall piece. Those who didn't could stay in the dark.

Her girl tribe was waiting for her to join them across the courtyard, and she was eager to walk into their welcoming fold. A small crowd of people continued to mill around DK, most of them people she knew who were happy to pat her on the back and exclaim over the intricacy of intersecting lines and planes in front of them. Slowly, they dispersed, and she had a minute to stand alone and appreciate what she had done through their eyes. They didn't see the missing top, cleverly hidden in her additions to the barrels and bottles portion. Inspiration still eluded her, but at least it wasn't obvious that it was incomplete.

DK wasn't sure how long she'd been lost deep in thought about the missing inspiration of passion. But she felt eyes on her, someone staring intently enough to penetrate her consciousness. A tall man stood a few feet away, almost blocked from view by the sculpture. His eyes were hidden by sunglasses, but he was definitely staring in her direction.

Fighting the urge to turn around to see if someone else was behind her, DK pulled in a breath and tried to hide how pinned she felt under his gaze. He was dressed in slacks and fancy loafers, a collarless white shirt with a top button open, and a summer weight sports jacket in a gray fabric that looked expensive. It all covered a body that didn't look fit, exactly, but well put together and imposing. His blond hair was long enough to catch the breeze but still stay in place, and she wondered what color his eyes were.

For the first time in a while, DK felt a desire to lick her lips and say yum.

He deliberately turned his gaze to the sculpture while he walked towards her. Or maybe it was more like a prowl, DK thought, and she shivered. Wow, maybe this was just because she'd been thinking about that passion she needed for inspiration, but she was definitely attracted to this guy.

"So what do you think of this?" His voice was low and husky, sexy in its intonation. Or at least that's how it felt. As silky smooth as the dress sliding over her body.

He'd asked her a question. She wasn't tracking very well at the moment, and all she could do was stare at him.

A quiver settled in her stomach and a shot of electricity went up her spine. Yes, most definitely a reaction to the man who was now towering next to her and staring down into her face.

"That good, huh? No comment on the art?" His inflection on the last word made it sound like he was putting the word in quotes with more than a trace of sarcasm.

"I, ah, I think it's great. It captures the journey of wine from grape to glass very well." DK was relieved to find she controlled the stammer in her voice. She didn't want to blurt out that she was, in fact, the artist. She could make her comments cool and impersonal.

"Really? You think that?" His voice held a tone of disbelief. "It's not very realistic."

Not very realistic? Well of course not! DK's estimation of the guy was quickly falling. Did he think himself an art critic? Of course barrels don't grow on top of vines…

"…and the grapes and the wines? What was this artist," he put a lot of negative emphasis on that last word, "trying to achieve here? This isn't how grapes grow. I mean, really? Is this supposed to represent wine-making?"

He'd spread his hands on that last comment to emphasize his point, and DK noticed that despite his derisive remarks, he had been enjoying a glass of something white, probably the signature Witch Hill blend.

"And those barrels and bottles? I don't think they're very representative either." He crossed his arms now, clearly waiting for her to agree with him, or to argue. It looked like he would enjoy either one.

Damn, DK wished she could see his eyes. She wasn't sure if he was playing with her or serious, but his rudeness was beginning to piss her off.

"Art is about representation, not necessarily copying reality completely. Maybe the artist is setting a mood, or suggesting the meaning rather than trying to replicate nature exactly." No hint of a stammer in her voice now, DK was finding her earlier attraction to the tall blond fading quickly.

He snorted. "You can't believe that. Art is all about creating something to evoke a feeling, sure. But if it's representing nature or anything real, it needs to look like whatever it was intended to be. If it's meant to evoke a feeling, it needs to do that. This? This is missing something, that's obvious." He took a sip of wine, paused to look into the glass with a small smile of appreciation, then returned back to stare at her.

It pissed her off that he was right about the meaning of art, or at least what she considered art to be. It made her mad beyond belief that he picked up on the fact that something was missing, mainly, the link of passion that should be the topper. At some level, she was probably embarrassed about that, but right now she decided to go with mad.

She hated art critics, doubly so when they were right but she couldn't admit it. And this guy had just pushed her buttons.

"Not every piece of art is complete, you know!" She made an effort to lower her voice, which she realized was starting to get louder with her anger. "Sometimes it's left to the audience to decide how to interpret and complete it." That part, at least, was true. The fact that it wasn't exactly true in this case? Too bad! She was feeling pretty protective of her work at this point, though there was no way she was going to admit she was the artist to this guy.

He snorted again. She realized that it was a surprisingly attractive sound, and she froze for a second with a sudden curl of desire in her belly. It had definitely been too long, and this provocative stranger was setting off sparks and smoke. Then he opened his mouth once more and ruined it.

"It's something done by an amateur, that's clear. If I wasn't drinking some fine wine right now, I'd be wondering about where else these new owners cut corners to get something on the cheap." He was still looking into her face.

She was livid, and she wondered if her face was as red as her hair because he had her Irish up. Her anger rarely rose to heights like this, flaming through her to the point where she could feel her blood boil. She'd examine that odd occurrence later. If she considered him a legitimate critic, she would have been embarrassed by the accuracy of some of his comments. But he just made her mad.

"I know that everyone thinks themselves to be an art critic, but sometimes, something is just meant to be enjoyed for what it is without any hidden meanings. And I doubt, sincerely doubt, that the Dawsons got this or anything else on the cheap as you put it." She was trembling with rage now, and she tried to remember her mother's words about acting like a lady and not giving in with harsh words.

DK squared her shoulders and pulled herself up as tall as she could, annoyed because she was still only just past his shoulder even in her heels. "It's too bad that you can't appreciate art for what it is, something to enjoy. For that, I really feel sorry for you. And if you think that you can do better, feel free!" She waved an arm at the vineyards surrounding them, taking a half bow to encompass the sculpture too.

She turned on her heel and stalked off, glad that for once she made her exit without doing something stupid like tripping over her shoes or bursting into tears. She needed a drink and grabbed a wine glass from a passing waiter. She needed her friends, who were standing and staring at her, clearly watching the whole exchange with great interest and probably able to hear it too.

Really, who the hell did the man think he was? Damn him for noticing the missing piece despite her best efforts to hide it. And damn him for making her insides curl up and want to find out more about him despite his rudeness.

*****

Hell and damn. Cassidy took another sip of the excellent white in his glass and watched with appreciation as the petite redhead stalked away, grabbing a glass for herself from a passing waiter and meeting up with a group of women and one man across the courtyard. He watched, interested, when there was a short energetic exchange, surprise and confusion evident on some faces, and then the man spun and steamed full speed down the driveway followed by a chestnut-haired woman. The remaining group, including Red, closed ranks and were in deep conversation, watching the two walk away.

There was a story there. He might be inclined to eavesdrop and find out what had happened, but the conversation with the little woman in the killer green dress had left him feeling unsettled and heated up. Damned if he wasn't sure why he wanted to get Red keyed up, but he was happy he'd done it.

It was easy to give her that nickname. The flaming curls on her head were spectacular in the sun, and the bright green eyes and sprinkling of freckles across her face gave away her Irish heritage. The fact that she had a compact body and muscles that screamed hours in a gym added to her allure. Funny, she wasn't his usual type.

He turned back to the sculpture. It was an artful piece, the intricacy of the welding capturing his attention now. He wondered about the process, which method was used, how long it had taken. There was something unsettling about it too, and the feeling that it was unfinished stayed with him.

But the artist who did this was clearly talented. He'd felt compelled to be disparaging when he faced Red, wanted to push her buttons if for no reason other than he liked being the bad boy and doing the unexpected when he wanted attention. Besides, she threw him. He hadn't expected someone looking like her in this backwoods area, and an electric shock he recognized as desire shot down his spine and left him twitchy.

He moved around to read the artist's plaque to see if he recognized the name, because this level of expertise was the work of someone with a following. DK McGiven – not someone he knew, but he made a mental note to look the name up. It was probably a big bulky guy with an attitude, or at least that had been his experience when it came to metalwork. A big guy with a soft spot for wine and the finesse to make the fine tendrils of vines intertwine like lovers. Interesting.

He looked back at the clutch of women, his eyes fastening on Red again. That emerald dress looked like it had been poured on her slim body, and he felt a new stir when he thought about how well that color brought out the deep green of her eyes. She looked like an elf, skinnier than his usual flavor of the month. But the pull in his groin as he continued to gaze at her had him wondering what was making her so attractive.

She was certainly prickly enough, Cassidy thought. He usually didn't like that either, preferring his women to hang on his every word. He never wanted to get into deeper conversations with them anyway since he rarely stuck around for anything that approximated a relationship. He was like teflon where relationships were concerned. He was better off that way, free to take off when the next assignment called him.

But there was something about Red that caught him up. He liked the fact that she'd argued with him, and if the flags of color heightening her cheeks were any indication, he'd pissed her off. That was okay, he thought. She wasn't going to let him talk his way past her with nonsense. He wasn't sure why he'd felt the need to goad her, but it had been fun to see her rise to the bait and get all worked up over some metal.

Maybe he'd follow up and find out if she was local. He was going to be here for a couple of months, and it might be fun to have someone to help him pass the time. She certainly wasn't his expected taste, but maybe it was time for a nibble of something different. That's what this was about, after all. A time to recharge, get rid of the boredom, try new things.

Cassidy smiled and considered following her right now and introducing himself. But the circle of women around her was tight and their attention was elsewhere. And there was work to do today. He should search out his winery hosts to learn more about the story of their rejuvenation of this place.

His eyes lingered on Red's back, and as if she could feel him staring, she glanced over her shoulder. She met his eyes with her mouth slightly open in what looked like a gasp. With a quick shift that changed her lips into a thin line of disapproval, she deliberately turned away.

Chapter 11

"Good morning, Vince. How is the writing going?"

Cassidy's landlady Lisa was sitting behind the desk of her office, her companion Dannie missing from the matching work area across the room. They amused him. They were completely at ease with their relationship and didn't hide the fact that they were a couple, but they didn't make it an obvious in-your-face point either. This town was very accepting of everyone's unique differences, he was coming to find, an unexpected surprise to him.

He'd spent the last few days writing down his first impressions of the area, something he always did when exploring new territory. He'd found that his first sense of a place was often accurate and he rarely had to edit that much as he became more deeply entrenched in the stories and the lives of those who lived them. He'd spent a day writing about the Dawsons and Witch Hill alone. His mind drifted often to Red and their encounter over the metal sculpture, but he hadn't had a chance to dig more deeply into that artist's background. Or learn more about Red either.

"It's going. I've been spending some time wandering around the area."

He rarely liked to be identified as the internationally known lifestyle writer that he was, since he'd found that people too often then tried to impress him or direct him to what they wanted written about their area. He just introduced himself by his real first name, which he never used in his byline. It wasn't until his articles came out that many people connected the names and realized who he was.

His cover was in place here too. The house had been rented by his agent, so there was no direct tie back to him individually. He was a writer looking for some new ideas for a book. He was interested in learning more about the area while he was there, since all work and no play, blah, blah, etc. Lisa and Dannie were a fountain of knowledge about what to do and where to go in their foothills.

"That's good! Anything you need at the house?" Lisa had pen poised over paper, waiting to accommodate his wishes.

"No, the house is great. It's a terrific set-up to get my creative juices flowing." He smiled disarmingly, feeling safe in the knowledge that he wasn't her type and being charming would have no effect other than their continued great service for his rental.

"Excellent! We like our guests to feel at home, so if there's anything you need, just give us a call." The woman smiled again and turned back to her computer.

Cassidy flipped through the various brochures and fliers for events laid out on a long table in the office. He'd seen information about the Witch Hill opening here last week, and it had proven to be an unexpectedly enjoyable afternoon. The Dawsons were engaging and personable, and they had been more than happy to tell him the story of their acquisition and renovation of the vineyard and the building of a winery.

They'd introduced him to their winemaker, a tall beauty with a French accent named Marguerite, and she'd walked him around the stainless steel tank room and the crowded barrel room, explaining the state of the art processes that were in use at the winery. The woman did little to start his engine humming, but even to his jaded eyes, what they were achieving was impressive.

The wine was indeed fine, and it would be interesting to see how it continued to develop in the coming years. The food had been surprisingly great as well, catered by a place called Roxy's which the winemaker had assured him was definitely worth more than one visit. Music was subtle in the background, a local group that played a broad selection of genres, ending their last set with a rousing pseudo-rock piece. Both food and music offered more story opportunities.

The one thing he had not had a chance to learn about was the sculpture in the courtyard. Every time he tried to ask a question about it and learn more about the artist, his hosts took him in a new conversational direction. It wasn't until he was walking back to the convertible with the evening light fading after sunset that he realized he'd never been able to quiz them on it.

And on the redhead too. He wanted to know more about Red, and he thought that they might be able to tell him who she was, since she was a guest at the event. Of course, not everyone there was specifically an invited guest. Many people showed up after seeing an announcement some place. But he'd never gotten a chance to follow that line of questioning.

Cassidy considered asking Lisa, since she seemed to know everyone in town. Red wouldn't be hard to pick out in a crowd, with that curly bright hair cropped close to her head and her elfin build and Irish features. But he also didn't want to appear too eager or obvious. The right time would come to ask more questions, he was sure.

Thoughts about her flashing green eyes made his groin harden, surprising him. His reaction to her was so uncharacteristic. He didn't like to give any woman power. He selected his conquests because they would be happy with short tangles or one night stands, and that suited him just fine.

But those green eyes had looked too deeply into him, and that made him both uncomfortable and strangely hopeful. He had wanted to lean closer and learn how she smelled, wanted to put his lips on hers and she how she tasted.

Enough about Red. If he fixated on finding her, he wouldn't get any work done. And the sooner his work was done, the sooner he could leave this town. Red would only be a temporary, though attractive, distraction.

He found a glossy trifold advertising an upcoming event – open house weekend at studios of many of the artists in the area. The list of artists was long, but one name jumped out at him – DK McGiven, the same artist who created that metal sculpture at Witch Hill. He hadn't had a chance to research the guy but going in cold allowed his first impressions to have free rein. He could meet him in person this weekend.

"Hey Lisa, what do you know about this studio tour this weekend?" He turned back to her desk.

"It's a terrific event, an opportunity to meet the artists where they work, see them in action. Most will be working in their preferred medium while you visit so that you can experience the creative process up close and personal. In some cases, you can even try your hand at something, like working with some clay on a potter's wheel or painting on silk." She smiled enthusiastically.

"So, who would you recommend going to see? There are a lot of names on this list."

"What kind of art interests you?" Pen was poised over the notepad again.

Cassidy thought quickly. He didn't want to point her in the specific direction of his interest. He'd come up with a list and see how she responded.

"Let's see, I'm interested in pottery, and in metalwork, not so much in painting or weaving. Does that limit me too much?"

She'd been jotting as he spoke, and she got up to take the brochure from his fingers. Efficiently marking off some names, she said, "You have a lot of potters to choose from, but I'd highly recommend Thomas Brunner. He's a gnarly old guy, gruff as can be. His studio looks like a hobbit house, all weird slopes and angles and wood shingles. He's got a number of different kinds of kilns and he works in varied ceramic styles. Once you get past the gruffness, you'll learn a lot from him."

She'd checked the name DK McGiven too, he'd noticed. "And metalwork? What about that? Isn't this McGiven a metal artist?" He didn't think that was too obvious.

"Oh yes, DK is a must-see too! The studio is an old barn, and the space is incredible. It was part of an old homestead and it dates back almost a hundred years. DK's kept the outside of the barn and most of the inside like it was when it was built, no changes. And if there's welding happening, well, there will be sparks flying!"

She chuckled at her own joke, and Cassidy had to smile. Her enthusiasm for all things in the Flynn's Crossing region was infectious, a one woman tourism bureau.

"Well that should get me started. I'll check out some of these other names you've marked too. The map looks decent, so I should be able to follow it. I've always got GPS if I get lost."

Lisa laughed harder now. "Don't rely on that GPS system too closely up here, Vince. While it's good for the main roads, once you hit the smaller lanes and such, it isn't worth much. Once, we had to send a tow truck out to a cattle pasture because guests followed the GPS voice's instructions to the letter and ended up in the middle of a herd of longhorns, up to their axles in mud." She laughed at the memory. "They were lucky they had cell phone coverage!"

Cassidy smiled along with her, a picture painted in his mind immediately based on her words, something too good to pass up for his series on the area. He made a mental note to capture the idea as soon as he was out of sight.

And ignore his GPS, definitely ignore his GPS.

Chapter 12

Saturday morning was another bright blue sky and perfect weather sort of day, the kind that encouraged him to explore the rural roads with the convertible taking a few turns on two wheels. Some of the two lane blacktop led through thick pine forests and vining underbrush, while other turns brought him to heart-stopping vistas of open meadows, oaks heavy with contorted branches, and meandering streambeds.

The streams were dry now and would remain so until the rains began. The lowered angle of the sun dappled the ground as leaves already dried from the summer heat floated to the ground. Cattle and horses grazing in large fields and wine grapes already tinged with fall colors brought a peaceful lazy feel to the day.

Then a steep rock outcropping would force him to stand on the brakes for one more picture, trying to capture the feelings of the land. In some places, the panoramas made him think about the descriptions he'd been reading in the history books quoting early settlers. Some things hadn't been altered by the passage of a hundred years.

Other things were very different. He'd seen some of the mega-mansions Randy had mentioned, the fancy SUVs and high end trucks with wheels that had never seen dirt parking at the end of long paved driveways. With the money came security fences and tall gates, acres of mowed lawn where chaparral used to stand, and a more aggressive attitude on the roads. Even he could tell the new money people, just by the way they hurried.

He'd sent a preliminary article off to Randy to review, his write-up on Witch Hill Winery. It hit the right note and he was sure that Randy could sell it to one of the wine magazines. In his latest research, he'd learned that the dozens of high quality wineries in the area were frequently ignored or overlooked. Once his byline hit the stands in a few months, though, that was bound to change, and he'd be contributing to the upcoming craziness.

People tended to follow his stories on new areas with trips of their own, shining a spotlight on a region that might have been previously obscure. On more than one occasion when his true identity had become known, he'd been actively courted to lend his name to a story about an up-and-coming chef or winemaker or designer to help them launch a national presence. That was one of the reasons he traveled incognito now and his picture never appeared with his byline. Anonymity allowed him freedom of movement.

He stopped at Brew Bank Bakery for breakfast, a small establishment by the bell tower on Main Street that sold incredible pastries, savory baked goods, and gourmet coffees. He liked the quirky owners, Stuart and Sarge, another interesting couple in this very unique town, and he'd already become addicted to the spinach and feta croissants and dark, rich brew.

Like everyplace around here, there was a story behind the shop. Back a couple of decades, the little local bank that had been around since it assayed nuggets during the Gold Rush was gobbled up by a national competitor, a logical takeover at a time when regulations made stand alone institutions difficult to keep profitable. Big brother had no need for the quaint little location, abandoning it for a modern structure on the highway leading into town.

A series of retailers had tried to make the former bank space work, a prime location in the center of Flynn's Crossing with a large but unused outdoor seating area adjoining the courtyard. No one could find the right combination to make it a success.

Then ten years ago, someone got the bright idea to turn it into a small restaurant. A kitchen was built in the back next to the old vault, the original behemoth door still visible from the indoor tables. After morphing into it a coffee shop, that owner had failed in the last economic downturn, and the current couple had taken over the shuttered space. And since then, they'd been busy keeping the residents and visitors in the area full of rich, gooey and delectable baked goods and coffee concoctions.

Cassidy had to admit, he'd expected a lot of redneck intolerance and perhaps rifles in the windows of pick-up trucks. This was not the wild west and rough living he had disparaged to Randy when the assignment came his way. In fact, so far, people were welcoming. It was nothing like what he had expected.

"We have a lot of old time families too," Stuart had told him, in response to his casual questions about all of the newly rich who seemed to be moving in. Sarge had added, "Native Californians, and proud of it. That's me and Stu too, though neither one of us was born right here."

They'd shared some tales about the new folks, as they were known, and their surprise when they found that they'd need to make a half hour drive to find a Starbuck's or even longer to shop at a big box store. Things didn't seem to change much from the independent way things were way back when. Cassidy found himself hoping that this didn't change with all of the new blood moving in.

"Nope, I don't expect it will." Sarge had waved a hand to wipe aside the voiced concern. "People move here for the peace and quiet, and they discover all of the little joints have exactly what they need 'round here anyway, like us." His laugh was like his body, round and full and jolly. "And then they don't care about those fancy chains anymore. Besides, they can always buy online and have it shipped."

And that, evidently, was that.

Heat began to build as the day aged, though it wasn't overly oppressive with the breeze of the moving convertible ruffling his hair. He'd found the roads well-marked and the map was easy to follow. After a couple of stops along the way, he decided to concentrate on the two names that intrigued him the most, DK McGiven and Brunner, the potter.

Thomas Brunner proved to be as gruff a character as Lisa had described. When he showed off his studio and his kilns to a group of younger children, though, on a field trip for school with tablets in hand and a list of questions at the ready, he had softened his booming voice. The kids and their long lists had given Cassidy time to look around and come up with some questions of his own.

"You're not from around here," Thomas said, looking at the car first and then at him up and down, eying him with suspicion. "You got a funny accent and look too pretty."

Cassidy fought the urge to grin. He wanted to be offended and tell the old man that he wasn't exactly welcoming the tourism trade or potential customers if this was how he treated most people, but he sensed that it was all a ploy to see what he was made of. Besides, he liked the guy's attitude.

"No sir," he replied politely, "but I heard you're the best potter around here and I wanted to see your work." He wasn't cozying up to the guy, exactly, but the pottery was more like sculpture than just plain old pots, truly amazing.

Thomas harrumphed. "You must be talking to them gay ladies, aren't ya? They set you up in one of their houses for your visit?" He was walking away as he spoke, and he either intended to leave Cassidy standing in the doorway of the studio or wanted him to follow.

"Ah, yes sir. The ladies have been singing your praises."

The sound that came from the old man could have been a bark of laughter or a cough of phlegm, hard to say, but Cassidy followed him into the weirdly shaped structure. Inside, the roof sloped at odd angles, the effect being one of wonder and charm rather than disorganization. Different styles of stoneware stood on shelves all around. In the back, three different wheels for throwing pots, tables, and pedestals all held work in various stages.

"Ya, sure. What other kind of nonsense they been filling your head with?" Thomas moved to a wheel, grabbing a lump of gray from a table to the side. He slammed it on to the wheel a couple of times until it resembled a pointy peaked mountain. Then he started pedaling the spindle to make it turn, and put his wet hands to work on the damp clay. No wimpy electric wheel for him.

Cassidy was quiet, drawn to the rapid creation of a pot from what had been a lump of nothing. The potter's hands might appear gnarled and misshapen, but he caressed the clay as a man might his lover and the resulting shape was extraordinary. It formed a ball, then flat sides. Keeping his hands flush with the clay and working his fingers into the center, a vase formed. Sides were smoothed with a flat tool, and a design began to appear when the skilled craftsman set a corner of it to the work.

Then, as soon as it looked complete, Thomas stopped the wheel, stared at the piece for a few heartbeats, and squashed down the artful cylinder until it was again a lump of gray.

Startled by the creation and destruction, Cassidy looked up at Thomas's face to find himself being watched carefully.

"That was amazing. Why did you destroy it?"

The old man regarded him solemnly. "Because it wasn't up to my standards, is why. Gotta be perfect, otherwise I'm not gonna bother firing it. Gotta put my name on it, it's gotta be perfect."

Breaking the steady gaze, Cassidy looked around. Every piece he saw was, in fact, perfect. Randy would love this stuff, he realized, because it wasn't the usual stoneware vases and plates that any potter formed or threw. These were exquisite works of art.

One piece in particular drew his eye, a sculpture of a woman, naked with arms raised as if she was stretching upon awakening. It reminded him of something, he wasn't sure what, and it made him restless. The facial features were intentionally blurred, but it was the sense of hope that came from the movement that was special.

He might have to come back and examine this piece before he left town, he realized. It caught him like nothing else had in quite a while. The dainty body and an innocence in the pose enchanted him.

"Do you mind if I take some pictures? I have a friend who's an agent and handles artists, and he'd love…"

Thomas got up quickly, faster than Cassidy thought that old body could. "Pictures, take all the pictures you want. Agent, hell no!"

The old man headed out the door of the studio, and with only a second's hesitation Cassidy lifted his camera on its strap and started shooting. At least he could hope to get permission to use these shots in an article, but he was sure that Randy would be interested in the pieces too once he saw them. Maybe he could convince Thomas that he needed representation.

He made sure he got a few shots of the statue of the woman. It would give him some inspiration as he wrote the article.

He found the old man outside, fussing with the front of a brick kiln, muttering. "No agents. Don't need 'em, never have. Do my own thing. Be like DK, always having to work for someone else, not something I'm going to do."

Cassidy picked out the name DK in the continuing rant. "You know DK McGiven? I've been looking forward to meeting him."

The man stopped, glanced back inside the studio, and turned to stare at Cassidy with a sly smile. "Yup, rented some space from me before that fancy back east agent got all of them assignments lined up." He'd spit out the word assignments like it was dirty.

"But the guy does great work, I saw it at the winery, Witch Hill. He's a great artist too, just like you. Sir." Cassidy decided that if he wanted information, a little respect wouldn't hurt.

Thomas was now staring at him fixedly, his gaze changing from speculation to amusement. Cassidy felt like there was something he didn't understand.

"Yup, great work, no doubt about that. Told DK the same myself. Works hard, does DK. Shows in galleries and art shows and stuff all over. Makes people things to order for their fancy big homes down in the valley. Yup, great work." Then he gave a little laugh and shook his head, clearly enjoying his thoughts.

Cassidy still wasn't sure what was going on, but he was getting prickly about it. "I'm going to visit DK's studio today too, on this tour. Don't let him know that I'm coming, will you? I want to surprise him, see what else he's working on."

Thomas continued to chuckle. "Nope, won't call ahead a you. You go have yourself a nice little visit." Still chuckling, he turned away to fuss with the kiln again.

Feeling his anger rise at being the butt of some unknown joke, Cassidy turned back to the car, the loose stones of the walkway crunching and scattering underfoot with his less than leisurely pace. He wondered if the old guy was crazy.

His fast path to freedom brought him past the door to the weird little studio and his eyes fell on the statue again. He had one more question.

"That statue of the naked woman, the one inside near the wheel. How much are you selling that for?"

Thomas didn't turn back. "Not for sale. Kind of fond of it myself." Then he chuckled again. "Reminds me of good times, yup, it does. Good times, you know what I mean." His grin was sly and he winked when he finally looked up. It was as close to a leer as Cassidy had seen on at least three continents.

Now Cassidy was pissed. The guy does all of this work and then it wasn't for sale? A nutcase, that was for sure. What was it, a statue of his mistress? Not for sale, huh? Well maybe he could change the potter's mind.

And with that, he turned and steamed back to the red convertible. Here he was trying to do the old dude a huge favor, get him an agent so that he could make some money and take care of things around this pitiful hole in the wall, and the guy didn't even want to sell his fucking work. He couldn't understand the continued chuckling he heard as he stalked away.

Slamming the car door, he revved the engine and took the gravel drive with enough speed to kick up a constant ping of stones on the side panels. The car rental company would just have to deal with it.

Chapter 13

A character to visit again, Cassidy reflected when he'd calmed down. Maybe he could convince him to sell that statue. He wasn't sure why he wanted it, but he did. And he'd still use the photos for his story about old Thomas. He'd make a great subject for a piece about artists and their quirkiness.

When had he last gotten remotely excited about a place? He thought back as he maneuvered the car over the twisting backroads. Had it been southeast Asia, or maybe Tanzania? New Zealand before the earthquake?

He wasn't sure anymore. It had become a blur of airports and planes, hotel rooms, and helpful women to pass the time. The stories ran together in his mind until he wasn't sure if the characters he recalled were actually from the parts of the world he associated with them. In and out, often in a handful of days, and no time to dig any deeper than the superficial take that his readers, or at least the publishers, seemed to want.

There were plenty of stories here, he knew. Some of them could be funny, and some might be poignant. He was finding something to intrigue him multiple times every day. The place was beginning to draw him in to a degree he hadn't felt anywhere else in quite a while. He shook his head. He was getting soft. That, or he was so tired of the jet set lifestyle he'd been leading that this was a balm to his frayed nerves.

He liked himself better when he was jaded and distant. He didn't get angry then, could instead be sarcastic and feel above it all. Cassidy always tried to hold himself apart from the people he was writing about, believing that it gave him the objectivity that was necessary to write about a locale without passion. He needed to steel himself against that, or his work would turn out to be a soppy love story about a town instead of the cutting-edge review that his international readers expected.

An opportunity to put his game face on was coming up, though, with the artist DK McGiven. He'd drawn a mental picture of the guy, big and meaty, and he was looking forward to quizzing him about the Witch Hill piece. Yes, the work was intricate and detailed, but something was missing, and he could recognize that even if others didn't. Cassidy wanted to know what it was.

A brightly painted sign planted next to a mailbox marked the long driveway for McGiven's studio. The last name was on the mailbox, along with the street number, though the street itself was little more than a wide one-lane holey blacktop path. On the opposite side of the road, a very rundown house stood at the end of an equally long drive. An old woman in a loose dress stood at that mailbox, watching him with suspicion. His nod of greeting was met with a tighter frown.

The land on the welding artist's side was flat with a few huge oak trees, gnarled branches never touching in the wide spaces between them. A ridge rose a short distance to the back of the property, and in between stood two barns. One was obviously almost new, and while designed to mimic its neighbor, it had windows that marked it as a house.

The other barn was much older, with weathered boards and the classic door on the second level to bring in hay for storage. It looked like it had been sitting in its place for decades, so much at home that it was less a structure and more an organic feature that had sprung from the earth. Another colorful poster pointed the way to the entrance.

This should be interesting, Cassidy thought. He didn't pick up his notepad, preferring to set a picture in his mind of what he was seeing. He could remember things very well without it and could jot those impressions down once he returned to the car. No, he was just going to go in and introduce himself and ask all of those questions about the metal sculpture, and maybe he'd solve the little mystery about what was missing too.

*****

DK was grateful for the help today. Gabby had volunteered to serve as hostess, greeting visitors to the studio and offering them refreshments. Her son Jeremy was welcoming people at the door and handing out fliers, even pointing out DK at work in the middle of the barn as if he owned the place. When things were slower, he'd run off to play with Fusion, boy and dog having a predictably great time with a ratty tennis ball and lots of running. DK had promised Jeremy a swim in the pool later on when the heat would make the barn a less inviting distraction in his day.

She shed the thick leather welding gloves and shrugged out of her protective long sleeve jacket. She was dressed, as she always was for welding, in heavy-duty coveralls and steel-toed work boots. With her short hair plastered to her head from the helmet and sweat, she knew she'd pass for a guy, albeit a short skinny guy, to people that didn't know her. That was okay on a day like this, though. It was fun to surprise visitors about who she was, and even that she was a she! Most people expected welding to be done by a man, especially when her use of initials instead of her first name didn't give her away.

"Thanks again, Gabby, for helping me out this weekend." She stopped at the makeshift desk they'd set up in the open doorway. A slight breeze was rising, and she hoped that it would continue to build throughout the day. She felt compelled to provide the studio show visitors expected with welding sparks flying. It got hot, though, when the sun was at its most merciless.

"No problem, sweetie. Jeremy is in heaven, being a host and getting to play with Fusion. I really need to think about getting him a dog. But with a condo, it's hard to even consider. Maybe a hamster would be better."

She grinned up at DK. "You're looking pretty hot, and I don't mean that in a good way. Can you take a break and cool off for a while? Maybe dunk yourself in the pool?"

DK considered the tempting idea, but there were cars coming up the drive, the last one a sexy little red convertible with its top down and its driver hidden in the dust of the first vehicles. Too bad they were eating dust, she thought. Obviously someone not from around here. People used to gravel roads would have delayed their progress until there was some distance between the offending dusty monsters in front and the open car.

"Wonderful as that sounds, we have more company. Time to suit up and get to work again. You and Jeremy handle the opening remarks so well, I can concentrate on the fun part, the welding demonstration." She smiled at Gabby and moved over to the pedestal that held the piece she was using for show. Shrugging into her jacket and putting the helmet back on, she fired up the arc welder, lifted some wire into place, and went back to work.

*****

He coughed and took off his sunglasses to rub his eyes. Note to self, Cassidy thought. Back off on unpaved roads when there's traffic in front. A dust bath was not a pleasant experience, and there was no place to hide from it in an open convertible. He should know better, but he was intent on his own thoughts.

Doors in the other cars opened and disgorged chattering people, the occasional laugh ringing out in the quiet. He sat, letting them head into the barn. He wanted to have a conversation with the artist in residence, and that would only happen if the other visitors had already done their bit. He'd noticed that in most cases, people didn't stay for very long in any one place, so he should have a clear line to Mr. DK McGiven in short order.

A boy stood in the doorway handing out brochures to people walking in. When they were past him, he scuffed a toe in the dirt and rubbed the head of a big black monster laying just off the path. Cassidy didn't like dogs. Or maybe it was not really dislike, since he wasn't around them much. He didn't get the attachment someone would have to an animal. Of course, he was detached from people, too, so who was he to say. Boy and dog took off with what looked to be a very slobbery ball, and Cassidy made a mental note to avoid the brochures if he was offered one.

The spot was very peaceful, he realized. Other than the hum of voices from inside the old barn and something that sounded like metal dinging from time to time, there was only peace. Or rather, other than that and the laughing boy and barking dog, and a whole bunch of creatures he associated with nature but couldn't identify. The air smelled good, though, something like sage and spice mixed with the minerally tang of dirt.

A pretty woman who looked vaguely familiar came to stand in the door and look out at the boy, smiling indulgently, clearly the mom. Probably the wife or other half, he thought. He would be charming to her, get an in with DK. That usually worked well, at least in other places. It would give him an introduction, he hoped a good one.

The two carloads of people finally came out of the studio. They were consulting the same map that sat on the seat next to Cassidy. After much pointing and a long debate, they came to some conclusion and piled back into their cars. They backed out and headed down the driveway, leaving the woman in the doorway regarding him. She looked pleasant enough, but he realized that continuing to sit in the car would make her suspicious.

Cassidy unfolded his long body out of the convertible and made sure his sunglasses were secured on his nose. He didn't want to give anything away, and he knew that part of his charm lay in his compelling eyes, or so women had told him. If he wanted to win points to get in good with DK, he needed to be charming to this lady gatekeeper. Some people up here were a little bit protective and not so fond of outsiders, he'd learned.

"Hello, and welcome to the studio of DK McGiven." The woman's smile was broad and appeared to be genuine. Time to turn on the charm.

He took off his sunglasses and put a big smile on his face. "Hello yourself! I've been looking forward to this stop all day. I've heard so much about DK and saw the piece at Witch Hill. Extraordinary!"

The woman's smile became wider and she extended a hand. "I'm Gabby, and I'm helping DK out today. Studio tour days get so busy, and if there's an official greeter, DK can concentrate on the welding demonstration."

Helping out, huh? Cassidy suddenly realized that his assumption about this woman being DK's wife might be off. But there was a wedding ring on her finger, and there was the boy, still playing with the dog out in the field.

"Hi Gabby, I'm Vince." He shook her hand and looked out to the field, gesturing with his chin. "That your boy?"

She laughed. "Yes, that's Jeremy. He loves coming to visit DK because he gets to run around with Fusion – that's the dog. And later, he gets to play in the pool!"

Visiting, huh? Still, maybe having her on his side wouldn't be so bad when he wanted to ask some tough questions.

Gabby had moved to the table at the barn's entrance and picked up a brochure to hand to Cassidy. He was grateful that it looked to be slobber-free. "Here's some information on DK's work and on DK. Feel free to wander around. And there's welding underway. You'll probably be able to tell the subject right off!" She smiled at him and waved a hand inside.

Without wasting time to glance at it, he put the brochure in his back pocket for later review. Cassidy took two long strides inside and set his sunglasses on top of his head, waiting for his eyes to adjust to the dimmer barn. Along the walls, boards had been set on sawhorses to serve as display tables, and those tables were covered with metalwork of various sizes and styles. The range was exceptional, everything from a fanciful display of metal flowers in a vase and what appeared to be an intricate bonsai tree, to a large hulking modern work that looked almost industrial. Large and small, they surrounded the area with a spectrum of reflection from the light coming in windows set high above.

In the center of the room, a pedestal held a work about three feet tall that was, in fact, very recognizable. It was a boy and a dog, connected by a ball in midair. The engaging quality came from the poses of both creatures and the laugh that was evident on the boy's face, the answering grin on the dog as it tried to grab the ball.

Cassidy was intrigued by the piece, immediately recognizing the boy and dog outside as the subjects for this whimsical work. It brought a grin to his own face. Even he could appreciate the fun and humor in it. It made a spot glow inside him, a feeling that was unfamiliar. He seemed to be finding all sorts of things that touched him today, highly unusual for him. It made him feel itchy and uncomfortable.

He was so intent on his examination of the work in progress that he didn't see the person behind it right away, welding arc and metal rods in hand. When he did, Cassidy gave a little start of surprise. It had to be DK, but he wasn't what Cassidy had expected. His mental picture was a big beefy guy based on the size of the Witch Hill work. And since it was welding and lots of metal, after all, someone strong.

This guy, hidden as he was under the helmet, jacket and coveralls, didn't look to be very tall, and certainly not beefy. In fact, the guy looked tiny and hardly capable of handling the piece on the pedestal, much less the mass of the Witch Hill project. But the sureness of his moves, the rapid competence of the welding, could only mean that this was DK the artist.

Cassidy realized he was staring, and his stillness finally stopped the welding activity. Setting aside the arc welder and rods, gloves were pulled off and the helmet faceplate was pushed back. And the guy stopped still.

"What the hell are you doing here?"

The voice stunned him into stillness. His mouth was gaping, he knew that, but Cassidy couldn't stop himself. He knew that voice. The face looking back at him from inside the helmet was familiar, the eyes bright green and very angry right now. And the hair, he knew, would be flaming red and tightly curled to her head.

Red. It was Red. Red and DK? He couldn't wrap his mind around out. He'd been so sure of his mental picture that the reality in front of him was a shock.

Red took an angry step back and threw the gloves on a table before pulling off the helmet and heading to the back of the barn. Cassidy found he couldn't move. He was trying to think very fast about what he'd said back at Witch Hill to someone he thought to be another guest, albeit a gorgeous one. Could this be the artist he had mocked so thoroughly that day?

"Hey DK, I'm going to make Jeremy some lunch. Do you want anything?" The greeter Gabby called from the doorway.

Red's muffled "No thanks" came from the back, and Cassidy heard Gabby move away from the old barn calling to the boy. He was still locked in place, realizing that he'd been rude, exceptionally so while he was trying to get her attention at the opening, and now he wanted to make nice and learn more about the artist, the one he had so blindly criticized.

And it was because of the woman, the one he'd wanted to find so he could have some distractions while he was here. The one who unexpectedly was hitting all of his hot buttons. The woman he'd been calling Red in his mind was actually DK McGiven.

No wonder Thomas had laughed at him.

Chapter 14

DK shrugged out of her heavy jacket and ran her hands through her hair. It was stuck in places, and helmet-head, she thought angrily, was not the best way to meet an adversary. But right now, she was too mad at her visitor to care how she looked.

The coveralls joined the jacket on a chair and she took a deep breath to steady herself. She wanted to march back in and yell at the guy, but she already knew what he thought about her work. He'd told her about it that day at Witch Hill. Clearly he thought himself to be an art critic and clearly he also didn't know what the hell he was talking about.

She wanted to chase him out. And she wanted to ask more about him too. He'd been on her mind, a nice distraction dwelling on her initial impressions. Damn him for looking like a page out of a sleek urban magazine, with the little red car and his bad-ass attitude. DK felt a curl of desire settle low in her body. Damn him!

Settling her tank top straight, she hoped that she didn't look as sweaty and hot as she felt. She wanted to put this dude in his place with disinterested detachment and cool reserve. It was hard to feel confident about pulling that off when she was sure she looked like a half-baked lobster.

He was still standing behind the pedestal with the work in progress, but he was looking straight at her. His eyes were a deep brown, she could see as she got closer. His sunglasses hid them at Witch Hill and she had been too shocked and mad to notice when she'd stormed out of the room before. His blond hair was a touch windblown and he carried off the urban casual look, stating without a doubt that his clothes were expensive.

Her reserve starting to slip, DK steeled herself to be objective and stay out of any discussions about art or her work. She'd just introduce herself, find out who he was so that she could stay out of his way, and then send him down the road. Even if her stomach was doing back flips and she wanted to see if that stylish haircut would feel as good under her fingers as it looked.

Putting a fake smile on her face, she walked forward and extended her hand. "I'm DK McGiven, the artist here and the one you so pointedly shot down at Witch Hill. And you are?"

He was still staring at her, his eyes on hers for a time, before his gaze moved down her body and back up, settling finally on her outstretched hand. She fought the urge to squirm and returned his gaze, an eye for an eyeful. He moved forward.

"Hi, I'm, ah, I'm Vince." His grip was firm and hard on hers. He added a smile to his rugged features and it lit up his face. He looked a little embarrassed.

Good, she thought.

"Well Mr. Vince, what can I do for you today? We've already established what you think of my work when we met at Witch Hill. I don't think we have anything else to say to each other, do you?" Her sideways glance took in the unfinished piece from that work sitting off in a darker corner of the barn. His presence was another reminder that something was missing there.

DK was proud of herself though. In the flip-flops she'd rushed on when she'd shed her work boots in the back, she didn't even come up to his shoulder. But she pulled a couple of extra inches out of her spine and put her nose in the air, brushing past him for the open door. Freedom and sunshine beckoned. She hoped he got the message.

She waited for him to follow her, not wanting to look back into the barn to see what was taking him so long. Impatient, she turned around, and found him staring at her backside with a bemused expression on his face. She wasn't sure whether to be angry about it or flattered, but it brought back the shock of electricity she'd felt before.

"Mr. Vince?" She waited for him to shake himself free of whatever was holding his rapt attention. A huge grin slowly broke across his face and he looked into her eyes again, moving towards her now. She refused to feel dwarfed by his height, though it was hard when her feminine side was appreciating their differences.

"Thanks for visiting today – feel free to avoid stopping by again in the future."

God, what was making her so bitchy to him? She wanted to slap the smile off his face and at the same time pull it down to hers to see what his kisses would feel like. Hormones, she thought. It had to be hormones, that and the need to finish that last piece of the Witch Hill installation. It made her grimace.

"Look, we got off on the wrong foot. I got off on the wrong foot." He'd come to stand next to her in the midday sun, and she noticed he kept his sunglasses on his head, staring intently into her eyes.

"Yes you did." She waited to see what he would do. Besides, it was really hard to look away from those chocolate eyes. They made her melt in response, and right now, she hated herself for that feeling.

"I'm sorry, I don't know what else to say. It was just that I was floored by what I saw, really impressed. I was an ass that day."

He was smiling at her, and she realized that he was either putting on a very good act of looking sheepish or he was really sorry he'd acted so rudely.

"Apology accepted. Still, I don't think we have anything else to say to each other." She forced herself to look away to a spot in the sun where Fusion lay on his back, paws all in the air, tanning his tummy.

"Can we start over?" He stepped back and put out his hand again. "Hi, I'm Vince, and I'm visiting the area for a couple of months. I'm a writer, and I'm spending my free time away from the computer learning about this fascinating part of the country."

She looked at his hand, and then at him with suspicion. "A tourist, huh? What do you write about?"

He slowly dropped his hand, clearly disappointed that she wasn't willing to play along with a fresh start. "I write about the history of places, you know, the background that travelers might not know about when they come to visit an area. And there's a lot of interesting history around here."

He was watching her carefully. She was sure he wanted to see how well she was buying the story. She wasn't buying it, much, but that didn't make it any easier to avoid noticing the lines at the corners of his mouth or between his eyebrows. Frown lines, probably, though his smiles hid them well. He didn't look like a man who smiled often.

"Look, Mr. Vince, there's a historical museum and a reenactment club and a visitors bureau if you want to learn more about the area. There are plenty of people who will be very willing to tell you all the stories you want to hear and then some. I bet you can find some books about the region in the used bookstores on Main too. Have a nice visit to Flynn's Crossing."

She turned away and headed for the refuge of her house, wondering when the walk had become so long.

"Hey, hold on, okay?" He caught up to her and put a hand on her arm to stop her.

The spot he touched tingled and another flash of fire went through her system. She had no idea why she was reacting to him like this, and she wasn't sure she liked it. On the other hand, it had been a long time since any man had sparked her interest. Way too long.

DK looked at his hand on her arm and then meaningfully up at him. He seemed to be shocked into stillness and he was searching her eyes for something. She felt a wave of uncertainty, her mask slipping. She found herself staring at his lips and wondering what his kisses would feel like.

"Yes?" Her voice was low and had turned husky. Giving herself a mental head slap, she forced herself to look into his eyes again. Mistake.

"Look, I don't know many people in town. And I'd really like to get to know you better. Could I take you out for dinner, or at least coffee?"

She speculated. He was going to be here for a couple of months, a short timer. He was attractive, appeared to be single, and he turned her on, no doubt about that. He was critical of her work, but he'd apologized about that.

And he picked out the fact that something was missing, a fact that she couldn't avoid thinking about. He probably didn't know what was missing, but he'd recognized it when so many others had not.

She eyed him carefully. "I'll think about it, Mr. Vince, maybe for a very long time. Right now, though, the studio is closed for lunch."

He dropped her arm and she turned, proud of herself for walking away with her head held high. She was most proud, though, about not turning back to look at him one more time – and not running flat out in the opposite direction for the safety of the house.

Chapter 15

Tess tossed the salad while Gabby put the finishing touches on a cold pasta dish. Marguerite came back in from setting the patio table, and the three of them dropped their voices so that DK could barely hear them.

"Are you sure it's the same man?" Tess turned to Gabby, who had been filling them in on the activities of the day.

"Positive. They talked, then DK came back in and he stood on the walkway for a while. Finally, he went back to his red convertible and drove away. DK wouldn't talk about it, just said that he was a writer and that he was doing something related to the history of the area."

"What's his name?"

"She didn't say. She didn't want to talk about it, changed the subject every time I tried and then would sit there completely silent. She ate a peanut butter and jelly sandwich and then went back to work." She paused, then looked between the two women. "The thing is, she doesn't even like peanut butter and jelly!"

Tess chuckled and Marguerite wrinkled her nose.

"So she was very distracted by this interesting man. Good for her. It's been too long and she deserves to have some fun. God knows it might give her the inspiration she needs to finish that piece." Tess turned back to the salad.

"We need to find out more about what happened," Marguerite added. "He seemed to be very nice the other day when Davinia and Marcus gave him the winery tour. I never caught his full name. But he was quite handsome and charming." She winked and wagged her eyebrows, and the others giggled in response.

DK had heard enough. She entered the room, hair wet from her shower and a storm cloud on her face. She stopped and looked from woman to woman, expectant faces all beaming at her.

"Yes, and... what?" Her eyebrows raised, and she glared at them. "You were talking about me!"

Marguerite moved up smoothly and put an arm around DK's shoulders. "Of course we were, darling. None of the rest of us had a handsome and gorgeous man fawning all over us today, now did we?"

Closing her eyes, DK shuddered and allowed herself a small grin. "He was that..."

*****

Jeremy was settled in the house with a movie and Fusion for company, and the women were draped across various chairs out on the deck surrounding the fire pit. It was too deep into the dry season to light it, but it offered a place to put up their feet. Sweatshirts and jackets had come out as well, the night air having fallen much cooler as an indication that fall would soon truly begin.

"So he asked you out, and you said...?" They had finally coaxed the story out of her, and DK did feel some relief in explaining what had happened. She even brought up the strange attraction she was feeling for Vince.

"I told him I would think about it. Then I left him standing there."

"At least he knows how to find you." Tess seemed to be almost lighthearted in her response, and that had DK puzzled.

"He does, and the phone number is on the tour brochure, and it's not like people in town don't know how to find me too. I don't get it, Tess. Why are you so cavalier about this? Do you expect me to go out with him? He was brutally honest about his opinion on my work."

DK really didn't get it. Her friends had been almost giddy in their excitement that she had met a man – they had used that same phrase about five times now and she was getting sick of it. That same man had very little respect for the work that was so much a part of her.

"It's your choice, you know that. I just want what's best for you." Tess sat forward and got more serious. "It's been a long dry spell for you, you've said it yourself. You don't even feel the inspiration to finish the Witch Hill work."

Marguerite joined in. "It's passion, darling, that's what you need. And that Vince, based on what I've seen," she winked and grinned, "could definitely fit the bill for you."

Gabby had been quiet. She was always the most conservative of all of them, least likely to jump into anything that wasn't safe and secure. It was probably the mother in her, DK thought. Right now, though, she wanted to know what Gabby was thinking.

"Gabby, you saw him today. You saw him at the unveiling and you saw how he acted, both times. What do you think? Should I go out with him?"

Gabby looked a little guilty. "Okay, so I watched the two of you when you came out of the studio. He was so darned cute and I recognized him from the winery and all. And I wondered what you were going to do."

DK and the others waited for whatever she wanted to share. Gabby cleared her throat. "It was like there were sparks coming off the two of you, you know? Like I could feel the energy all the way in the house."

Tess smiled and Marguerite's laugh boomed out. DK could recall the feeling of those sparks without any difficulty, and that was not helping matters at all.

Yes, he definitely lit something up in her, something that melted and heated and reminded her that in addition to the long dry spell, her life skills when it came to sex were awfully meek and lacking in any real breadth of experience.

She'd need pointers on how to act with someone who was clearly out of her league in terms of lovers. As least she assumed he was out of her league. He seemed so worldly.

"Yes, but he's a stranger, not from around here, and not sticking around." It made her slightly nervous, thinking about how out of her depth she was. Damn the man for looking so good and for her own sorry deficiencies in seduction over the years.

"So what?" Marguerite got up and literally danced over to the wine bottle. "He's perfect for a fling. A little passion and a little fun, what hurt is that? He said he is leaving in a couple of months. You enjoy each other, you get the passion fill-up that you need to finish the piece, and you both go your own ways when you're done. No harm, no foul."

DK stared at her in awe. "Sometimes, Marguerite, you are just so damned French!"

Chapter 16

"Honest to god, Randy, the art around here is pretty frigging surprising."

"Yeah, I'm looking at the picture of that statue of the naked girl right now. Great piece. Does the guy have an agent?"

Cassidy could hear Randy shuffling papers on his desk, then clicking on his computer keyboard. The man never concentrated on only one thing.

"No, remember? The potter was grumbling about how he didn't want to end up like DK, and that's how I knew he knew DK. Except he let me think that DK was a guy. It was something of a shock when I met her. And I'd met her already at the winery – she was Red, the woman I told you about."

Randy chuckled on the other end, focusing back on the conversation. "So you met DK McGiven and talked to her and stuff, eh? What's she like in person?"

Cassidy stopped playing with his pen and sat up straighter. "You know her?"

"Well yeah, seen her work. It's incredible the detail she can do. And all with metal. So what do you think of her, I mean really?"

Not knowing where to begin or what to say, Cassidy stood up to pace the dining room he'd taken over as an office in the rental house.

"She's cute, Irish-looking, kind of on the pixie side. Short curly red hair and big emerald green eyes, very expressive eyes. They get emerald bright when she's mad and sea green when she's not." Where the hell had that come from?

He could almost hear Randy's brain churning over the cell phone connection. "So not bad to look at. Single?"

And what kind of a line of questioning was that? Cassidy got a little more cautious. "I think so, since she didn't tell me she was married or dating anyone when I tried to ask her out." A sudden flash of disappointment at the thought of Red being connected already fired through him. "She's not my type," he added defensively.

"If she's female and not shitfaced ugly, she's your type Vinnie. You tried to ask her out? And...?" Cassidy could hear the anticipation in his friend's voice across the continent.

"She didn't tell me yes, but she also didn't tell me no. I think she is as attracted to me as I am to her, that was the vibe I picked up."

"Attracted, huh? You haven't used that word in, god, I don't know how long, college? Attractive, yes. Attracted, no." Randy laughed and Cassidy could picture him, cranking his chair back and settling in with a chuckle.

"Give me a fucking break here, will you? I'm just saying that Red's a good looking woman and I'm liking what I see, and I'm only here for a short time anyway. May as well have some fun and enjoy each other, right?"

"Hey man, whatever you say." He heard Randy's voice get more serious. "Just be nice to her, okay? She seems like a good person, you know? So don't leave her with a broken heart or anything, okay?"

Stopping abruptly, Cassidy pushed the Bluetooth device further in his ear. He was sure he hadn't heard right, because it sounded like Randy knew DK.

"Are you holding something out on me, man? Because it sounds like you know her."

He heard paper moving again in Randy's office. "You know I never leave the city! Just saying that I heard she's a nice person, so be nice to her."

Cassidy shook his head, because something wasn't right.

"I'll be on my best behavior, I promise. You can tell whoever you know that I'll be very nice to her. I just want to get to know her a little better, pass some time while I'm here." He paused. "And if it goes further than that, well, we're both consenting adults, right?"

He heard Randy chuckle again. "Yup, two consenting adults. I have nothing to do with this, you remember that. You just complete your assignments and then you can come home."

Cassidy signed off the call, still puzzled by what his friend had said. If he didn't know better, he'd say that Randy had engaged his agent mafia to find out who was being represented by whom in the area. Maybe DK was agent-shopping. Thomas had said she had an agent. Maybe she wasn't happy with that agent.

It wouldn't hurt to ask her, Cassidy thought. Maybe he could hook her up with Randy. The guy was a great agent, and he'd take good care of her career. He wasn't sure why he was suddenly feeling so protective over a woman he didn't really know except to fight with. But if Randy represented her, he'd be able to keep an eye on what was happening with her no matter where he was in the world.

Now why the hell was that suddenly feeling like such a good idea?

Chapter 17

The morning had dawned cool with a hint of fog wisps coming up from the Sacramento valley. The calendar said fall was officially here and the weather was finally catching up to it.

DK was grateful for the cooler temperature since she was moving some pieces into the cooperative gallery. It was her turn to work here today. Each artist on display took their turns, hers coming every two weeks. Today she'd work with Bettie, an active woman in her late sixties who crafted ornate ink drawings and some fanciful watercolors.

She had an hour of peace yet before Bettie arrived, which gave her just enough time to change around the pieces she had left in her displays and add the new ones sitting in the back of her truck. Most could be moved to a dolly and rolled in without a problem. The boy and dog piece, though, would take a little more effort. She could winch it out of the car, but the gallery display was another story.

"You're just too skinny, no meat on you at all for all that metalwork, and that's all I'm going to say about it." DK had smiled at Sarge's greeting when she stopped in Brew Bank for her coffee earlier. He'd insisted that she take a cannoli too. She'd loved them since the Italians who owned the bakery in the neighborhood growing up had slipped her some as a child. A large mocha coffee and that pastry were going to be her treat once she shifted the statue into place.

How she was going to do that by herself, though, she wasn't sure. She had plenty of muscle. There was no way she could do the work she did without it. Still, the piece was heavier than many others she had done because of the smooth solid surfaces.

The wheels of the dolly caught on the broken sidewalk by the gallery's back door and DK cursed. Forget getting it on to the display pedestal. At this rate, she wouldn't be able to roll it into the shop by herself.

"Want help with that?" She blinked her eyes into the early morning sun, a tall male body silhouetted against the brilliant slant of light. If she was right, she recognized the voice, and it wasn't someone she wanted to see this morning, particularly when she was struggling to get her work in place dressed in holey jeans that had seen a better decade and an old stained t-shirt.

Two large hands joined hers on the dolly's handle and an arm touched her shoulder. She didn't want to look up. Together they lifted the wheels over the bad patch of concrete and into the back door of the shop.

"Thank you, though I could have done it by myself." DK stood up to look into Vince's face. Then she had to laugh. He had clearly been to Brew Bank too, and a bear's claw pastry was gripped in his mouth. He had needed somewhere to put it while he helped her, and he'd found a spot.

Vince pulled the partially eaten pastry from his mouth and laughed along with her. "Wait, let me get my coffee. I set it down in the alley." He disappeared a moment and returned with an extra tall specialty something in a paper cup.

"Good morning DK, how are you?" He took a munch of his pastry and chewed while he looked at her. His gaze swept up and down, taking in the jeans and shirt, and his smile got bigger.

God, he looked so normal today. He had on a sweatshirt that advertised something in Hong Kong and faded jeans that had a couple of holes in them, not too different from hers. His running shoes weren't new, though she doubted he used them for running. His hair was mussed and he had his usual sunglasses on, right now perched on top of his head. So normal and so delicious, much more tempting than that flaky pastry.

"Ah, good morning yourself. I see you've found one of our fine bakery establishments."

She watched him take a swig of coffee and close his eyes in appreciation. She watched the liquid as he swallowed it, and felt herself heat a little as his throat moved. He was looking just as good as that cannoli this morning, maybe even better.

"Look, I'm still very sorry about the other day at the winery. I don't know what came over me. Blame too much great wine." His apologetic smile was magnetic.

She couldn't figure out a single thing to say.

Finally breaking their gaze, he looked around with interest, still munching and sipping. "I haven't been in here yet. It's an eclectic mix of work in this gallery, isn't it?" He moved away from her to stand in front of a large bright oil with a stylistic hummingbird painted in its center.

DK was glad he had moved because she was feeling herself get pulled into his orbit, and the strength of that pull was egging her on to do something she shouldn't. That pull of lust was back. She needed to reassert control over her own body, even if she couldn't do anything about him showing up here.

"Yes, Sierra Shining is a cooperative gallery. Anyone who shows here takes a turn working. Today's my day and it seemed to be a good opportunity to bring in some new pieces." She looked back at the boy and dog in metal and realized that she would still need to wrestle that into place. Then she looked back at the man who had finally finished off the bear's claw and thought, why not.

"Do you think you could help me get this on the display over there?" She pointed to an empty pedestal near the front door as she moved back to roll the dolly over.

"Sure thing, absolutely, on one condition." The tall blond turned to watch her over the rim of his coffee cup. He paused to sip again. "Have dinner with me, tonight."

DK stopped in midstride and caught the rolling dolly just before it ran into a display of Thomas's pottery. "Dinner? You'll help me move this for, what, five seconds and for that I have to have dinner with you?"

He was smiling at her, clearly enjoying himself. "Come on, it won't be so bad. You can take me to one of your favorite places here in town after you get off work. Then you can go home, no strings attached. Just dinner, Red, and some conversation."

He'd moved closer to her while he was talking, and DK found herself staring up into his chocolate brown eyes again. He was ruggedly attractive, and her friends were right, it had been a while. The advantages were that he was a stranger, and by the time they got to know each other and her own insecurities kicked in big time, he'd be ready to leave. She could keep all of her flaws hidden for a few weeks, right?

Just light, uncommitted but passionate sex. It would be easy to move from this casual flirtation to something more, since he seemed to be at least as interested as she was based on the spark in his eyes as he watched her. She licked her lips and decided that he fit the bill.

"Okay, I'll have dinner with you, as long as you help me get this into place. Just dinner and conversation. You can meet me here at five when we close."

"Deal!" He toasted her with his coffee and she wanted to wipe the self-satisfied grin off his face, but she was pretty sure she was wearing the same one, reluctantly, on her own.

*****

The day lagged, minutes seeming like hours. Cassidy stared at the byline on the article he was trying to complete on Thomas the potter. V. M. Cassidy. It sounded so pompous to him. It sounded like he should be writing history books instead, the kind that few people read unless they were forced to by a malicious professor.

He'd been trying to write steadily throughout the day, waiting for the tempo to click into gear and the words to flow. All day, though, it had been a chore, something that writing very rarely was for him.

It was DK's fault, he knew. When he'd been walking back from his morning trip to the bakery for breakfast, he'd seen her from a block away, her red hair flaming in the morning sun. She was wearing snug jeans that outlined her petite body. A long sleeve shirt that she'd pushed up to the elbows showed tanned and toned forearms, leaving him no doubt that the work she did made her physically stronger than she appeared. He'd intended to come up and engage her in some idle chit-chat and try once again to get her to go out with him.

But opportunity had presented itself in the form of that big sculpture of the boy and dog, the same one she'd been working on when he'd visited the studio. It had turned out to be amazing. He wondered if, like Thomas, she ever squashed back any piece to molten metal because it wasn't perfect. He hadn't seen anything she'd done that would be considered less than perfect.

Except that Witch Hill piece. There was a story behind that, and hopefully he'd be able to get it out of her tonight at dinner. Or on some future night, because he intended to get to know DK McGiven better, a whole lot better.

His mind kept returning to her licking her lips, a simple enough gesture but one that set his blood racing through him, just before she agreed to have dinner with him. Heat rose a few degrees at that point. She wasn't his type, and yet that compact body and those big green eyes did things to him. They left him wanting to do things to her.

He shook his head again and tried to focus on the computer screen. It was just that he'd been on something of a sabbatical since he'd gotten to town, he thought. It was unusual for him to stay away from casual relationships for so long, but being in the same place for a while made him cautious.

It was time to forget about that caution and live a little, he reasoned. His brain got stuck on his memory of the scent of her, something spicy and floral that he picked up when they were moving the metalwork, something that had his jeans tightening uncomfortably. Tonight, he'd get to know the mysterious DK McGiven better and find out if that fiery red hair was a match for the passionate woman he assumed she'd be.

His smile was a little bit wicked as he returned to the keyboard and slammed his fingers down with new determination.

Chapter 18

At five o'clock on the dot, Bettie turned the sign in the front door to closed and locked it up tight. DK had dropped the days' receipts in the safe's slot and locked the small change they kept in the register in another desk drawer in the office. She'd been disappointed that Vince hadn't come back late in the day, and now she was surprised that he wasn't here yet. She'd give him a little more time, and then? Well, then if he didn't show, she'd head home. DK sighed.

"So where is this nice young man, DK? I don't see anyone out in front." Bettie craned her neck in the front window to peer up and down the street, then bustled to the back of the shop and did her usual triple check of everything that DK had already done. She was obsessive that way.

She was also nosy and had unfortunately shown up just in time to see Vince leave with a friendly wave to DK and a promise to see her tonight as she stood in the back doorway of the gallery. Caught off guard and staring at his retreating back, her defenses were down when Bettie started to pry. All day the woman kept asking about DK's dinner companion. Here it was, finally quitting time, and it appeared he'd forgotten her.

"I don't know, Bettie. He's a writer. Maybe he got caught up in his work and he's running a little late. You can head out. I'll wait a few minutes and then if he doesn't show up, I'll go home. It's no big deal."

No really, it was a big deal. She was glad when Bettie took her at her word and walked out the back door. DK turned the lock on the door just to be safe, but left the lights on in case Vince came by and thought she had left too.

She examined her make-up again, cursed her red hair that was determined to curl in every direction, and reminded herself again that she needed to make an appointment for a haircut. At least she'd had a change of clothes with her that would work for a casual evening out, and the slacks and sandals were a big improvement over the work duds she'd worn this morning to complete her gallery organization work. Bare of make-up and in smudged and torn jeans, she was surprised Vince had even stopped to say hello today. She had not looked her best in those early sunrise hours.

She straightened the papers on the desk as she'd done more than once during the long day. It had dragged on forever. Curls of anticipation had teased her insides and brought secret smiles to her face. Now that quitting time was here, her reason for being on edge all these hours should be here.

And he wasn't.

The clock hands moved at a glacial pace to five-fifteen and DK decided that he wasn't going to show. He'd had second thoughts. Unreliable, that's what her mother would say. A man should always be on time for a date, it was a sign of the kind of person he was. It was a sign of respect. Why did her mother show up in her mind at times like this?

DK knew why. It was like the nail-biting that she still found herself almost doing from time to time, a sign of her own uncertainties flaring up to remind her of the person she had been trying to shed all these years. Right now, she just felt deflated that Vince had abandoned her, obviously having second thoughts. Maybe she should have second thoughts too.

*****

He'd seen the older woman come out, bustling across the alley into the parking structure and heading up the stairs to where he assumed her car was parked. A couple of minutes later, she came down the ramp in an old SUV. He couldn't figure out what was taking DK so long, since more than ten long minutes had passed since then.

Cassidy sat watching the lights finally turn out through the shop's back door. DK appeared, shifting a huge ring of keys in her hand, setting first one lock and then another. She didn't look up. God, didn't the woman have any sense? She could be mugged in a second and she would never see it coming.

He didn't understand what he was feeling about DK. First he was nasty at the winery, which he admitted he did just to get a rise out of a beautiful woman. Then he wanted her to like him at the studio, which was so unlike him. He wasn't a people pleaser. He preferred to lay things out there, and if they didn't like him, that was okay with him.

Then he was Mr. Good Neighbor this morning, helping her out with the sculpture, though granted, he had ulterior motives. And now he felt protective, and that made him angry. He didn't want to feel protective of anyone, least of all a woman that he planned to take to bed a few times between now and whenever he could leave this boondocks town. She had some kind of power over him, and he hated that.

It was like this town. It was beginning to grow on him. The old man who walked his dog on Main Street when Cassidy was heading down for his coffee and breakfast now waved hello. Sarge at the bakery caught him up on gossip about people he didn't even know. The roads were no longer completely unfamiliar and he'd even found some favorite foodie hangouts to buy his meals. And everyone was friendly to him.

It was growing on him like a fungus, he thought viciously.

Cassidy kept his position leaning up against the driver's door of her truck. She'd replaced the jeans from this morning with sleek slacks and heels that added a few inches to her height. She still hadn't looked up, and her expression was a little sad. It made his heart turn, and that made him mad all over again. He wasn't going to give up any power to her. He'd had all day to stew on this, and he needed to set some ground rules in place before they jumped in the sack.

He didn't develop feelings for the women he got involved with. Hell, he didn't even really get involved. Love 'em and leave 'em with a big smile on their faces, that was his motto. If he was going to be stuck here for a few more weeks, he may as well find a way to enjoy it.

*****

She'd head home, DK thought. Maybe she'd stop at Roxy's gourmet grocery store for a treat for dinner, or maybe she'd even stop in at the restaurant, have a glass of wine and some kind of decadent appetizer oozing cheese and better humor. He was just a guy, granted an incredibly good looking guy oozing sex appeal like a very tempting appetizer. But she'd get over it.

It wasn't the first time she'd been stood up on a date. Why, the first time she was fifteen and her mother had set her up for the school dance with the son of her parents' friends. He hadn't shown up either. Lack of respect, that was her mother's opinion. Not worth even thinking about. But she'd missed the dance just the same.

DK was so deeply into her memory that she walked right into Vince's tall frame. He was scowling as his arms came around her to keep her from falling. He was warm, very warm at each and every point where their bodies touched. The shock of finding him here when she'd already convinced herself that he had blown her off had her staring up into his brown eyes.

He gave her a little shake. "Don't you pay any attention to your surroundings? Someone could come up and mug you, grab that big bag you sling over your shoulder and flap around behind you, and you'd miss the warning signs completely."

Vince felt good, hard in the places where she was soft, and strong in a way that his usual casual stance didn't emphasize. Up close, the lines at the corners of his mouth were accented right now by his angry expression. DK stopped herself in time from raising a finger to trace his compressed lips to see if the lines would vanish, if she could wipe the anger away along with the lines.

She didn't say anything. So he hadn't had second thoughts, or maybe he did and he was waiting for her here to tell her, figuring it was a quiet enough spot to lay on the disappointment. But then why was he so angry with her?

*****

Cassidy gave her another little shake. She hadn't said anything to him, and she was staring into his face with wide eyes and something akin to wonder. He didn't want her to look at him like that. It made him feel special, and he didn't want to feel anything other than lust and satisfaction, maybe a little fun and sheer pleasure. But nothing deeper.

He watched her carefully. Her eyes had dropped to his mouth, and she licked her lips. It left him with an overpowering need to find out how she tasted. His anger was dissipating, and the feelings that were flooding into the vacuum didn't feel gentle or protective.

DK raised a hand and he let her go abruptly. She took an unsteady step backwards and Cassidy found that the sudden coolness where her warmth had pressed against him was too big a void. He reached out again, putting his big hands on her shoulders and pulling her in.

And this time, he gave in to the feelings that were rioting untamed inside him. He needed to taste her, and he didn't want to wait any longer.

*****

DK had one short heartbeat to get her bearings before she felt his lips crush down on hers. A minute before, she could feel the anger coming off him in waves. His lips were hot with it, demanding a response from her. She didn't need any encouragement, meeting heat for heat and feeling her own demands rising.

He tasted like sin, all male and insistent purpose. He'd lessened his hold on her, moving the big hands gripping her shoulders into a persuasive caress. One hand moved up her neck to bury itself in her curly hair and the other traced her spine. He turned his head and slanted his mouth, using his tongue to trace the seam of her lips.

DK couldn't help herself, pulled in by the magnetism that radiated from him. She felt she should push him away, despite her own lecherous thoughts about him all day long. She heard her mother's voice in her head as if it was from a long distance away. Good girls don't act like this.

The hell with that, DK thought, with what little reason she felt she had left. She moved her hands up Vince's chest to rest one on his cheek and the other around his neck. She turned to get a better angle and let her tongue explore his lips, let her fingers smooth away the lines of anger that he'd had before.

A murmur of pleasure came from her throat, and an answering brief groan almost like a laugh came from Vince. His hands continued to explore her neck and back, pulling her more closely against him. DK had a single second of shock, realizing that he was aroused and feeling the press of him at her belly. Then her own hunger took over and she gave in happily to the spread of heat and anticipation.

*****

He needed to put a stop to this. They were in a fucking parking garage and all he wanted to do was lift her up on the truck's tailgate and lay down on top of her, covering her with his body and burying himself deep inside. He couldn't remember ever feeling a wave of longing like this, desire so strong that he was fighting it with his last conscious thoughts.

Cassidy took a deep breath, maybe a mistake given that it just brought DK's subtle scent of arousal slamming into his senses again. He wanted her badly. He needed to get control over himself. This was a hell of a way to start a first date.

He pulled away suddenly, looking down at DK's half-closed eyes and wet parted lips. The sheen drew him in, and he had to fight the urge to dive back. He rubbed his hands up and down her arms, her skin so soft it gentled his hands, waiting as she shook herself back to reality. Her deep sigh made him smile.

Dinner, he thought. They were going to have dinner. He needed to get his control back on track, damn it. She was pulling him into some kind of hold and while he didn't like the consequences of it, he'd be lying to himself if he didn't recognize that he certainly enjoyed the results.

Cassidy watched DK's face as she blinked twice, hard, as if she was clearing her brain. Know how you feel, he thought, and that gave him a lot of satisfaction. At least this wasn't one-sided. She'd been as affected as he was.

She stepped away from him, running a hand through her hair in what he thought was an attempt to quiet the curls. Or maybe she was trying to calm chaotic thoughts, which would again echo his own feelings. She licked her lips, seeming to linger there, and he fought the need to grab her and taste her again. Breath deep, buddy, he cautioned himself. You are so screwed, figuratively but hopefully literally too.

DK shrugged her shoulders and crossed her arms in front of her, not a protective gesture. There was defiance and a certain air of challenge in her stance. She was watching him carefully, as if she was deciding something.

It was making him nervous. This was like he was on display, a pastry in the case at Brew Bank awaiting a customer's selection. And he really wanted to be selected, he realized with a shock.

Finally she seemed to make up her mind, and a small smile came to those very kissable lips. Licking again, she opened her mouth to speak.

"So, was that a sampling of dessert?" And a big grin spread across her face.

Chapter 19

The restaurant had a comfortable feel, modern but intimate, all dark wood and stone and glass. The menu was non-traditional, filled with lots of comfort foods that weren't part of the normal fare eating out, and each one promising some little twist on the usual. The wine selection was local and extensive, and the full bar was hopping with people catching up at the end of the workday.

DK took a grateful sip of her zinfandel and watched Vince examining the place. He took in the busy bar area, the servers moving smoothly between tables, the subdued lighting making the whole place glow in the lowering dusk outside.

"I like this, it has a good vibe. Is the food decent?" He turned back to her and picked up his microbrew, taking a sip and closing his eyes in what she took for appreciation. She liked watching his throat work those swallows down. She'd like to place her lips there to see how they felt. Damn!

"The food's great. They have things you don't find in other restaurants, like the turnip fries with dipping sauces or the truffle mac-n-cheese. It's all great, and you can relax and take your time enjoying it too. Roxy loves to come here, and she would know."

"Roxy, as in Roxy's the restaurant? I saw an ad for it. Is it any good?"

DK felt a big indulgent grin settle on her face, and she twirled the wine glass by its stem before explaining.

"Yes, that Roxy. She's a good friend of mine, one of my girl tribe. I stop by her grocery store a couple of times a week, usually when I'm on my way home from a long day and I don't feel like cooking, which is most of the time. Or I go to the restaurant and have an appetizer in the wine bar. Why cook when you have a best friend who's an award winning chef?"

Vince was watching her intently. "Award winning, huh? So is she, like, nationally known or something?" He took another sip of his beer, his eyes now locked on hers.

She'd feel uncomfortable, she thought, if she didn't feel the same intense interest in him. She could happily dive into those chocolate brown eyes like they were a big bowl of sweet dessert. She shivered.

That kiss that went on forever had been amazing, nothing like any kiss she'd ever experienced before. She thought she'd been involved with some talented guys in the kissing department, but Vince was head and shoulders above the rest. It left her wondering what other surprises he had in store for her.

Back to the business at hand, dinner. Thoughts of dessert possibilities would have to wait.

*****

Cassidy was enjoying the stories DK had to tell. He rarely was this engaged with whatever his dates had to say, but her tales intrigued him. He learned about the circle of close girlfriends, the girl tribe she called them. He learned about Roxy, and based on the stories, he knew he'd have to visit the restaurant soon. It would make a good article.

Maybe DK would be willing to visit it with him on another date. He didn't want to think about the charge that idea gave him.

She filled him in on her own background too. He learned about how DK came to town a few years back, determined to follow her art even though she was not yet well known or able to sell much. Her friendship with

Thomas sounded so warm, Cassidy wondered if they were thinking about the same gruff old man.

"I worked as a checker at the grocery store, and I could afford the rent on my little condo, but paying for studio space was harder, just about out of the question. Thomas really did me a favor, taking me on. I could weld there in exchange for helping him with his work." She'd fallen quiet then and played with her wineglass, not meeting his eyes. Obviously there was more to this story too, he thought.

"How did you help him out?" He was curious, suddenly aware that he wanted to know a lot more about her, details that he never bothered with from the women he usually planned to sleep with.

"I, ah, helped him with some of his creative stuff, you know, inspiration – or at least that's what he'd say to me." She fell silent again, seemingly uncomfortable with the direction of the conversation. Something twinged at the edge of Cassidy's memory, but he didn't take the time to examine it.

"Anyway, I stumbled on the old barn one day when I was out riding around to clear my head. It was for sale, a rock bottom price, a short sale in the depressed housing market. It was perfect, and since my work was taking off then, I could afford to buy it. I lucked on to a good agent to represent my artwork. He got me known in some major galleries, helped set up some promotions for me. I couldn't afford to pay him at the very beginning either."

Her expression had grown distant and a little sad again, and Cassidy found himself wanting to wipe away whatever was causing her glow to fade. He reached a hand across the table, taking her empty one in his and turning it over to play with her lifelines. He waited.

DK's focus had dropped to the tracing of his fingers and she sighed, then put a bright smile on her face. "Anyway, it's a good thing I found people who were willing to barter to help me get going. But that's all in the past now. I'm riding a great wave of success, and my work is terrific, praised across the country." She looked a little defiant as she stared at him again.

He wondered if she was waiting for him to challenge her on it, and he thought back to the Witch Hill work and his nagging feeling that something was missing from it. Suddenly loath to ask more about it, he let the challenge drift away. He didn't want to ruin the mood they'd struck, the one that was sucking him in even as he knew he should fight it.

"So, Mr. Vince, how and where do you do all of your writing? Would I have read any of your work?" She had pulled her hand away and settled back in the chair, taking a sip of wine and licking her lips.

It would be his undoing, those little licks of her pleasure. It made him shift in his chair and wonder what her lips would feel like ranging over his body. Her scent, that spicy richness, settled on him again and he felt his groin twitch in anticipation.

Cassidy's guard was down. Talking with Red was easy, too easy. He'd shared his love of writing about places, learning more about the history and what made them special or unique. He found himself sharing some of the more ridiculous snafus that international travel was today. She laughed, and he watched her, enthralled with the musicality of it and the way it lit up her whole body.

He was definitely out of his element here, unusual for him. Some part of him kept saying that this was wrong. He shouldn't be getting involved like this, feeling pulled into something deeper than the casual flings he'd had for years. He was only going to be here for a few weeks, and then he'd be flying off to someplace else on the globe. He found he didn't want to hurt her feelings when he left.

What was up with that?

*****

Once their dinner plates were removed, Vince took DK's hands across the table, turning them over to trace the calluses that were the scars of her profession. They'd shared a dessert, and she'd fed him a few bites of the chocolate cake before he insisted on turning the fork around and feeding her. She thought that he missed a couple of times on purpose, using a finger to wipe off the gooey mess and then licking his finger.

By the time they were done, she was sure she would combust, the glow inside her a barely banked spark ready to flame with the smallest gust of wind. She wanted to fan those flames and let herself become molten, welding herself to him.

But DK also knew she should slow down. It was one kiss. Okay, maybe technically it was multiple kisses at one time, but still. If she gave it all up now, she'd hate herself for it in the morning. She was shocked to see that they'd spent almost three hours by the time Vince was signing the credit card receipt for dinner. She'd wanted to split it but he'd refused.

Somewhere in the back of her mind, her mother's strictures about dating protocol came up. Of course, her mother didn't really have a rule about how soon it was appropriate to rip a guy's clothes off and engage in wild, passionate sex. In her mother's eyes, never!

Vince's hand was at the small of her back, guiding her out the front door of the restaurant and into the dark and almost empty street. He'd walked to the gallery from his rental house up on the residential hill at the end of Main. They'd taken her truck and parked it up the block. He took her hand as they strolled slowly towards the vehicle. It felt so natural that it seemed like they'd been doing this for years.

She was ready, she realized. She wanted to slam him back against the brick building, grab his face and pull him into a sizzling kiss, and then she wanted to spirit him away someplace, either his place or hers, she didn't care. And she wanted hours of him, hours that she knew somehow would fulfill the passionate promise of those kisses.

They stopped next to her pick-up facing each other. She watched him turning her hand over in both of his, tracing the shapes of her fingers and rubbing the rougher spots on her palms with subtle determination. He was so tall, and she barely came up to his shoulder. Her mind wandered, wondering how they would fit together in bed. Quite well, she suspected.

"So," he hesitated, "this has been great." He wasn't looking at her face, just continuing to play with her hands, now toying with both in his. "Can we do it again?"

DK felt a moment of confusion. She was wrapped up in a heavy cloud of lust and anticipation. And it sounded like, what, this was the end of their evening?

"Sure, sure we can." She took a step back, which brought her up against the passenger door of her truck. In the dimmer light away from the street lamps where they stood, the expression in his eyes was unreadable.

He was staring at her now, and she wondered if her flustered feelings were evident on her face. Disappointment might have showed there too. She was ready to move forward, and he seemed content to call it a night.

"Would you like to get together again this week?" She was happy her voice didn't squeak. She was being a whole lot more forward than her norm, but she also heard that clock ticking. He would only be here for a few weeks, and she didn't want to miss a bit of it.

His smile made desire curl in her belly again. He had a great smile. "I'd like that, a lot. Can I call you tomorrow and we'll set something up?"

"Tomorrow would work." Her inner self did a fist pump of happiness and she began to run through some scenarios, seduction being a primary activity in all of them. She was intent on her inner dialogue and missed all the signs.

He moved in fast and pressed her back into the truck. His mouth dropped, and his lips traced hers, gently this time. It was so different from the kiss before, and DK was sure something was sizzling circuits in her brain.

She raised her arms around his neck as he held his body against hers. Sparks and flames raced along her nerve endings. He started to pull back and she wanted to draw him in again, not give him a chance to think but only feel the way she was.

She felt some satisfaction when his shallow quick breathes mirrored her own. He was staring at her, his eyes too dark to read. He traced her lips with a finger that she swore might be shaking.

Then he stepped away from her, gave her a quick wave of salute, and headed up the street into the evening.

And damn him, he was whistling.

Chapter 20

"Kisses, as in multiple? Were they amazing, awesome, inspiring?!?" Gabby was on the edge of her seat next to DK's pool. Tess was watching her with heightened curiosity too.

DK wasn't sure how she wanted to respond to that. Yes, it was amazing. No, it was disappointing, but not because of the heat those kisses enflamed. Because they had ended.

Was she inspired? No, not yet.

In all the years that they had known each other, DK had never held back on the gory details of her love life. There hadn't been much to tell most of the time. And now that there appeared there might be something to start to say, she wasn't sure how to frame it.

Roxy got up to pass some stuffed mushrooms and stopped in front of DK. "You don't have to tell us, honey, if you don't want to. We'll find something else to talk about, honest." She was sympathetic, but DK could see the question marks of curiosity in her eyes as well.

DK sighed. She really did want some input here.

"He's turning out to be not what I expected."

Gabby jumped on that comment. "How so? Is he boring, dull, a bad kisser, what?"

Smiling, DK began to get into the explanation. "No, he's not boring or dull. He has a lot of interesting stories to tell about the places he's visited." She paused, seeing the expectant expressions on her friends' faces. "And he's definitely not a bad kisser!" Now she was grinning.

"So what's the problem?" Tess had a perplexed expression on her face.

They had all agreed that Vince, with his good looks and short term visitor status, would make a great target for DK's flirtation with her wild side. After all, no one expected that the affair would last more than the few weeks he would be in the area. DK was attracted to him, and it appeared that he returned the interest. It was safer than, say, someone who lived in town that she would run into all the time after she worked the itch out of her system.

Shifting uncomfortably again, DK tried to figure out how to put something so, what, indelicate? She cleared her throat. "So here's the question. How exactly would you suggest I ask him if he'd just like to sleep together for the next few weeks while he's in the area? You know, telling him it's just to get my passion mojo flowing?"

Silence fell so completely that the birds and breezes were suddenly a cacophony of noise. They could hear Fusion snoring in the shade next to the house. Even the muted bubbling of the pool filter was audible. No one said anything for a full minute.

Gabby was the first to recover. "You know, sweetie, there was a time when Doug was alive that I could remember how that level of sex drive felt. It's been a while. I need to rewind for a couple of minutes to catch up." She sighed deeply and a slightly dreamy expression settled on her face as she stared out over the distant fields.

Tess was still staring directly at DK, and the subject of her examination was feeling like a bug on a pin. Hadn't they discussed this, that she needed to have a good hot fling to understand what passion was supposed to feel like, no strings attached?

Roxy recovered her voice next. "I think you should entice him to your lair, or in this case, your barn. Ply him with good food and fine wine, then kiss him until his toes curl – and yours do – and haul him off to bed." She looked very pleased with herself when she finished. Tess now turned to stare at her, her gaze even wider, much to DK's relief.

"I don't want to be a slut and I don't want to trick him into anything, but I think he's as interested in me as I am in him. I'm not worried that he's leaving in a few short weeks. It would be like short term friends with benefits, right?" DK thought she had the reasoning worked out in her head and only needed a plan to implement it.

But maybe she did need to think this through a little further. Her old uncertainties started to rise to the surface again. What experience did she really have in seduction? Zilch, nada, nothing. And what if she'd been reading him wrong?

She fought the urge to chew on a fingernail and took a sip of wine instead. Waving off Roxy's offer of another stuffed mushroom, she got up to pace the length of the pool deck. "People do this kind of thing all the time, right?" Damn, talking about it in fun was one thing, but thinking about it seriously was taking all the fun out of it.

"Look, I'm not in a place to want a full time relationship. Vince is only going to be here for another couple of months, tops. He's gorgeous, kisses like a dream, and is interesting to me even out of bed. I mean, we talked for hours. I need to experience some serious passion, and he seems to be a good candidate. Anyone else have any other prospects for me to consider?"

DK came to stand in front of the women, one hand on a hip and the other gesturing broadly to encompass all of El Dorado County. She realized that this whole discussion was getting to sound more ridiculous by the minute, but now that she was in it, she felt suddenly committed. Her decision was made. She needed to figure out what piece of her passionate make-up was missing. And she knew that Vince would be just the man to help her figure it out.

Tess finally seemed to find her voice. "DK, it isn't that I don't agree with you on all counts. He's a good looking guy and he's into you based on what you've described, no doubt about it. But do you really think, I mean really think," she emphasized, "that you're going to experience that kind of passion with a friend with benefits?" She put the label in air quotes.

Good question. But somehow, DK thought she knew the answer. "No one's lit up my fire like this in – well, in forever. Maybe forever, period. Or maybe I'm just extra needy right now, it being a long dry spell and all. Whatever it is, I'm game if he is. I just need to know how to approach him."

*****

"Love the article, Vinnie, just love it." Cassidy paced his make-do office with his cell phone in hand while Randy's voice boomed through the Bluetooth in his ear. "That old guy, what's his name, Thomas – he must be a real character." A chuckle followed, and then the sound of clacking keys.

"Focus, man, I really need you to focus." Cassidy was frustrated and wanted to grab Randy by the front of his $300 shirt right through the phone. He needed some advice, and since this was his supposed best friend he was talking to, he hoped to get some honest feedback.

The clacking continued. "Randy, damn it, step away from the keyboard and listen to me!"

The keys fell quiet. "Okay, sorry man. Didn't know this was a national emergency! What's up?"

Cassidy sighed and tried to steady his nerves. "I told you." Honestly, did the guy listen to him, ever? "I met a very interesting woman here. An artist who works in metal. DK McGiven, we talked about her, remember? She's really great at what she does. And she's very attractive. I'm interested."

He waited, still pacing. Randy wasn't responding, but at least he wasn't typing.

"Did you fucking hear me? I said I'm interested in her." He was trying not to shout, though he wondered if the connection was still working since things had gotten so quiet.

Randy finally harrumphed at the end of the phone. "And you need me to say, what? Congratulations? You find an interesting woman in every city, if you don't mind me saying so, and often in between stops too if you know what I mean. None of them ever mean a thing. So what do you want me to do, put another mark on the tote board?"

Cassidy felt himself getting defensive, but what Randy said was true. He wasn't necessarily proud of how women seemed to latch on to him no matter what country he was in, but it was the way things were. He was careful never to make any promises, and he was equally careful to use a condom without fail so that there were no little versions of himself running around the planet. And he took himself off to the doctor regularly to make sure he wasn't picking up any strange diseases along the way.

So why was this any different? Damn, this town and its laid-back acceptance of life was getting to him. He was becoming a little too comfortable in his routine here. Usually his bags were packed and he was off to another lifestyle spot and new assignment long before any settled feeling had a chance to grow roots.

He stopped pacing. "Listen, she's different from other women I've, ah, dated." The fact that he would consider he and DK dating at all was different. "It's just that. She's petite and Irish, or at least her parents were, and the art she creates is incredible. I like her stories, and we have some things in common to talk about."

God, even to his own ears he sounded pathetic. On instinct, he headed a different direction.

"When I leave, I know she'll be disappointed, but those are the rules of the game. My game, my rules. Just friends with benefits while I'm here. That's all."

He wasn't sure who he was trying to convince, Randy or himself.

He could hear his buddy breathing on the other end of the line. Cassidy was beginning to think this was a really bad idea. After all, Randy had been divorced three times, had used his couch for more than seating space in his office, and was currently dating a model who was barely legal age. She looked good on his arm, but Cassidy doubted that they ever had conversations about anything that dipped deeper than her cleavage. Any forthcoming advice was bound to be a problem.

Randy started typing at his end of the line again. "Look, Vinnie, who am I to give you advice on women? I'm lucky they like my money because I don't have what you've got in the looks department. I'm an agent, I can get them gigs and I control some nice purse strings. But I hate to travel, hate to leave New York and barely ever leave my office for that matter. I'm not the one to be asking for relationship advice." He paused. "Maybe write to Dear Abby instead, ya know?"

Cassidy considered grabbing the Bluetooth out of his ear and hurling it across the room, then stomping on it where it landed. He knew he was taking a risk trying to get any help from Randy. But he was unsettled and he felt like he had no one he could talk to about this.

The distance he'd designed into his life and the lack of close friends other than Randy suddenly seemed like a very bad idea. He didn't do relationships, didn't do friendships. He thought of the distance between his parents and wondered if he'd ever find some good role models to follow in that department. No one stuck around or stuck close together in his world.

This was all so different, strange in a way that had nothing to do with being in a new place. If it was just that, he was used to it. Hell, he was in a new city nearly every week or month. He met new people, new women, all the time. Rarely did any of them capture his attention for more than a couple of nights. It was the way he was wired. No strings, no attachments, no commitments.

And he liked his life this way, right?

He heard Randy sigh on the other side of the country. "Look, Vinnie, I asked you before and I'll say it again. Be nice to her, okay?"

What was this nice to her shit? Clearly Randy was working an angle, probably trying to become her agent and rep her around the world. But that wasn't Cassidy's problem, now was it?

Cursing again, he filled the line across the country with a string of colorful language. Randy laughed. "That's my boy! Come on, you're only there for a few more weeks, right? Get a feel for the place, turn out a few more terrific articles like you've sent me already, and wrap things up. If you meet a few willing women, the kind you usually date, along the way, so be it."

The implication was clear. But not DK. Screw him.

The forced joviality coming through the phone was grating. "You'll be home in time to enjoy all of the holiday craziness, the decorations, the ho-ho-ho and presents and all. You know, the things you love to make fun of? All of the tourists gawking at the big tree at Rockefeller Center and the people falling down on the ice rink and the leggy Rockettes? You'll feel better in no time!"

Holidays at home. Cassidy stopped and looked around the small rental house, comparing it to the stark condo he inhabited whenever he was in New York. The differences were blatant. Where his condo was stripped down, devoid of personal touches and signs of him, this little house was full of charm and a sense of place. Copies of faded photos on the wall represented what Flynn's Crossing had looked like over the decades since it had been founded at the beginning of the Gold Rush. Other photos and some drawings and paintings depicted rural scenes that he already recognized from the area.

The house was warm, just like the people here were. It all made you feel accepted, invited you to stay a while and put up your feet, engage in a long round of story-telling about the history of everyone in town.

His condo, on the other hand, invited you in for a drink, made polite conversation and then handed you your coat in short order. Or dragged you off to the bedroom for some quick release before sending you out the door.

That was the problem, Cassidy realized with another curse. He was getting drawn into this little town and its surrounding region, the warmth of the people, the stories that were everywhere, just waiting for the telling. He wanted to dig deeper into the place, and he wanted to dive deeper into one of its charming inhabitants in particular.

Chapter 21

She had been more adventuresome in the past two weeks than she'd been in ages, DK thought. At least, she'd been a whole lot more forward in the relationship arena than she had been in ages, maybe in forever. And she liked it.

Vince called her for another date, and they'd taken a drive through the region to taste at some wineries that DK hadn't visited before. She'd brought a picnic from Roxy's and they'd spent a couple of hours arguing the merits of art mediums to represent various emotions to an audience. They hadn't agreed, but they'd agreed to disagree.

When he'd dropped her off, she'd taken the initiative to move in and wrap her arms around his neck, kissing him with more feeling than she even knew she had. She was ready to invite him in, ready to seduce him with whatever charms she could muster, when he'd set her away from him, tapped a finger on her nose, and said he'd call her the next day.

True to his word, he did, asking her for another date. They'd taken a drive to Lake Tahoe. They'd hiked to an outcropping of rocks that gave them a view of the whole lake, from casinos and hotels to the remote cliffs of wilderness and deep blue waters. Hawks keened overhead, and in the distance, the roar of motor boats competed with the wail of the wind. They'd had a heated discussion about the value of new development versus the need to maintain pristine wilderness. Vince didn't seem to have a strong opinion about it one way of the other, but he did appear to enjoy baiting her. When she got riled up about his apparent uncaring attitude, Vince had grabbed her and kissed her. When they'd come up for air, neither one of them cared about the discussion anymore.

DK fiddled with the flowers set on the patio table while she thought about the rest, the coffees and pastries Vince had brought her at the gallery on the days she'd been working. They'd taken a drive to Sacramento for a visit to an art museum and an early dinner at a new local hot spot. He'd surprised her with lunch at the studio one day, though he'd spent most of that meal eying Fusion with suspicion as the dog sat in front of him waiting for a hand out.

"You like him, don't you big boy?" DK gave the shaggy black head a good rub and the dog rolled over and presented his belly for continued attention. He made her laugh with his antics, and now was no exception.

"Come on, we don't have time right now. I want to make sure everything is ready." She headed for the kitchen with Fusion jumping to his paws and following.

Since nothing she'd done so far seemed to be moving the relationship along on a physical plain, DK had called in the girl tribe for reinforcements. At a quick breakfast meet-up, she'd laid out her proposal.

She needed help in figuring out how to seduce Vince into her bed.

After the teasing laughter had died down, Roxy looked at Serena, who frowned. Serena turned to Tess, who shrugged. Tess looked at Marguerite, and their smiles were suddenly too broad and too knowing. Marguerite looked at Gabby, who turned back to DK with way too much eagerness.

"I think we can get you on track, girlfriend. Between us, we've got all the skills and prerequisites to help you set up a night he's always going to remember. You'll knock him back on that bed in no time!" And with that, she raised her coffee mug in a toast to DK's future success. Then she quieted a bit. "Of course, what happens after that is up to you."

She had to appreciate everything her friends had done to stage her house for her big seduction scene tonight. She was tired of waiting for Vince to make the next move, though every time they wrapped themselves around each other, his desire for her was obvious. If she waited any longer, he'd be ready to leave.

Tess had done the flowers, providing a bouquet for the living room, a smaller low presentation for the patio table where they'd eat, and a couple of subtle fragrant sprays for the bedroom. Serena found books on the area, since Vince always seemed to be intrigued by the history and stories of the people who settled the region. And she'd throw in a couple of current guide books, new copies that DK intended to give to Vince so that he could continue his solo explorations. Marguerite coordinated their wines with their meal, with a promise that the bubbly by itself would be enough to make him DK's slave.

It was Gabby and Roxy who'd really knocked themselves out, though. Gabby had insisted on new towels for the bath and racier sheets for the bed.

"Really, isn't that a little... obvious?" DK had stared at the pale green satin as it flowed out of the packaging. Gabby's full grin had gotten even wider.

"What's wrong with a little satin among friends with benefits? It will feel sensuous, and he'll know you're serious. Besides, you deserve it!"

Now the bedroom did look like a boudoir, the pale green a nice offset to the cream colored walls and deeply shaded brocade drapes left open on the loft's windows. Candles were set on every level surface, ready to light at the right moment. And even now, DK could smell the light scents of Tess's small flowers overflowing the vases.

Gabby hadn't stopped there, insisting on taking DK shopping for a filmy cream sundress that complimented the bedroom display. She had planned to wear a fancier white t-shirt and her usual denim shorts, but she'd been overridden by her friends on this too. They all agreed that she needed to dress up a bit, maybe even bother with some make-up, and to that end, she'd spent the last hour with Gabby fussing her hair and adding eyeliner and other touches of color to, as she had put it, "...accentuate your already great positives – those big green eyes and that terrific red hair!"

Something else drew her inside, and it was the savory aromas coming from the oven. Roxy had outdone herself, and she'd prepared an amazing round of appetizers that were heating right now. A light salad of local greens and flowers sat in the fridge, along with a luscious dessert that she had encouraged DK to "...share, like you know, feed each other, and maybe not use silverware either." It would be much more fun that way, she had been assured, forcing them to sit closer together.

Like they ever needed an excuse for that.

DK thought back to the many kisses she and Vince had now shared. In her opinion, each one was getting better that the last, and the evening they'd spent draped over each other in the front seat of the convertible after the Sacramento trip had been particularly hot. His hands tracing her breasts through her shirt had almost sent her up in flames. She'd felt her own need sizzle along nerve endings that were in serious jeopardy of fraying, and by the erection she could tell Vince was sporting, she got the feeling he wouldn't need much encouragement to move their relationship along.

Still, a hint of insecurity popped up. If he was as hot for her as she was for him, what was he waiting for? Or did his body have a physical reaction but he really wasn't into her that much? He kept calling, kept going out with her. Why did he keep pulling back when she clearly sent signals that she wanted to move forward?

At least she thought she was sending the right signals. She wasn't sure.

Tonight was not the time for doubts or she'd sabotage the whole effect herself, DK realized. Yes, the stage was set, and the leading lady was all costumed up, just waiting for the leading man to arrive. Now if she could only get her lines right...

*****

The twenty-minute ride from town to DK's place seemed to be taking a whole lot longer today, Cassidy fumed. He'd run into traffic in town as he'd left, weekend folks starting to make their way up the hill to enjoy the apple farms and wineries or on their way to Lake Tahoe. He'd stopped at the flower shop, Buds and Blooms, which he knew was owned by one of DK's close friends. The striking Native American woman, Tess, had helped him pick out a live plant that she assured him would be a great selection as a hostess gift of sorts. She'd eyed him with what he thought was speculation and the humor of some hidden joke, but then he shook it off, thinking he was being overly sensitive.

He was prickly again today, a feeling that seemed to be with him more often than not most days recently. He didn't like the pull he was feeling towards DK, and it made him angry to think that she could be something more than only a fling. He'd never waited this long to get a woman into bed, but for some reason, he kept telling himself he didn't need to rush it, that he had weeks yet before he left town.

Weeks to go, but most days it wasn't feeling like long enough. Something was changing, and he wasn't sure he liked it. He felt this need to take care of DK, and this caretaking urge was getting harder to shake each time he touched her. He was protecting her, waiting until she was ready, he assured himself.

Even Randy remarked on it. "You got a new voice going here, my boy, and I'm telling you, some of the review group likes it." He'd gone on to comment on the expansive story lines, the human interest, greater depth and history that was bleeding through what had previously been superficial venue reviews.

"They're eating it up! Course, some of them are complaining too – saying the old Cassidy who could spit nails has gone all soft and wimpy, but most of 'em love it!"

Maybe that was it, Cassidy thought. He was getting soft on a woman and soft in the head, soft on the little town and its friendly inhabitants too.

He hit the steering wheel and pushed his foot further to the floor, the curving two-lane road almost forcing the car up on two wheels. He wasn't sure what kind of sign he was waiting for, or even why he was waiting. The other day after their Sac trip, he wanted her so badly, but he wasn't willing to get out of the car and walk with her through the door to her house to seal the deal. What the hell was up with that?

Now he didn't want to wait any longer, and he thought that DK was as willing as he was to move their relationship to the next level, the one where they both got naked and horizontal and enjoyed exploring each other for hours on end.

Relationship. That was the word that he got him. He didn't think he wanted a relationship. He wanted the sex, but that's as far as it would go. He was leaving in a few weeks and she needed to realize that, not get stuck on him like he was sure that she would.

Trouble was, he was the one getting stuck, damn it. He'd already agreed to an additional month on his lease, staying now past Thanksgiving. He'd told himself it was so that he could get a chance to explore a few more places for the series of articles that seemed to be coming up so fast that he could barely get one out before the next demanded his attention.

He'd been seduced by the region. There was so much to write about here that he doubted even a year would be enough to tell all the stories he knew were waiting, willing and eager for his consideration.

But even more, he was seduced by Red.

He hit the steering wheel again and swore out loud, shocked at the vehemence in his voice. It was all pulling him in, DK and the town, and he didn't like it one bit. He needed to take control of his situation again. He needed to go back to being the bad boy with the cruel tone that was his writing voice, the guy who could have sex with a different woman in every city, seven nights a week. Tonight, he'd show DK who he really was and set down the rules for the rest of his visit.

Chapter 22

"Okay, I have to admit that dinner was amazing. Your friend Roxy definitely knows how to cook."

DK allowed herself a mental high five at the choice to have her seduction dinner catered instead of cooking herself. Other than grilling the seasoned steaks and portabella mushrooms, she'd given in to the offer and she was glad that she had. She was an okay cook for basic meals, but Roxy was a genius chef, and for a world-traveled guy like Vince to be sitting back, hands on stomach and eyes half closed with compliments flowing off his tongue, caving was so worth it.

"We should go there some time. It's not far. It's pretty busy right now because it's in every guidebook and linked to so many great reviews that every visitor to town wants to try it. The locals love it too."

His eyes popped open again when she'd mentioned the reviews. Hadn't he said he wrote occasional reviews too? Maybe he didn't want to go. He'd feel obligated to write something nice.

She backtracked, suddenly a little nervous again. "No pressure, though. You don't have to review the place. Roxy won't expect anything from you."

Vince got up to pace the length of the patio, staring down at the pool for a few moments before raising his gaze to the clouds that were gathering in the sunset and out to the big oaks spaced in the fields. He didn't say anything, but she could feel the zing of energy radiating from him. She'd stepped in it bringing up work, she thought. This wasn't leading down the road to seduction. She was reminding him about why he'd come to town in the first place.

DK busied herself picking up the dishes. He still hadn't moved, watching the movement of the clouds coming up from the southwest, coloring brilliantly with the setting sun. Rainy season was almost here, and the weather prognosticators were dancing with excitement over the possibility of waves of wet tomorrow. She thought of his little convertible, sitting open to the elements in her driveway. He'd left the top down, but maybe he didn't plan on staying long enough to worry about the interior getting soaked. That thought led to feelings of disappointment.

Stacking the plates in the dishwasher inside, she felt her confidence deflating. Vince told her some fun new stories as they'd eaten, things he'd discovered about some of the town's early bawdy inhabitants. They'd laughed, and then his gaze had fallen serious and intent, like he was trying to read something important in her expression. They'd eaten in silence after that.

Why was she so willing to let him take the lead? She was an accomplished artist, a woman with her own successful business, independent and completely capable of making her own decisions. There was no reason she had to wait for him to catch up. She planned to seduce him tonight, expecting to find the passion she wanted to fill those voids inside of her. Why was she so willing to step back and wait for the first sign from him?

DK knew he wouldn't wait if he was interested. He'd swoop in and take what he wanted. It was evident in his stories about his life. She knew he was interested, even if it was only a physical reaction. But that's all she wanted, right? She wanted an exciting and passionate fling to satisfy her curiosity and feed that creative part of her that she felt still missed something.

She squared her shoulders. The stage was set for this seduction, and damn it, he was going to get seduced, like it or not. And where the hell was he, anyway?

*****

DK had been gone for the past few minutes, and he could hear her through the open windows clinking dishes in the kitchen. The clouds seemed to be building, but there had been some debate on whether or not they meant the beginning of the rainy season. Some of the old timers said that all the signs were there. The woolly caterpillars' stripes meant that it would be a long, cold and snowy winter, starting early, maybe even before Thanksgiving. Few relied on the televised weather predictions that cautioned the rain would probably miss the area completely.

The top was down on his convertible. He wondered what kind of message it would send if he put the top up and closed the windows. Would DK see that as an expectation on his part?

That prickly feeling was back, setting up the hairs on his neck and making him antsy. He wasn't sure he liked this sense of hesitant expectation. It made him nervous, and damn it, he was never nervous. He was always in control. He called the shots. He wanted, and when he wanted, he took what he wanted.

It was time to lay down those rules and let DK know how it was going to be. They'd take each other to bed and enjoy the friends with benefits options over the next few weeks, and then he'd be gone. It made him feel better to believe he could set things on the right path.

He'd close up the car, then he'd go inside and find DK, and give her the plan. The sun colored the clouds orange and magenta, and he took a moment to tuck a description into his memory for an upcoming article. Then he spun around, so intent on his direction and his own thoughts that he nearly ran into the huge black beast that blocked his path.

Fusion sat on the patio between him and the house, watching him with what Cassidy thought was suspicion. It stopped him. Fusion opened his big mouth in what Cassidy hoped was a grin. There were lots of teeth in there. DK had insisted that the dog was a lover, not a fighter. Right now, though, he looked pretty intent on taking a piece out of Cassidy's flesh if he made a wrong move.

It was silly, Cassidy knew, to be afraid of a dog, especially a Lab that played with little boys and swooned onto his back for a belly rub whenever DK was close by. But the dog wasn't moving. He was eying the man in front of him with the same speculative gaze that Cassidy was sure people use when they regarded the selection at the butcher's counter.

"Ah, good dog." The dog's tail flicked in a wag, then stopped when Cassidy tried to move forward. "Good dog, good doggy. I'm just going to go close up my car, okay boy? Just need to button it up in case it rains, okay Fusion?" The dog wagged when he talked, but stopped and showed off more teeth whenever the man tried to move.

If he wasn't sure he was looking into the jaws of death, Cassidy would be laughing at himself. He was talking to a dog, explaining what he was going to do and why. He was trying to reason – with a dog.

*****

Minutes passed, and with each second, DK felt her fire banking hotter. Vince was just going to stand outside and expect her to clean everything up, then what – come outside and sit on his lap meekly waiting for his next move. No way!

She glanced out the window at the bright colors of the sunset, aligned so closely with the flames of anger that were licking up her insides. Deciding to ride on those waves rather than think herself out of the mood, she spun out of the French doors to the patio and saw Vince standing at the end of the patio, Fusion sitting not far away. He seemed to be talking to the dog.

"I think it's time, don't you?" DK didn't want to second-guess herself and brushed by the dog to stand in front of Vince. He looked relieved, and she had a fleeting thought that she should try to figure out why, but the anger was stronger. Her voice came out louder than she intended.

"We've walked on eggshells around each other for the past few weeks, Vince, and I for one am tired of it. Let's just acknowledge the pull we have for each other and act on it. I'm ready. Are you?"

Then she didn't wait for a reply. She registered the surprise on his face as she grabbed his hair and pulled his mouth down to her. Fusion gave a happy yip, but the sound of it was lost on her in the quick fire of the moment.

She didn't give Vince a chance to respond to her question, any opportunity to say no. She worked her lips over his and used her tongue to trace the seam until he opened his mouth to her. His arms came around her in a strong vise and he lifted her to fit her more tightly to him.

This was what she wanted, DK realized, this heat with sparks flying, uncaring about what was igniting around them. It was just the two of them, the pull so strong that there was no way to separate them.

She buried her fingers in his hair, loving the rough bristly texture against her skin. The scrape of his teeth on her tongue, the thrill of nerve endings on fire when he moved from her mouth to nip at her neck, banked the flames even higher. They would be consumed, she realized, and it didn't matter.

He pulled her higher against him, and she felt his hardening erection press against her middle. The big double chaise was only a few steps away. The bedroom was too far right now, too many steps that required them to separate and walk. She wasn't sure she could navigate those few paces, her legs feeling shaky and unsteady.

"The chaise," she whispered, wondering if he could even hear her. He had a tight grip on her, pulled so close that she could feel each fast breath he drew in and the quick hard beat of his heart. His scent, the woodsy aroma with some underlying tang that she'd come to think of as uniquely Vince, wrapped itself around her.

He pulled back and looked at her face. "We need a bed, not a chair." His voice was raspy, catching on rough pants of air. His eyes were so aroused that DK shivered. Fire licked at the edges as he stared at her.

Vince released her only long enough to slide down his body, tucking her tightly against his side and turning them to the doors to the house. "Which way?"

Chapter 23

DK couldn't speak, so she pointed the way past the living room and up to the big loft of her bedroom. Proud of herself for not stumbling, she pulled him up the stairs. The candles hadn't been lit, and she didn't care. The last bright radiance of the sunset shown through the windows, but she didn't think Vince noticed. She barely registered it herself, so caught up in the almost desperate intention in his face that she had a difficult time drawing a breath.

His eyes were on her face, purpose and fire warring there with something that looked like uncertainty. Was she projecting her own trembling feelings to him? She shivered from the impact of it, unable to look away and suddenly unable to move. He raised a hand to cup her cheek, and she could swear he was shaking too.

He couldn't be as moved as she was, could he? It was like the torch she held in her hands almost every day. The blue flame was barely visible, and yet it could melt metal and mold it into something new. She felt like that blue flame was licking all around her.

She pulled his lips down to hers, and his hands were brushing down her back to cup her buttocks and pull her tight against him. There were too many layers of clothes between them, and she was sure they'd melt away, as hot as she was.

She put shaky hands to the buttons of his shirt, and his long fingers covered hers to stop her. He pulled back, hesitating. "Red, we need to talk."

It was the last thing she wanted, time to think and time to remember that this wasn't her way. He knew much more about this fine art of seduction than she did, she was sure of it. She didn't want to hear his arguments one way or the other.

She went back to work on the buttons. "No talking, just action," and she was proud that her voice didn't shake. In fact, she sounded strong and demanding, and the fire burned hotter, insistent on finding new fuel.

Vince's unwillingness was evident in the hard lines of his body and way he held his arms to his sides. After another moment of hesitation, his arms snaked around her and his mouth came down on hers again with a curse. She smiled into the kiss, knowing that she was driving him crazy. It made her feel reckless, the same heady kind of energy when metal was coming together exactly as she had envisioned it.

His hands were rougher now, more urgent and more insistent as they teased the sides of her breasts. He broke the kiss to pull on her earlobe with his teeth, then he gave her neck a soft bite.

"You're such a tender thing, so little that I have to remember I could devour you in a single bite." His words in her ear made her shiver, the heat she was feeling going straight to her core and making her wet. His mouth moved to her shoulder and he pushed aside the strap of her dress to nibble. His hands cupped her breasts through the sheer material, rubbing her nipples to full attention and then moving more urgently up to her shoulders.

She felt exhilarated, like she was on top of bonfire that would burn for hours. "We have too many clothes on," she breathed with a laugh cut short to a gasp as he bent to put his mouth on one taut nipple through the material.

"Damn it, where's the zipper on this thing?" There was no hesitation now. He was unrelenting, and she felt a new surge of power at how fast and far she was driving him. She laughed and stepped back, reaching to push down the stretchy fabric. His eyes were burning hot on her, and he stepped forward to cover her hands, taking over with such authority that she felt more needy than before.

"Turnabout's fair play," she said and stepped deeper into his embrace to return to the buttons on his shirt. Now she was the one shaking in anticipation. Soon she had the material open and ran her hands over the light chest hairs that narrowed down his stomach and disappeared into the straining jeans. She loved the feel of him, the bristle of coarse hairs an echo of the styled cut on his head. He sucked in hard when her hands wandered to the button on his jeans and she felt the quiver of his muscles contracting under her fingers.

God, what energy there was in this soaring feeling! Her mind was emptying, her senses surrounding her with the unique heady aroma of aroused male that was Vince, and the exhilarating touch of his hands on her everywhere. His skin was smooth and rough at the same time, and her palms tingled as they ran over the muscles that held such strength and promise.

Her dress was past her hips now, and he knelt in front of her to push it down her legs. His mouth nibbled at her hip and she felt herself sway. His hands came around to grip her buttocks and he nipped playfully at the waist of her lacy panties. When he finally stood up, his eyes were alight with mischief as they roamed over her.

"You don't look like a welder," he growled, his voice as rough and demanding as his hands. Then he cupped her face and dove in for a deep kiss.

When his mouth wandered to her neck, she gasp out, "And you don't look like a travel writer."

And he didn't, DK realized. For a man who was a self-proclaimed hater of exercise, his body was lean, muscled and fit. She wanted to see all of him, run her hands and her lips down the length of him and let the fire consume them both.

"Jeans," she said, not wasting words as his mouth teased her nipples again through her bra. She cupped his erection to make her point, and he lifted his eyes to stare hard at her, cursing again. His reaction to her boldness made her smile.

He stepped back, his arms straight to hold her at a distance. His gaze wandered over her and where it touched her, DK could swear she could feel the sizzling burn of it. Then his eyes were staring into hers again and she saw some of his hesitancy returned.

"Red, are you sure? Sure this is what you want?"

She couldn't understand him at first. Wasn't she almost burning the place down with this feverish heat? He was as consumed as she was, she could see the evidence of that. So what was the problem?

She cleared her throat and tried to speak, but the words were stuck on a tongue that was suddenly dry with anticipation. Yes, she wanted him, even knowing he was leaving and already sensing that it would be oh-so-hard to feel okay about letting him go. The past few weeks had brought them close on all the levels that didn't involved sex, and it was time. She swallowed again and shook her head yes with certainty, hands coming up to run along his arms in slow caresses.

Something seemed to snap in him then. He cursed repeatedly, but his arms dropped and he stopped fighting her. Stepping back, he slid down the zipper and stepped out of his jeans in one easy movement.

She had two seconds to admire the size and length of him, and then he pulled her close again, seeking out the clasp of her bra and getting rid of it in an instant. DK pulled his mouth down and walked backwards until she felt the bed behind her knees.

"No more talking. Action." She fell back on the bed, pulling him with her. She needed something to quench the fire that was raging through her, something to satisfy her throbbing core and fill her.

He seemed to lose all interest in whatever he had wanted to say as her hands wandered to his throbbing erection. She rubbed the tip through his briefs and his breath hissed out. Her body was waiting for him, and she pushed up restlessly, the invitation nothing conscious in her mind but a movement driven by her desire alone. His fingers pushed roughly at the lace elastic of her panties. She lifted her hips to help him pull them off, and dimly realized that he'd thrown them someplace across the room as he fell on top of her hungrily.

It was probably a good thing the candles weren't burning.

His hands were rough and demanding now, as driven as she was. She felt a sense of triumph as his fingers pressed into her wetness and her body involuntarily curled upward to meet him. Vince's control seemed to be slipping as fast as hers. His hand cupped her mound and he snarled again, putting his lips to a nipple as he rhythmically worked her core.

She felt the orgasm rising like a flash fire inside her. It was so fast, too soon, and she wanted this to last for hours. But her body was adamant.

Vince's mouth came to her lips. "Let go," he whispered before his tongue dove between her teeth to ravage her mouth again. His fingers were resolute, teasing and tormenting her incessantly until there was only the incredible tightness and sense of standing at the edge of a very high cliff, waiting to drop.

His lips moved to her neck and he bit gently. "Let go, Red," he said again, his raspy voice now more demanding.

And let go she did. It was like a volcano, something extinct and brought back to life. She'd never felt like this before, even in those moments when she thought she knew intense satisfaction. Vince's hand stayed on her, continuing his insistent motions until she fell back on the bed and melted into a mindless puddle.

She should move, DK thought dimly. She should return the favor. She wanted to get her hands on him, have him experience the same kind of mind-emptying release that she had. For now, though, her bones were molten, and she could barely move her eyelids, much less lift an arm.

Her breathing finally slowed and she opened her eyes to find Vince eying her warily. His hand was on her breast, but it wasn't moving. His watchfulness made her feel a little self-conscious.

"I need to get something," he said finally. She gave him a puzzled look. He was decidedly uncomfortable, she realized.

"Get something?" She wasn't sure she'd heard him right. What did he need at a time like this? Her hand wandered to him, and she felt his throbbing erection through his briefs. He had everything he needed right here.

Then it dawned on her. She smiled and reached across the bed to a small cloisonné box on the nightstand, silently thanking Gabby for her brilliance in discretion. Flipping it open, she pulled out a condom and held it up in front of him.

"Is this what you need?"

She wasn't sure why he looked so surprised, but she decided to go with the energy she felt rising again and be bold. She pulled his mouth down for a teasing kiss, her hands busy at the waist of his briefs. He pushed them away and got rid of the last clothing between them.

Taking the wrapper out of her hand and ripping it open, he got over whatever was bothering him as he suited up and pulled her more fully underneath him. In seconds, he was between her legs but pulled back once more. "You're so petite," he started, and she raised a finger to his lips. He pushed it away. "I don't want to hurt you. I feel like even this," he raised his hand, held snugly around her wrist, "will leave you with bruises."

"I'll be fine," she assured him. She was ready again, ready to take the full length of him inside her and experience that joining that would take their passion to new heights.

And she knew it would be passion. This was much more than sex. It was a meeting of their minds that she could see as she stared into his eyes. Those brown depths still held some concern, something he probably wanted to share with her when he'd stopped them before. But they could talk later.

DK lifted her hips in invitation, running fingers down Vince's face and along his lips. He bit down on her thumb, and the sensation created a new zap of energy to her core. His mouth came down to tease one nipple, then the other. His hands were gentle now as he traced her body, seeming to memorize her muscles much the same way she had his. Time stood still, and the sensuous feeling that overcame her left any concept of its passing hazy and unimportant.

He finally lifted his head. "I want you, more than I've wanted any woman in a very long time." His voice was gruff, and his dark eyes bored into hers. He shifted, teasing her with the tip of his length at her opening.

"I want you too, more than I've wanted anything in a very long time." DK shifted to take him in further, feeling herself expand in that lovely stretch that meant filling and fulfillment. He reached a hand between then to play with her again. Her legs came up of their own volition to grasp his hips and pull him closer as she gasp at the multiple waves of sensation. Her hands traced down his belly to the base of his erection as he pressed into her, each inch another layer of incredible pleasure.

He braced his long length over her on strong arms, lips coming down to tease hers as he set a quickening pace. She traced the tense features of his face. Every thrust brought him deeper, and that sense of almost desperate tenseness rose in her again. He pulled back, keeping them joined and maintaining the urgent rhythm.

"Diane, I..." he started, then seemed to catch himself. He held her eyes with his, and increased the pounding rhythm instead. DK couldn't look away, didn't want to, lost in the depths of chocolate brown that had gone wide and intense. Her legs were wrapped tightly around his hips, meeting him stroke for stroke, her own fire banked so high that she was surprised that the room wasn't in flames.

Her hands caressed his neck, straining with his building tension. The pace he set had her bound up in a knot so strong that she felt she might never break free. She wanted it to last forever but knew that there was no way she could bear it.

"Vince." She sighed his name in the wonder of it. Their eyes stayed locked together, and in that final instant, he tightened and bucked over her just as her own orgasm sent her flying again.

Chapter 24

There was a soft steady sound at a distance, and another more rhythmic and insistent one closer by. Cassidy wasn't sure what either one of them was, and he was too sated and content to care anyway.

His hand still cupped a small breast, what Marie Antoinette would have considered a perfect champagne glass shape, he mused. He wondered what dark recess of his brain that little factoid had come from. Yes, DK's body was the perfect description of what was expected of ladies who enjoyed their pleasure back in old Marie's time.

He smiled as he thought of all of the pleasure the two of them had enjoyed last night. That first climb for the both of them together had left him with ears that were ringing and a fierce need to pull DK against him and hold on for a long time. He'd been unwilling to let her loose, his arms tight around her as he finally rolled them both and held her close to his heaving heart.

She started to speak a couple of times, and both times, he'd covered her mouth with his until any thought of talking was long gone. He knew he should say something, lay down the rules, get things out in the open and an agreement set between them. He was suddenly leery of doing it, unwilling to break the novel contentment he felt.

This wasn't him. He liked to get his kicks, leaving the lady plenty happy as well, and then roll over, dress and head out the door. Or point the lady to the door, depending. The urge to cuddle closer to DK and run a hand through her hair until he'd laid all of those crazy curls straight was new to him. New and scary. Running fingers along her silky skin was enough to mesmerize him for hours.

They slept, and he'd wakened to find her hands roaming over him. She'd lit the candles around the room, and in their glow, her hair was like red flames. It made the green of her eyes even more intense, fired as they were when she was rising to a climax. The small sly grin that played at her lips told him she was enjoying her exploration, and his answering smile must have given her whatever encouragement she needed to let her hands become even more bold.

He'd learned so much about what pleased her in such a short time, what teased her until she begged and what made her writhe with pleasure. She'd driven him to a fine edge of distraction too, so desperate to have her that he'd flipped her off him and pinned her, letting his mouth roam even as he held her hands still. He'd settled on the apex of her thighs and stroked and sucked until she'd levitated off the bed beneath him. Then he'd quickly donned another condom and entered her in one fast stoke before the quivers of her climax had even subsided.

She was such a little thing, and he was surprised that the size of him didn't disturb her. The feel of her around him was like a tight fist, and even now, the thought of it was making him hard again, after what, three times last night? He wasn't sure if there had been some kind of aphrodisiac in last night's dinner or if it was just Red that was driving him.

Cassidy pulled her closer, tucking her head into his shoulder and marveling at how well they fit together. She was a good foot shorter than him, and yet they fit like two pieces of a puzzle. Like they were meant to be.

He started. He didn't like that direction of thinking. A couple of times last night he'd wanted to stop her, stop the pace of their intimacy because they hadn't set any boundaries. A playmate, that's what he wanted. Right? He was going to be gone in a few weeks.

Why did that idea suddenly depress him? He never got tied down, never let any woman lure him into the comfort that could mean longer term commitment and, god forbid, domesticity. He wanted to be footloose, ready to head out at any moment for a new adventure, a new assignment. What he didn't want was hearth and home and enjoying only one woman for all time forward, even if the pleasure she was bringing him was beyond anything he'd imagined he'd find.

He should have been angry, but instead, he felt confused. DK seemed to have it all together. The puzzles of last night didn't add up to the woman he thought he'd been getting to know. She'd been demanding, insistent in grabbing him and hauling him off to her satin-covered bed. The condoms in the fancy box by the bed – so convenient. Did she do this all the time? She'd challenged him with her words and with her body. And she'd made it pretty clear that she wanted him without ever expressing a single word of commitment or care.

He shifted uncomfortably. She sounded an awful lot like him, he realized, and that did make him mad. She was supposed to be better than this. She had standards, and she shouldn't be taking just anyone to bed, particularly him. It was such a contrast to the woman he thought he knew, the beguiling woman who had such passion for her art and commitment to those she cared about.

And innocence. He didn't think he could be so wrong about that, but last night had him questioning his understanding. He thought DK was a woman who wanted the whole white picket fence fairy tale. Hell, deserved it as well as expected it. But he was leaving in the near future and she knew it, damn it, and there were no commitments coming up on either side of this relationship.

Like before, the word stopped him. What in his brain kept bringing that up? She wasn't asking for a relationship. Why did he keep thinking about it?

His hand wandered lower to the curls that covered her mound, red as the hair on her head and equally intriguing when lit by last night's candles. He thought about her cries of passion during the night as his mouth had teased her there. He had been unrelenting until she had begged him to fill her. He'd obliged, finding his release as she had come yet again. She was too uninhibited to be an innocent, and the idea made his blood heat.

Uncertain or not, angry or not, he wanted her again already. He opened an eye to try to gauge the time.

The light in the room was low, a bright gray that he couldn't read as any distinct hour. The distant noise had become more insistent. The closer one was the same. He opened his other eye to try to figure out what was happening around them.

And came eyeball to eyeball with a big black face and grinning fangs that were incredibly white.

Things came back to him in a flash. Fusion sat next to the bed, watching him with a wide grin that could mean he was happy to see him in his mistress's bed – or that he was happy to have Cassidy as a quick snack if he so much as moved. The close up noise was now easy to identify, his easy panting now joined by the brush of his tail on the floor, wagging and delighted to see someone paying attention.

Cassidy lifted his head and squinted out of the windows. The distant sound was now more like a torrent, and he swore as he realized that the semi-promised rain was indeed pouring down outside. And pouring into the seats of his convertible, sitting with its top down out in the driveway.

He vaulted out of bed, forgetting the fierceness of Fusion's teeth in the rush to find his jeans and his keys. The jeans were easy, left in a pile where he'd pushed them off so urgently the night before.

His keys, where had he left them? He had a vague memory of his jacket on the back of a chair in the kitchen. Yanking on the jeans alone and heading down the stairs without even bothering to zip up, he spotted the denim and dove for the pocket. Fusion was now happily barking at his heels, delighted with this new game of play.

He pulled open the front door and stopped, taking in the rain that was coming down in sheets between him and the car. It must have been raining for a while because there were big puddles covering the ground. The car looked forlorn sitting open to the elements, its insides soaked.

Fusion barked again and ran past him, stretching his front paws out in front and his head down, tail up in the air and wagging, ready to see what Cassidy would do next.

"You could have warned me, you know?" Fusions yipped and wagged harder, then leaped up and ran in short circles, whirling around in place like he couldn't wait for someone to join him in the fun of the soaking rain.

Cassidy looked at the sky. It clearly wasn't going to stop anytime soon, the slate clouds seeming to go on for miles. The car was already a mess, and he grimaced as he thought about the explanations he would have to make at the rental car counter now. Still, maybe it wasn't too bad yet, and maybe he could clean it up if he got it covered soon.

Fusion was now running around the car, uncaring that his shaggy body was now slick with the wet. "You stay there, okay?"

God, he was talking to the dog again.

Zipping his jeans and putting the ignition key in his fingers, Cassidy sprinted to the driver's door and opened it. He had a brief regret that he hadn't thought to put on his jacket, because the rain was freezing on his chest and back. Gravel pinched his bare feet and the puddles were icy on his toes. He was so distracted that he didn't think about the consequences when he dropped down into the flooded seat. Glacially cold and deep enough to soak through his jeans in an instant, the puddle made him think that any fire he felt for Red would be quenched for quite a while as everything shrank to hide inside the denim.

The trill of laughter a split second later shocked him almost as much as the drench of water. He looked over at the front door to see DK framed there, wearing his button-down shirt and holding her middle in hysterics at the sight of him. He grudgingly realized the picture he must make. The rain had already slicked down his hair, and the act of sitting in the seat had displaced a large splash of water, at least what hadn't ended up soaking through his jeans.

She stood just out of the drops, holding on to the doorframe to steady herself as he kept watching her. He put the key into the ignition and started the car with as much dignity as he could muster given the situation, and raised the convertible's top. Then he pressed the buttons to raise the electric windows. Still she laughed, the green of her dancing eyes evident even from this distance.

Fusion ran between the two of them, barking happily. Cassidy stepped out of the car, gently closing the front door of the soaked car. He could feel the water run down his legs from the butt of his jeans, and the unceasing rain was making him shiver with cold. Still, he took his time. Just to make a point, he locked the car before walking with careful slow steps to keep the gravel from causing his feet permanent damage.

DK had a hand over her mouth, but it did little to contain her laughter. Cassidy stopped in front of her.

"So you think this is funny, do you?" He tried for a solemn and stern tone. "Well, let's see how you like it."

And he grabbed her, pulling her out into the rain as peals of laughter burst from her again and the dog's joyous bark rang through the downpour.

Chapter 25

Pulling DK into the downpour with him had effectively drenched almost all of his available clothes, and while Cassidy could complain about this, he liked the vision of her with his shirt clinging to her every curve in the rain. When he finally released her mouth and let her slide to the ground, she was as soaked as he was. She shoved some too-small flip-flops at him and told him to pull the car into her studio, and ran ahead of him to open the double doors to the old barn.

There the rain sounded even more persistent, the pound of it on the roof echoing in the large open space and wind gusts blowing through unseen holes in the board walls. She found some old towels and together they dried out the interior as best they could, both shivering with the cold by the time they'd made some progress.

"There's a detailing shop in town, and they're open on Saturday morning," she said, once they stood back to examine their work. The car's rug was a sopping mess, and the leather seats showed dark marks from the puddles that had graced the space for hours. His notebook had been in the glove box, luckily, or that would have been a useless sponge as well.

He eyed his shirt clinging to her and watched a shiver of cold lick goose bumps up DK's arms.

"First, we need a hot shower to warm up. And then I need dry clothes." Though, Cassidy considered, the idea of slipping back into bed and warming her up in a different way was very inviting indeed.

"I have a drier. We can throw your things in there while you warm up in the shower."

She looked so appealing standing there in bright pink clogs, obviously something she used in the garden or walking to the studio, his white shirt hanging halfway down her thighs and hiding nothing of her perky breasts. He felt himself stir again.

Why did she have this effect on him? Usually he would be tired of a woman already, bored and ready for her to get her things and exit his room to leave him sleep off their pleasure in peace. Instead, he wanted to carry DK up the stairs to make love to her for hours in the loft, with the rain cascading down as a pleasant symphony playing in the background.

He shook his head to get rid of the thoughts, things to consider much later when they weren't both shaking with cold. Throwing an arm around her shoulders and pulling her close, they dashed back through the rain to the house.

*****

She hadn't expected him to pull her into the hot shower with him, and the long interlude of slippery soap and pulverizing heat brought them both to another release after a quick dash for a condom. She'd have to buy a bigger box next time, she thought in a haze. The idea brought another lick of heat, perking her up so fast her eyes snapped wide open.

Where did she get this sudden sexual energy? She had always been somewhat reserved, and even when she did find pleasure in a man's arms, she rarely wanted him to stay. She rarely wanted a repeat performance right away either, and here she was, wanton and almost begging in Vince's arms.

She enjoyed the odd sight of him sitting at her kitchen table in black briefs that left nothing to the imagination and a green terrycloth robe of hers that barely tied above his waist. He was scooping up scrambled eggs and devouring toast with homemade jam like it was elixir of the gods, all the while watching her.

It felt nice to have him here, still here after a long night and morning that left her feeling pleasantly loose and lax-muscled. She'd told him stories of her neighbors, like old Mrs. Bellechois who lived across the way, alone now that her husband had died and her kids lived in other states. He seemed to like her tales, asking questions to bring out new things she hadn't considered.

They felt so normal, sitting like this and discussing the neighborhood. Conversation then trickled off. Vince suddenly turned serious, and when the last of his breakfast was gone, he wiped his mouth carefully, folded the cloth napkin, and set it aside to line up precisely with the placemat. Then he cleared this throat.

"Last night, this morning, were, well, pretty incredible." He wasn't looking at her now, intent instead on creating a perfect crease in the napkin. He seemed to be waiting for a response.

"It was." She realized her voice was soft and decided that a stronger tone would be more appropriate. "I enjoyed myself too."

She winced, glad that he wasn't looking at her. It sounded like she was thanking a host for a nice time at a barbeque, so cool and detached. Squaring her shoulders, she decided that if she was going to carry this whole power-for-passion thing off, she'd better step up and be bold.

"In fact, I enjoyed myself immensely, as I'm sure you could tell." She put a mischievous grin on her face and waited for him to look up.

Vince did, the expression on his face puzzled and disappointed before he dropped a curtain and made it unreadable. "DK, you know I'm leaving in a few weeks, right after Thanksgiving in fact." He was watching her carefully again.

There was a pang somewhere that she associated with her heart, but she decided to ignore it. She let go of the grin and let her expression get as cool and distant as his. "I know." She paused a minute, trying to find the right words to make it sound like this was all going to be just fine with her.

"So, friends with benefits, okay?" She waited, holding her breath as Vince considered her words. "No strings on either side. We can just enjoy each other."

He seemed to be a little baffled by her direction, but that look raced quickly across his face to be replaced by an easy smile that didn't quite reach his eyes. "Friends with benefits sounds good, Red."

He stood up and crossed to her with his dishes in hand. Placing those in the sink, he turned to her and put warm hands on her arms, rubbing gently. "Are you sure that's okay with you?" His voice had softened to a near whisper.

DK pulled herself up to her full height, having to tilt her head back to stare into his eyes. She wanted to pull this off.

"Of course it is!" She realized she needed to match her actions to her words, and quickly reached up on her toes to pull him into a quick kiss. "There's a lot I haven't had time to show you about the area, still a lot for you to learn for your articles."

He looked at her strangely, the kiss he returned almost absent-minded. He let her nestle into his chest, bringing his arms around her and rocking her back and forth. Then he pulled away and his eyes were expressionless when they bored into hers again. "And that's fine with you? No strings, no commitments?"

She swallowed and almost lost her resolve to keep things light. Why did he keep pestering her about this? If he did, she'd give in and admit that she was already more involved than she'd counted on.

A new smile plastered on her face, she looked up at him and tapped his cheek gently. "Absolutely fine with me, no strings, no commitments."

There was nothing to read in his face now, no sense of what her words meant to him. He kissed the top of her head and turned to the laundry room to pull his clothes out of the drier, dressing where he stood.

*****

Her friends, thankfully, waited until the early afternoon to start calling and quizzing her. Tess was first, and DK let the house phone go to voicemail as she heard her friend identify herself as Buds and Blooms and ask if the flowers had proven to be acceptable for the occasion. It sounded like she was talking to a client, and DK realized that Tess was being discrete in case Vince was still there.

She was unsettled and unsure of why. She'd gotten exactly what she wanted, hours of passion unlike anything she'd ever experienced. Vince had proven to be an incredible lover, demanding, considerate, and willing to let her please him as much as he pleased her.

So why was she feeling more than a little let down?

Work was always a good distraction, and DK pulled a waterproof slicker on over her sweater and jeans to walk through the still pouring rain. The old barn was empty of his car now. Vince had called the detailing shop, and the owner had agreed that he could try to tidy up the convertible today if it was brought in immediately. The sound of rain on the roof was soothing, a welcome relief from the long months of perpetual sunshine that marked the dry season. It would have been better to have it start out slowly, giving the ground a chance to soak up the moisture, but even the runoff would be welcome.

DK built a fire in the woodstove and let its heat warm the small office before shedding the slicker and heading to her desk. Her mind was on the Witch Hill work. Maybe now, drowning in emotions and saturated by a night in the arms of a man who could definitely light her up in so many ways, she could find the design that would make the work complete.

An hour later, she'd about given up. The sketch pages were full, but not of the sculpture. Instead, she'd drawn Vince, his various expressions, animated or at rest, even one with him sleeping as she'd stared at him last night.

Her cell phone rang, and it pissed her off that her heart did a little dance thinking it might be him. He said he would call once he figured out how long it would take him to come back here tonight.

She almost groaned when the caller id brought up Gabby's name. But she needed to talk to someone, and Gabby seemed to have the best handle on all of this emotional romantic stuff.

Pressing the green button, she put the phone to her ear. "Hey Gabby."

"Hey yourself! So is he still there? Or are you alone?"

"He's gone into town. It's a long story. But he said he's going to come back tonight."

"And?" Gabby was waiting, and DK knew it was for a full report. But she was at a loss what to say next.

Her friend tried again, her voice suddenly sympathetic. "DK, how was it? Oh sweetie, is he a dud?"

DK barked out a quick laugh. "Not a dud by any stretch of the imagination!"

She could probably have heard her friend's woohoo scream all the way from town even without a phone connection. Putting the cell away from her ear, she waited until things quieted down, then brought it back.

"So it was amazing, huh? Everything you hoped for, dreamed about? Did you find all that passion you wanted?"

DK sat still and closed her eyes, pictures of she and Vince entwined dancing in her memory. Oh yeah, all the passion she wanted and a whole lot more she really wasn't prepare for.

She sighed. Gabby was unusually quiet on the other end too. Finally, she filled the silence.

"DK, are you all right?"

Sighing again and putting her head down on her arm across the drawings on her desk, she said, "Oh Gabby, I am so completely and totally screwed."

Chapter 26

Vince stood in front of the bakery case staring not at the pastries but at his soaked shoes. They, like the interior of his little convertible, were not made for punishing downpours. He was leaving a puddle between the water seeping out of the leather and his dripping umbrella.

"You want something, some soup maybe, or maybe a hot pasty?" Sarge was behind the counter watching Cassidy thoughtfully. His partner Stuart was at the cash register, quiet and waiting as well.

"Yeah, soup sounds good." Cassidy tried to bring himself back to the present.

"What kind?" Sarge was waiting by three big cauldrons, a large to-go bowl in his hand.

"Whatever, man, whatever you think is best." Too many decisions, Cassidy thought. That was his problem right now.

The detailing guy was blunt. "Ya knew that it was going to rain, right? These cars, they're not made to be left open out in the rain."

Cassidy alternated between wanting to punch the guy and wanting to disappear. "Yeah, it kind of came up suddenly though, you know? Unexpected." He didn't have to explain himself, did he?

The guy then proceeded to launch into the long story of the woolly caterpillar and its rings and Cassidy finally raised a hand to stop him. "Yeah, I heard that one. I just didn't expect it all to come down in one night. So, can you clean it up?"

The guy rubbed his chin and looked at the car again, shaking his head. "You should really call the rental company, ask them what they want to do. They might want to put their own guys on it, ya know?"

He walked around it, bending over and shaking his head twice. "And ya know, once the snow starts, this ain't gonna be any good anyhow. Too low to the ground. No clearance, can't put chains on it. Won't be able to get around these hills."

Cassidy knew the guy pegged him for an outsider when he'd explained that the car was a rental. One look at his denim jacket, damp despite the umbrella DK had given him, and the expensive but squelching leather loafers, and he definitely looked like he didn't belong in these mountains.

"Ya might wanna get yourself a different rental, is all I'm saying. Something like an SUV, ya know? Then ya don't need to worry about it." Then the guy laughed and slapped him on the shoulder. "Besides, them's have roofs on 'em, ya know, so the rain can't get in!" And he laughed as if he'd just delivered the greatest punch line in the world.

Cassidy agreed that this would probably be a good idea. He didn't add that he expected to be long gone before the snows blew in sometime in the winter. He would be tucked back into his New York condo, writing away to shrink the accumulated backlog of stories that were building up from around here.

And missing a woman with flaming red hair that matched her passionate personality and the fiery green eyes of a witch.

Which brought him back to right now, standing in Brew Bank Bakery under the considerable weight of its owners' gazes, leaving an ever-growing puddle in front of cases of baked goods oozing sugar and temptation.

"Here you go Vince, nice and warm to fix you up on this wet day." Sarge put a cover on the big take-out bowl and pushed it into a brown paper bag. He filled the bag with toasted baguettes that smelled of garlic and olive oil, and he threw in the spoon and napkins before moving it all down to the register.

"That's eight forty-three," Stuart intoned, and waited. The two men looked at Vince, then each other. "Ah, earth to Vince? Eight forty-three?"

With a start, Cassidy realized that he was still standing in front of the display case, and he shifted the umbrella to dig into his pocket for money.

"So how long are you planning to stay? In town I mean? Lisa mentioned that you extended your rental on the house." Stuart made conversation as he handed bills and coins back.

How long did he plan to stay? He thought he knew the answer to that one, but now he wasn't so sure.

"Until right after Thanksgiving I think. I have some research I still want to do and I've heard that the holiday is interesting around here, and then the Christmas parade is right after on the weekend." It sounded kind of lame, really.

The bakery was quiet of customers and the two men lounged behind the counter, regarding Vince with curiosity. "Yup," Sarge replied, "the parade's a hoot and everyone comes down for it. We light up that big old oak tree at the end of the Main, the one you can probably see from your house. I assume you'll be at the girls' big celebration, right? They always put on an incredible spread, and this year it's at DK's house. We all get invited, and we like to go. It's like a survivor's Thanksgiving – you know, anyone who doesn't have someplace else they'd rather be." Sarge and Stuart both grinned, trading stories about past years' shindigs.

He didn't know, Cassidy thought. He didn't know if he was invited. He didn't even know what would happen past this weekend. He assumed, when he called DK to give her the status on the car, that she'd ask him back over, but maybe not.

Maybe she'd think about what they'd said right before he left and decide that a short term fling wasn't for her. He found himself hoping that she didn't make that choice.

"So, if you're going to stick around for another month, you're going to need some different clothes." Stuart pointed to the soaked leather on his feet. "Boots, the waterproof kind, and a heavier jacket." Then he circled his wave to encompass all of Cassidy's attire. "You look like a city slicker, my friend, and if you want to hang around much longer, you really need to start looking like a local."

*****

An hour later and a few hundred dollars added to his credit card, and Cassidy was outfitted for the weather. The rain still hadn't stopped, but now he had a jacket that shed it like Fusion's coat. His leather shoes may or may not recover, given time to dry completely. In their place, warm waterproof boots with a set of short laces were surprisingly comfortable.

He'd stocked up on some shirts and jeans while he was in the sporting goods store up the street from the bakery. The store clerk had happily wrapped everything in plastic bags, chattering away about how the rain wasn't scheduled to let up for a while and bringing up the rings on the woolly caterpillar yet again.

He definitely was going to have to look up this woolly caterpillar story.

Walking back up the hill to the houses overlooking town wasn't bad now that he was dressed for it. He even felt like a local now, despite the bags of shopping hanging off his arms. Others were out walking too, he noticed, unfazed by the rain and dressed as he now was. A little rain didn't bother these folks.

The house felt different too, he realized. The dining room table where he had set up his laptop and tiny printer was covered with books about the history of the area, a few dating back to the founding during the early immigrations across the wilderness and the boom brought on by the Gold Rush. Cassidy loved to read about those times, imagining what the people would be like and what stories they had to tell.

He fired up the laptop, intent on capturing words to explain the feel of the torrents of rain, the way it ran down the hilly streets and filled the ditches on the sides of the rural roads. The sound of it was everywhere, even here in his little place. He was sure that at some point, people got tired of it. But as so many had explained to him, the long dry months and the need for rain to both protect the area from raging wildfires and provide for agriculture made it welcome when it arrived.

His mind wandered, and the words came slowly. He typed, then stared off into space, remembering something DK had said or the way she pushed at the curls on her head. It made him smile. She was so soft everywhere, and it was hard to reconcile the woman who could bend metal to her will with the petite dream she became in his arms.

She seemed like such an innocent, despite her bold assumption of control last night. She was demanding, but at times she waited, almost as if she wasn't sure what to do next.

But the loft had been designed for seduction and sex. The satin sheets had slid over him, almost as soft as DK's skin. The candles danced in soft puffs of air that came from somewhere and lit everything with a fire that was both tempting and wanton. The stash of condoms disguised by the lovely box on the bedside table spoke of experience and significant expectations.

He wondered again at the pile of contradictions that he was coming to learn about, the more he got to know DK. First she was as ruthless as he was, and then she was this lovely sprite who was tempting in her very tentativeness. His emotions wanted to peel away the layers and learn everything about her even as reason chimed in with decisive regularity that he was leaving soon.

The dining room was cozy, but not as much as the great room at DK's. Despite its expanse, she'd created welcoming warmth by placing a rug just so under the dining table or circling a nest of seating surrounding the large fireplace. He wondered what it would be like to sit there, deep in the big chair wide enough for DK to tuck against his side, and type out tales of those early pioneers and settlers.

He wondered what she was doing right now. Was she sitting by that fire, reading one of the hundreds of books she had filling shelves everywhere? Was she working in the studio, the flame of the torch molding something unimaginable out of mere metal?

Or was she thinking about him, just like he was thinking about her?

Where the hell had that come from? Cassidy shook himself to try and get rid of the thought, the longing. When had it become longing, exactly? It wasn't last night. No, it had happened before that, sometime in the past weeks of exploration and conversation.

He couldn't fall for her. He couldn't. He swore out loud, surprised when his voice reverberated around the room. This wasn't him, his life. He belonged on the road, touching bases in New York in his sterile apartment with the wide view and clean rooms. He belonged with a different woman in every city, his heart unattached and his mind clear.

His cell jangled for attention in his pocket, and he started out of his reverie and looked at the display. Randy.

Unusual for a weekend, but not unheard of when he was traveling. He engaged the call and waited after a gruff hello.

"Hey, Vinnie, how are you? I thought I'd call, see how you're doing. I saw the rain was really coming down on the weather channel. Do I need to send you an ark?"

Cassidy held the phone away from his ear, amazed as always that Randy could sound like he was sitting across the table from him, booming voice all jovial and good humored, even when he was across the country.

"Ah, no, no ark, but I did need to buy new shoes, a new jacket, and almost a rental car."

"What happened to the car?" Randy sounded curious, and for once, he wasn't typing on his keyboard while he was on the phone.

Cassidy told the story of being surprised by a downpour that he wasn't expecting and how he'd left the top down. He left out the part about what he had been doing at the time that so distracted him from realizing the car was being flooded.

"But you got it covered, right? I could get you a different car."

Cassidy declined. He liked the little convertible, even if it didn't shed water easily. It suited him.

"So listen, I had a reason to call you. Travel International called. They want a series on the area. They want the quintessential V. M. Cassidy, you know? The biting commentary, the sarcastic tone, the places their readers could deign to enter, the places they can make fun of. You know, your usual hyper-critical snobby hip stuff."

Cassidy sat without responding long enough for Randy to ask if they were still connected.

"Ah, Randy? I'm not sure that this region lends itself to those kinds of articles." Cassidy surprised himself by saying this. He wasn't sure he'd articulated it to himself yet, but he was growing kind of fond of Flynn's Crossing, and he wasn't sure he wanted to make fun of it or its inhabitants.

"Aw, come on. It will be in Travel International for god's sake. In Europe. No one out west will shoot you on the street for it. They won't even friggin' read it." The clatter of keys was back on the line.

"How about I do a serious piece, the kind with some history thrown in? You know, educate them about this area, what makes it unique, what makes it special."

He put the phone away from his ear as Randy ranted about the editor, the publishers, the audience. They wanted vintage Cassidy, not some soft-in-the-head also-ran. And words continuing to that effect.

Waiting for the phone to fall silent, he rested his forehead on the table. This was not the conversation he wanted to be having right now, not when he was confused and trying to figure out some answers for himself. First he wanted his old life back, and then he wanted something completely different. He couldn't make up his mind.

Randy finally fell silent and asked again if Cassidy was still there. Wearily, he picked up the phone.

"Yes, I'm still here. Let me think about it, okay? Give me a couple of days, at least until Monday."

His agent-cum-friend bleated out his thanks, said he wouldn't regret it, could lead to an exclusive someplace in Europe for a couple of months, who knows?

Cassidy had a sudden flash in his mind, a picture of DK and him laughing on a cobbled street in Paris, sitting for an intimate dinner at a café street side after a day full of museums. Or maybe a sunlit beach after spending a couple of days wandering the Greek countryside. Or maybe…

He stopped himself. He was getting ahead of everything. He was here for a short time visit, only a month left now. He and DK had a friends with benefits arrangement, nothing more. She'd made it clear, and it was what he wanted too, right?

The thought of it, of adding an ocean and another continent to the upcoming distance between them, suddenly left him feeling shaken and cold.

Chapter 27

DK hid the drawings of Vince under a stack of sketchpads on her drafting table. She couldn't bring herself to throw them away. She realized that this was an indication of how far sunk she was on the guy, but right now, she didn't care.

Gabby had been sympathetic and her story came out. DK had feelings for Vince, feelings that were more than a month-long friendly but non-committed fling were supposed to carry. Yes, the hours of intimacy had been amazing.

And she wanted more of it, of that she was sure. Even if he left, when he left, she would hurt. It was a lot more fulfilling to imagine making the most of each minute rather than worrying about the future.

Her heart? It was already in trouble.

DK wandered back to the house, unable to concentrate on work and unwilling to sit and listen to the cozy sound of rain on the old barn's roof. It never let up, and Fusion came in more than once spraying a shower from his coat as he shook in the entry hall. The dog loved the rain since it brought up a million new smells for his over-active nose to follow. The wet reminded her of the puddles she and Vince had left behind coming in from the car escapade, on their way to a shower that lasted longer than getting warm required.

After a short interval, Tess called again. This time, DK took the call and explained the story once again. She left nothing out. Where Gabby had been high-fiving, Tess seemed to pick up on the problems right away.

"Have you fallen for him, honey?" It was less a question and more like a statement.

"I don't know. Fallen for him? Can you do that when you've only known someone for what – a little over a month? I mean, he's incredible intelligent, always looking at everything from a whole range of angles. He's got a killer sense of humor. He knows so much about so many different subjects."

"DK, sweetie, you're not interviewing contestants for a game show. This is the guy you took to bed, the man who according to you just about set fire to the sheets while you sang the alleluia chorus!"

She had to chuckle at that. Leave it to Tess to find a way to make her laugh and lighten the conversation, even when the subject was serious.

"I don't know what I'm going to do, Tess." She realized she was biting a nail and quickly put her hand in her pocket, as if her friend could see the nervous habit through the phone.

"Simple. You want him. He wants you. Your heart is already involved, so backing away now, while the sensible thing to do, probably isn't going to hurt any less. And you'll always be asking yourself what-if. You have a month yet to figure it out, or he does. Who knows how you'll each feel by then?"

Stated simply like that, DK had to agree. Telling Vince that it had been nice but thanks anyway would be hell, and she didn't want to do it either. He made her feel more alive, whether they were in bed or out of it, than any man had before. She loved to hear his stories, loved to see where his nimble mind would head when he was faced with a new inspiration. His humor could have a wicked edge to it, but she'd never been the subject of it, and in fact, he'd directed it most of all at the places and people he'd met in the course of his recent travels.

No, stepping back was not an option, and as long as he was in town, she'd do her level best to enjoy the time they had together and ignore the looming future when he was packed up and gone.

*****

The car detailer assured Cassidy he could get rid of the wet and make it look almost as good as new, as long he had a few more days to dry things out completely. He could rent another car from a chain in town, or he could call DK and see if she'd be willing to pick him up so that they could spend time together tonight.

He didn't want to think about spending the evening alone in his cold house. She'd never been here, and even so this place felt empty because she wasn't in it.

Yup, he was so fucked up, Cassidy thought. He was righteously screwed and it was all his own doing. He had rules, and he had broken them without even seeing the result coming. And he seemed to be damned pleased with himself for breaking them too if his physical reactions were any indication.

DK sounded happy to make the drive, even suggesting a place for dinner on the way back. Jeans were fine, he was assured – just like they were fine everywhere up here. No one, he suspected, ever went out for a dressed up occasion in anything else.

The rain continued its drumming insistence. Now the weather prognosticators were saying three days of the stuff, followed by an early and wet winter. The official start of the season was still a good six weeks away, but the ski resorts were rejoicing about the snow coming down up in the high mountains and the price of firewood sold in bins on the roadsides went up accordingly.

Promptly at six, DK's big pick-up pulled into his driveway, dwarfing the narrow space. When she got out, it seemed so improbable that she and the truck belonged together, and yet they fit. Kind of like the two of them.

The fleeting thought came and went almost before he sensed it.

He opened the door before she had a chance to knock, grabbing her in his arms and pulling her in tight for a hard kiss, her arm still raised to announce her arrival. After enough time to curl his toes and he hoped hers as well, he lifted his head.

"Hey Red. I missed you today." He was being sappy, but she was looking so gorgeous with that big brimmed hat pulled down over her curls and a gentle touch of make-up to accentuate her green eyes. Those eyes were laughing at him, and he hoped it was his kisses that put the tint in her cheeks.

"I missed you too." Her laughter died down to an intermittent chuckle, and she looked around the entryway. "This place is cute! Probably exactly like the little bungalow it used to be."

He looked around too, trying to see the place through her eyes. He released her, glad that he'd straightened up the piles of writing on the table, and feeling a little guilty that he'd made a start at writing the kind of article Randy said the foreign magazine wanted. It didn't feel right to be doing it.

"According to my landladies, the house dates back to about 1920. There was something else on this land before that, but a fire swept up the hillside and all of the wooden structures were burned to cinders."

"I remember that story. Tess's house is the only one that survived the fire, and that was because it was a bordello at the time and the men of the town couldn't bear the idea of their fine ladies having nothing shiny and satiny to wear, or a place to ply their trade. Or so the story goes."

She was laughing again, and he loved the sparkle it brought to her eyes. She'd taken the hat off and run fingers through her hair, though the curls were committed to springing up no matter what she did.

"Do you want a tour? It will take about two minutes. Honestly, the place is that small." And he took her arm to guide her around the living room, kitchen, bathroom and bedroom.

"My home away from home. See, two minutes flat." And in those two minutes, he realized now, he would see her in this space even if he ushered her out right away. He wouldn't even have to close his eyes to see how she lit it up with her energy.

They stood staring at each other in the small living room, then DK looked away and he noticed that her smile was now polite and sadly distant. She walked towards the dining table.

"So this is where you're working? At least you have plenty of room to spread out." She paged through a book on northern California history, one he'd marked with a number of tabs on pages that referred to the region.

"Plenty of room. But then, I'm used to working from almost anywhere. I don't need any kind of routine or ritual. I just write."

He hated the way that sounded, like he was a pompous ass and could set off around the world at the drop of a hat, productive and happy. Which is the way it was, of course. Or at least the way it had been.

He wasn't sure what it would be like now.

"I love the fact that you can look at the history of a place, the times and the activities, and then imagine what the people living in those times were thinking. You have such a gift for that." Her hand was still stroking the book, but she was looking at him with great sincerity on her face as she said it.

Cassidy suddenly wished that she was stroking him in that same way instead, her eyes so wide he could see the outer rings of darker green. Artless and unassuming, that's what it looked like.

The bedroom was only steps away, and he imagined what it would be like to lay her down on the intimate double bed and forget about dinner plans and welding work and writing schedules.

She made the decision for him, stepping to the door and putting the hat on again. "You'll want to bundle up. The rain is still coming down in buckets and the roads are a mess. There was some flooding coming into town. The ground can't absorb it fast enough and the runoff is making the streams something to see. Even the river on the edge of town is raging, and that usually doesn't happen until the spring snow melt."

She opened the door and stood waiting for him, keys in her hand, the pouring rain a slate gray backdrop. He gave up the mental picture of her in his bed, thinking somewhat wryly that it was better this way. He wouldn't be able to get anything done in this space if all he saw was her face in front of him every time he sat down to work.

*****

The pub was lively despite the weather. A big stone fireplace was blazing and the noise was spirited and fun. A darts board was set up near the bar, and a few people took turns in attempting to outdo one another with their accuracy. From what Cassidy could tell, they would all give an Irishman a run for his money in Dublin.

"This place is great. It reminds me of a few places I've raised a pint in Ireland," he related to DK as they settled in to a small booth with a view of the fire.

"Oh, don't let them hear you say anything about Ireland in here. Mallory's was founded by a Welsh gentleman, don't you know?" She leaned forward conspiratorially and did a fair approximation of the flat-edged accent from Wales. "The Welsh came to work the mines, after the gold had run its course and some of the smaller settlements were falling back into ghost towns. This used to be a righteously large place, was this town, almost as big as Flynn's Crossing back then. But after the rush, the empty buildings fell down and it disappeared from the map. That is, it all fell down except this place."

They both looked around at the tall brick walls and high beamed ceilings. The fireplace was a huge stone structure that rose a good twenty feet. There were some stuffed animal heads mounted on the walls but the dim lighting made them hard to see.

DK turned back with a wicked grin on her face. She continued on in a rough approximation of a Welsh brogue. "The miners, ya see, worked round the clock, shifts all day every day, even on Sunday. The clergyman they brought over from the old country to preside over services at their little white church was appalled that the mine owners didn't observe the holy day. He said that as long as there was no Sunday observance, every day was just like the other."

She leaned in closer on their bench, whispering now directly into his ear. "In the old country, the pubs were closed on Sunday, it being a holy day and all. But some enterprising Welshman, the aforementioned Mallory, decided that if the priest said one day was like every other here, there was no Sunday. So here he was open all day every day, just like the mine. A man could end his shift at six in the morning and come get his daily pint before heading home for dinner – in the early morning sunshine – and bed."

He liked the story, and he loved the way she told it, lit up from inside with the joy of the telling. They differed in their views on some things, but on more and more topics that they explored they found that they agreed. He still enjoyed baiting her, just loving the picture of her with her Irish up, but now, she was wise to him most of the time and teased him right back. She'd even made him get riled up more than once, only to collapse in giggles when he'd sputtered to a stop, indignantly realizing he'd taken the bait again.

It was another thing they'd found they had in common, the love of a good story. He was glad that they were sitting side by side in this darker corner, making it easy and natural for him to reach down and kiss her quick and hard. The desire to touch her, hold on to her, was getting overwhelming.

As he pulled back, he saw the confusion on her face. Did she think the only reason he kissed her is because she'd said bed? While it was fast becoming his favorite piece of furniture to think about, it wasn't the only thing on his mind.

He needed to lighten the moment again. He picked up her accent and continued the story. "So what did they do during Prohibition, do ya think?"

She blinked a few times, then pulled back in the small space and picked up the yarn. "Word is, the barkeep at that time was a law-abiding fella, but he didn't see any reason to go against what he saw as man's true nature and deny the miners their drink. He found some local brewers and stills who were willing to sell behind the law's back." She paused, then winked broadly. "And he found some local lawmen who got thirsty just the same and were more than willing to look the other way. Mallory's was able to stay open without a pause and still stands today, a testament to the commitment of men. To their drink, that is!"

She stopped and laughed, that sound like a quick flash of blue flame as he'd seen that first day in her studio. He watched her eyes, mesmerized as their green glow seemed to intensify and shift with her mood. The thought of leaving her, getting on a plane and heading thousands of miles away, hit him like a fist in the solar plexus.

Cassidy thought of the future, of DK sitting in this same pub and maybe even on this same bench with some other guy, telling the same story and laughing her quicksilver laugh again. She probably had told it more than once before, and the men in question had probably all been hypnotized by her eyes lighting up with the conclusion.

It hurt him to think that, and then he thought again to the well-planned seduction scene, the candles and the pretty box to hide the condoms. She was gorgeous and an artist, after all, and she probably found attractive men she wanted to take to bed and did so quite successfully all the time.

He felt himself withdraw, grateful that the waitress picked that moment to come up to the table with their drinks. His shot of scotch and pint of ale were set in the center along with DK's large glass of red wine and a basket of chips. Orders for dinner were taken. The waitress told them that things were busy but she'd bring something else for them to nibble on if they needed it, and then she left with a wink.

DK nibbled a chip and took a sip of wine, his eyes roaming the room. He wanted to reel her in, hold on to her and let her innocence speak for itself. But there was the siren, the firebrand that rose over him in the bedroom, demanding and confident that she would get what she wanted, what she needed.

Friends. Friends with benefits. Nothing more. She'd said so herself.

Ah, Red.

Chapter 28

"That fire is wonderful, don't you think?" DK stretched, full from the big dinner. They'd driven home in the still-pouring rain, Vince at the wheel this time. He'd insisted, saying he wanted to feel what it was like to drive something as tall as a building.

When he'd begun to sing truck driving songs on the few short miles to her house, she'd giggled. That made him sing in an even more exaggerated fashion, until she was laughing and wiping the tears from her eyes.

Everything was better each time they were together. At the pub, he'd pulled away for a while, his smile not reaching his eyes and the watchfulness that he sometimes got back in place. He'd asked her for more stories about the area then, and she'd obliged, happy that she had some to tell him that he found so entertaining.

Soon she'd had him laughing once more, and the waitress arrived with their big burgers on dark bread to find him doing an admirable mimic of what were supposed to be early settlers discussing the possible locations of a wayward cow. The waitress had looked at them strangely before leaving them to their own devices.

She tried to get up off the couch in front of her fireplace but Vince's arms tightened and pulled her back. The fire needed tending, another log to be added and the spark barrier put back in place.

"Stay here." His voice was a rumble in her hair. He kept his arms around her and kissed her ear, nosing her curls. It felt so perfect, so right. She could stay like this forever quite happily.

"The fire needs to be fed, even if we're full. I don't want to doze off and leave it open. That's how house fires can start." Okay, she sounded a bit prissy, but it was her house and it was made of wood.

Vince sighed and released her. Her body felt cold when his arms left her, even in the warmth of the blaze.

He'd been moody tonight. One minute he was full of fun, and then a cloud would cross his face and that watchful expression would return. She could joke him out of it, but part of her wanted to ask him what was the matter. He seemed so serious then, and sometimes, she thought he seemed a little bit angry.

He shifted on the couch as she fed the fire and put the metal cover in front. She'd made this too, something she'd done one winter day when she was out of inspirations for anything new. It had ended up to be a big hit with her friends, and those who had fireplaces wanted their own versions. Pretty soon she had added it to her catalog and she still made a few each year, customized to the design ideas of her clients' interiors.

DK traced a finger along the curve of the river represented on hers. She had taken pieces of her memories of the county, places she loved the most, and blended them here. The ridge of mountains behind her house, a curve of a road, the old wooden bridge crossing the high river that gave the town its name. To her, it meant home.

She stood up to find Vince right behind her. He had that serious watchfulness in his eyes again. She realized that these mercurial changes should probably concern her, but she never felt scared. Somehow, she knew that she was always safe with him.

He pulled her to him brusquely, and she had no time to gasp before his mouth came down on hers with hard passion. His tongue was between her lips and dancing with hers before she had time to gather a single thought, and once she had, all she wanted to think about was how the fire he lit licked along her nerves and sparked in every corner of her body.

She twisted to get closer to him, putting her hands in his hair to grip as his kisses became more urgent. It was like he'd been holding himself in check since that one hard kiss at the restaurant tonight, like everything since then had been a soft glancing pass awaiting this combustion.

If something was wrong and he was acting out because of it, she didn't care. It felt so right, wrapped so tightly to each other that the wind wouldn't have been able to come between them. She forgot about him leaving, forgot about her own resolve to hide her emotions until he was gone. She poured everything she had into the dance of her tongue with his.

He pulled away suddenly, his breathing hard. "I want you here, in front of the fire, watching its light on you." His gaze burned into her and her own frantic heart rate kicked up even more. Something of the urgency that was coming off him in waves leaped to her and she grabbed his hair to pull his mouth down again.

Their hands went to work on clothes at the same time, and they struggled with the layers until they let go long enough to toss pieces in every direction without ever unlocking their eyes from one another. Vince finished first and grabbed her, just in time for DK to find her hands trapped between them.

The heat of the fire was nothing compared to the scorch coming off their bodies. DK found that her hands were in just the right place, trapped at the perfect height to cradle the long hard length of him. He sucked in hard as she explored, feeling as powerful as the roaring flames from that new log.

"What in the hell do you do to me, Red?" He ground out the words as his teeth set to work on her neck. "I can't hold back, can't control myself when I'm around you."

He sounded almost angry, and that made DK all the more exultant. This power, it was so wonderful and so unlike anything she'd experienced before. She let her hands roam over the hard silky length of him, laughing when he hissed again and cursed. He finally gripped her wrists to move her away and bent over to suck the leaping pulse in her neck.

Why had she never known that making love could be as amazing as this? The heat of his body and the heat of hers were enough, she was sure, to send the whole house up in smoke. When he released her, she used her mouth on him, feeling him shudder when her teeth scratched over his skin in return. Her hands wandered lower again, and this time, he let her have her way, his arms rigid at his sides.

She pushed him back on to the couch, watching his face in the dancing shadows of the fire. She couldn't read his expression, but she could feel the race of his pulse and see the clenched hands he held still with effort. She gentled her touch, her mouth now setting on a path of kisses to his navel. His hands were shaking now as he rested them in her hair.

"God, Diane Kathryn, you're burning me to ashes." She could barely make out the words over their harsh breathing. She hated when he used her name like that, because it reminded her of too many things she would rather forget. It made her pause.

His hands were moving restlessly, caught in the curls on her head. This was Vince, this was now, and he wanted her. He pressed up, his erection throbbing where he rested between her breasts.

Something broke open inside her, some rocky cap on her emotions that she had probably set in place a couple of decades ago. This was Vince, he wanted her as badly as she wanted him, and it was as simple as that. Shifting back, she looked up into his face. He was staring at her with half closed eyes, and his expression was haunted. He looked so alone, odd given the intimacy of their positions at the moment.

"You do all of that to me and more," she whispered, and his gaze lasered in on hers. The emotional distance disappeared, and he gripped her hair tighter. When he would have pulled her up, she gave a little shake and he released her.

"I want to bring you some of the same pleasure you've brought me." He left his fisted hands where they'd fallen at his sides, and she liked the fact that she was making him fight for control. Her flash of power was back.

She smiled and slid her hands up his torso to toy with his nipples, then ran them down his belly lightly, feeling the shiver of muscles that she knew she roused in him. Then she let her head fall to rest on his inner thigh, and an unsteady hand moved into her hair once again.

"I want to taste you, enjoy you. I want to drive you crazy. I want to make you as needy as you do me."

Her hands came up to cup him and his hiss of breath was pure pleasure for her to hear. Her lips moved to trail kisses along his thigh, and she wrapped fingers around his length and moved them slowly. Her lips followed and she tasted his essence.

Vince pressed up from the couch and swore loudly, his hands suddenly tightening in her hair. It was a wonderful giddy feeling, this knowledge that she could spin him out of his careful control. She increased the pressure and soon he was pumping to match her rhythm. She reveled in the glory of it, the ability to take him to the razor's edge.

Abruptly, he pulled back and away from her, breathing in gasps. Picking her up by the arms, he dumped her without ceremony on the couch. He moved across the room to his jeans, digging in pockets until he found a slim foil package. He ripped it open with his teeth and he stalked back to her. He was magnificent to look at, but she had only two quick heartbeats to enjoy the view. He lifted her and slid her body down his until he'd filled her completely and fell back to the couch buried deep inside.

Chapter 29

"Bring him by the restaurant tonight. I want to see this guy, see if he's good enough for you, judge for myself." Roxy stabbed the air with her fork, making fast work of the omelet and potatoes in front of her.

DK looked around at the faces watching her. Gabby was out and out elated. Serena, who had been so wrapped up in her own love affair that she'd needed to cliff notes to catch up on the story, was smiling broadly. Marguerite sat back with a look of satisfaction on her face that could only be described as a cat having enjoyed the whole bottle of cream.

"See, what did I tell you? Some good sex, a whole lot of hot passion, and your artist's block is over," Marguerite said triumphantly.

DK shifted in her seat, a little uncomfortable that she hadn't come completely clean with how things lay between she and Vince.

The past few days and nights had been incredible, that much she had shared. The lovemaking that night in front of the fire had stretched on for hours, until they finally fell into an exhausted but happy sleep under a comforter as the fire burned low. She awakened with the sun high in the sky, a surprise after all of the rain, to find his mouth on her core in the most intimate of kisses. It was noon before they bothered to move from that old couch.

She might have to have it bronzed, she thought. She'd never be able to look at it without a smile again.

She popped out of her reverie when Gabby elbowed her. All three were watching her and laughing. "What?" She wondered if her hair was on fire.

"We've just been talking to you for the last few minutes. Earth to DK?" Gabby laughed indulgently and the others followed her lead. DK couldn't help but join in.

"Well, I'm not getting a whole lot of sleep," she emphasized the last word as the laughter got even more rowdy. "I might have dozed off a bit."

All four women laughed and it felt good to let loose of her emotions.

"I'm serious," Roxy started in again. "Bring him by tonight. I want to check him out." She took another bite of her eggs. "And I want to find out if he has a brother!" A new round of laughter followed, along with a lot of good-natured teasing about her sleep-deprived status.

Still, she wished she felt she could say what was on her mind. Vince was leaving in just over two weeks, and it was going to be hard. She went into this with a simple concept, planning on having a fling and then sending him on his way. She thought she could have her passion with no strings attached. But her heart had developed very different ideas.

Vince was a picture in contrasts these days. Times when his guarded expression dropped over him seemed to come more frequently now, in sharp contrast to the tender way he held her, always wanting to keep some part of them touching, even in sleep. Their lovemaking had grown as well, sometimes fast and furious and sometimes long, slow and luxurious. She now tripped over memories of them in almost every corner of her house and his, along with her studio, the patio, and even the chaise by the pool despite the cooler weather.

It was a good thing old Mrs. Bellechois across the road couldn't see back there!

True, there were times when she couldn't figure out what he was thinking. He would turn so serious and she'd want to wipe the concern from his face. The haunted empty expression that came to him now and then would fill his features and it was all she could do not to blurt out her own feelings in an effort to bring him some relief.

At least she hoped he would be relieved. Maybe he would just feel… trapped.

She shook herself and realized that she couldn't share the depth of her feelings, even with these closest friends, not before she shared them with Vince. She set herself up for this, and once he was gone, she'd just have to grin and bear it. There was plenty of passion now to feed into her art. Based on the way she was feeling, this would fuel the flames for a couple of decades to come or longer.

*****

The articles didn't feel right. He didn't like being snarky about Flynn's Crossing, hated the idea of even setting a teasing tone about the gentle people who were more accepting of each person's unique quirks before breakfast than those so-called sophisticated readers were in their whole lifetimes.

Maybe Randy was right. Maybe he was getting a little soft. Soft in the head most likely.

He paced DK's great room and thought about last weekend. He and DK had settled into her house on Friday night, not heading down the driveway again until midday on Monday. He'd brought his computer and some of his reference materials, intent on working on a piece that featured the history after the Gold Rush for an academic publication. It felt good to be working on something meaningful again, not that bringing home the big pay bacon in the international rags wasn't important too.

DK disappeared across to the studio as he typed, and when he got up to stretch, he realized that she'd been gone for almost three hours. He found her welding, surprising them both with a playful tussle on one of the empty pedestals she used for her work.

Time, he found, flew by whenever they were together. It was spinning by too fast.

He all but abandoned the little rental house in town, bringing more of his clothes and his materials to her space. She gave him a key, though since she didn't bother to lock the back door most of the time, he wasn't sure why he needed it. The symbolism wasn't lost on him though.

He didn't want to think about spending any of the time he had left in Flynn's Crossing without her. They had to separate once in a while, like her breakfast with her girlfriends in town today, or his occasional trips to some venues for writing inspiration. They considered it healthy – that was how they put it to each other. It was always best when they were close together though, close enough for him to wrap his arms around her and find her face lighting up with his kiss.

He and Fusion left the house. He still gave the dog a wide berth. He hadn't been raised with dogs, and he wasn't sure about big dogs at all. In some places he'd been to, dogs like this were trained to kill intruders. Despite DK's assurances to the contrary, he was still concerned.

Fusion, on the other hand, wanted to walk as close to his side as possible, which made for an interesting picture he was sure. The dog would walk close to him, and he'd inch away, and the dog would move closer again, until they were both walking at an angle to whatever straight path Cassidy had originally set.

The day was sunny again, the spell of rain now a memory except for the bright green it had encouraged in every direction. The old woman across the road that he now knew on sight as Mrs. Bellechois was at her mailbox, and he raised a hand in greeting. She didn't return the wave. DK said she never did for her either. But she still tried each time she noticed her neighbor, thin hair on end and whatever form of attire she'd selected that day blowing around her in the breeze.

Grass was growing and the trees looked clean again. Dust no longer spiraled up when they drove down the driveway, and deer had returned to what DK called their winter home. Colors painted the leaves as a reminder of the lateness of the season.

His stomach clenched when he thought about how quickly time was passing. It now almost made as much sense to count the days as the weeks, they were such a small number. Friday before the fabled Thanksgiving week, and then the following week he'd be gone.

It hurt, and he didn't want to think about it.

When he entered the studio, he heard the familiar hiss that meant DK was welding again. He'd become used to the sound and liked to watch her take seemingly immobile objects and make them dance into a new shape or form.

Today she was working on some mess that was beginning to look like a wine bottle, glass, and something else he couldn't distinguish. When he'd asked her about it last week, she waved him off, explaining it was a commissioned piece and she didn't want to discuss it.

Fair enough. He didn't want to discuss some of his work with her either, the articles that made him uncomfortable most of all. He'd need to call Randy about them again. He had promised to do a follow up with Thomas the potter and report in on whether or not the old guy would like to talk to Randy as a possible agent.

DK pushed back her mask as she turned off the torch. Hissing sounds subsided, and Fusion rushed forward for his greeting. She set the torch and mask aside, leaving her gloves in place. The dog got a good roughing up, and then she turned her face to Cassidy.

"Hi honey," she said, laughing already at his expression, "how was your day?"

It all seemed so normal, like something he could spend the next hundred years doing until they were both older than Mrs. Bellechois and could barely totter between house and barn. The clench in his belly got stronger and he heard the faint sound of a ticker counting down in his head.

*****

It was coming together, she realized, and she could see it in her mind's eye as clearly as anything concrete she had on hand. The passion she wanted to feel was all there. In fact, it was so much more. But soon he would be gone. She'd be left with the feeling of it, the memories and the dreams to wrap around herself as she created those next few pieces. And the raw new feel of it in this last segment for Witch Hill.

She had felt him rather than saw him, covered as she was with the mask, all noise obliterated by the flaming torch. It was as good a reason as any, better even, to quit for the day. He was standing in the doorway, the sun slanting behind him in what was becoming a rapidly falling autumn light. The dog looked between the two of them, wagging his big tail and waiting for someone to make a move and announce that the games had indeed begun.

She couldn't see his face, which was just as well since she was sure her own gave away too much right now. It was at times like this, when she was directing everything she felt into her work, that she knew she was the most vulnerable. If he was watching her with that lonely hunger in his eyes again, she'd say something she'd later regret.

He moved slowly across the space, waiting for some indication from her that she was done with what she was welding right now. She pulled off her gloves and reached out a hand to him.

"Hey Red. My day was good. Yours?" He didn't look at the work, just at her. She was suddenly conscious of the hair plastered to her forehead and the damp that coated her body under the heavy welding jacket, even in the cold weather.

"What time is it? I lost track."

Fusion yelped in happy circles around them, then ran off to explore a sound only he could hear in the corner of the barn.

"Almost five. I thought you might want to know that the sunset looks like it will be beautiful, almost but not quite as beautiful as you." He started to dance her around the barn, ignoring her welding clothes and honest sweat.

She smiled. What a wonderful line. Like what he wrote about, what she'd been allowed to read or what she'd snuck a peek at when he wasn't paying attention.

"I need a shower. We have reservations at Roxy's in an hour. And tonight I want to dress up. I feel the need to be more of a woman than all of this," she gestured around her, "let's me feel like during the day."

He smiled now, a full on glare of white teeth that reminded her of Fusion with a new toy.

"I can make up for that, you know." He trailed a finger down the rough buttons that closed the old scarred jacket. "You know, more than a woman…"

Chapter 30

They were late, but it was her fault as much as his. He'd learned all of the ways into her welding clothes, each button and clasp. The barn's office was warm and their joining was fast and furious. It reminded her of what underscored all of their days right now.

Countdown. She felt like it was t-minus something and she was holding her breath in the hope that there would be a delay. She didn't want to say anything about it. If she did, she was afraid he would race away from her.

After all, they had agreed to friends with benefits, right? They had both agreed. She couldn't suddenly change the rules because she had feelings for him.

And oh god, what feelings they were. They flashed through her unexpectedly and left her empty and full at the same time. In her mind, she told him she loved him a hundred times a day or more. She tried to infuse it in a look, a touch, a simple task like handing him a napkin or setting his pillow just so. She could only show him because she could never tell him.

The dress was one she'd been saving for a night like this. Roxy's was one of the few places in town that inspired attire other than jeans. He'd agreed, disappearing into town for what he labeled his 'city duds'.

She straightened the cling of dark brocade restlessly. Gabby had been her shopping maven for this buy, and she had to agree that her friend had picked a winner. It made her feel like a million bucks.

Checking her make-up one last time, DK turned and walked down the stairs. Vince had returned some time ago and set up his dressing area in the bath downstairs. They hadn't seen each other since, and she was nervous.

He was waiting for her, standing stock still in the middle of the great room. Fusion was sitting off to the side, intent on her clicking heals as she descended the stairs from the loft. His tail beat a very happy wag, which didn't mean much since he had absolutely no fashion sense whatsoever.

But the man was a different story. Vince's face was in the light, and his eyes held an intensity that had her sucking in air. And if that wasn't enough, the sight of him would have taken what was left of her breath away.

He was dressed in a suit, the first time she'd ever seen him in one. It fit him perfectly, obviously from an expensive tailor in a city far away and made from a fabric that looked like rough silk in the firelight. The shirt must have been tailor-made as well. The tie was the perfect width, the design subtle. His hand in his pocket and the deceptive casual stance added to his man of the world appeal.

She wanted to say to hell with dinner and haul him off to bed instead. She wanted to tear off that fancy suit like she was unwrapping a present at Christmas. She wanted to drag him to the airport and find the furthest, most remote destination in the world so that they wouldn't be found for years.

The look in his eyes let her know the dress was more than adequate. Her heels stopped their clatter on the steps and she tried for an elegant swoop down the remaining steps instead. His eyes got hotter.

"You look... amazing." His words caught, and it made her heart trill to hear that depth of feeling. He hadn't taken his eyes off of her, pretty amazing since Fusion was now leaning against him and he hated that.

"You look amazing yourself." She decided on nonchalance, not letting him know that each day that they counted down together brought her heart closer to breaking.

He held out a hand and she set hers in it. He brought it to his lips and kissed the back of it, then turned it over nestled in his larger palm. Then he licked it, bathing it from the curve of her wrist to the base of her thumb, his eyes never leaving her face.

Roxy would understand, wouldn't she, if they never made it to the restaurant tonight?

"Your chariot awaits, my queen." His smile was charming and teasing at the same time, and DK felt her insides relax and give over to the fun tonight. For one night, they were royalty in paradise and she was, in fact, the queen.

*****

He would have preferred the feel of the big truck tonight. It fit him, he'd found, and made him feel like he was taking care of DK in yet another way. He wanted to bring her to the restaurant in style, though, and he thought that their outfits were better suited to the little convertible.

The detailing guy had performed his miracles, and the car no longer smelled of damp. As he and so many others had predicted, though, it was a poor option once the roads turned wet. But he would be long gone before the winter's snow they kept warning him about would set in.

He would be back in New York, listening to Randy brag about how great a financial return he had gotten on the latest set of articles while he sported an over-decorated holiday sweater. There would some empty-headed blonde or brunette with big curves to distract him from the festivities. Cassidy would usually be content.

But now, he realized, it wouldn't be enough. The redhead next to him had changed all of his expectations.

He thought back to his day. When he'd run into town for his suit, he'd taken the time to call Randy. It was late night in New York, the three hours of time difference much more obvious on a weekend evening.

"Hey, Vinnie, how the hell are you?" Randy had taken the opportunity to take a couple of swigs of something, and maybe that was best. Vince wanted some answers.

"Good, man, really good." Cassidy decided to take a little risk. "DK's great too. She says hello." He waited.

"Hey, tell her hey from me too. You know her latest work is selling like crazy, right? She told you that?" A female voice rang out in the background of the call, and Cassidy heard the clink of glasses and a woman's laugh. Randy was clearly enjoying the beginning of his evening.

"Ah, yeah, of course she told me." Cassidy had to hold himself back. He was ready to jump all over Randy, since the bastard had never told him flat out that he knew DK. Cassidy had just suspected.

"So tell me again? How did you two get to know each other?"

Randy laughed across the continent and said something in the background to the crowd around him. Soon the voices faded away and his friend came back on the line.

"C'm on. She told you, right? I'm her agent. Been handling her work since before she was big. Now, hell, I can't get her to produce enough to make more than my price in ties in a year, but what the hell. She's a sweet little thing."

Cassidy could imagine his friend's lopsided grin and slightly leering wink. He'd seen it more than once when they were discussing women. It was okay when they were discussing someone else. But this was DK.

He also realized that Randy had no idea why Cassidy was even asking. It made him feel foolish, baiting Randy like this. But he needed to know.

"Hey, you never leave New York. How do you know what she's like?" He waited, unwilling to want to hear the reply he got and fearful about it all the same.

Randy guffawed at the other end of the line and coughed, then took a noisy sip of whatever he was drinking. "Hey, I know, ya know? A little redheaded firebrand, and I don't just mean the welding, you get my drift?" He laughed, and Cassidy felt sick.

He tried to imagine Randy and DK, and the image wouldn't work. His short and portly friend's head, bare of any remaining hair, next to DK's red curls? Her legs wrapped around his extra large waist, the same way she held him in passion so many times. It didn't make any sense.

And yet, maybe it did. DK had been more than cool about their arrangement, happy it seemed with the friends with benefits thing and unswerving in her acceptance of its casual and time-limited quality. She'd made no demands.

Still, there were things that didn't make a lot of sense. The satin sheets had been replaced by sensible soft flannel, and when he'd quirked an eyebrow at the change, she'd only shrugged and looked embarrassed before turning away quickly. He'd been assigned the job of loading up the fancy condom box, catching DK blushing a deep red when they came up to that aisle at the store. But her eagerness to step into his arms and meet him passion for passion was something else again.

The thought that others had experienced some facet of the passion he found in her arms over these last weeks was painful at a level deeper than he even knew existed. The very idea of DK wrapped around Randy was disgusting.

He shook his head clear, returning his concentration to the conversation. "No seriously, man, how do you know her?"

"Man, how do I know her?" Randy's cackle came through the phone, and for a moment, Cassidy hated his friend.

Randy finally got hold of himself and stopped laughing enough to speak. "Hey, ya know what they say, man, right?" The laughter started up again, and Cassidy thought again that he was an idiot to have an agent as a friend, doubly so since this friend was an ass.

"I'm her agent, man, have been for years. Know her better than anyone, if you know what I mean. Had to make sure she had the staying power, the passion to pull off the art world. Yup, she's looker alright, and when it comes to passion, well, you know yourself now." Cassidy could almost see the broad wink that Randy gave across the miles.

And it made his heart turn cold and stony.

Chapter 31

The table was intimate, a corner slot in the busy space that felt quiet despite the bustle. DK felt like the princess in an amazing movie. Vince was attentive, making sure she had exactly what she wanted throughout the meal.

They had seen Roxy once, a quick pass through when she gave DK a hard hug and shook hands assertively with Vince, clearly sizing him up but giving no indication of her determination on his worthiness.

DK felt the lull of wine and consideration wash over her. Vince's expression was intense. It was something she was used to by now, and if she was less tired, less uncertain because time was growing so short, she might have been more on her toes. As it was, she was cataloging every expression, every moment, for the years that stretched in front of her without the marvel of him beside her.

"So, tell me more about your agent. What's his name again?"

She took a minute to ponder the weird direction of the question. She was sure they'd talked about her agent before, the guy who kept encouraging her to expand the reach of her market, finding her exhibition spaces in San Francisco and distribution on the East Coast as well.

Vince wasn't looking into her eyes right now, instead tracing the lines in her palm as if they held the secrets to their future. It made her feel trapped in a layer of sensuous contentment. But the energy pumping off Vince had nothing to do with sensuousness or contentment, and that made her a little nervous. She closed her eyes and set her head back against the chair.

"His name is Randolph Gold. He handles a lot of different artists. I met Randy years ago at an art conference in New York. He was on the agent pitch slam at that conference, where you give your elevator speech to a horde of agents. You get about five minutes with each one. I probably talked to twenty agents that day, and he's the only one who bothered to return my follow-up calls."

She opened her eyes to look at Vince again, his face mostly hidden by his examination of the base of her thumb. His touch was a gentle caress repeatedly tracing her thumb with the tip of his middle finger. DK sighed.

"So how well do you know him?"

His questions felt more like an inquisition.

She sat back again, wishing that Vince would look up so that she could read his expression, maybe understand something about why he was suddenly so interested in such a mundane topic.

"As well as anyone knows their agent, I guess. I spent hours in his office, going over strategies and sales ideas. He's taught me a lot about selling in the art world, that's for sure. I'm sure I'm a very boring client to him. I've even fallen asleep on his couch more times than I want to remember." She chuckled at the memory of the all-night redeye flights she'd taken because it was all she could afford, just to meet with various representatives of the art world in Randy's office. But it had all paid off in the end, building her reputation and her distribution network.

Vince looked up suddenly, and his eyes were angry. She wasn't sure why he was so upset right now, but it made her pull her hand away. It seemed like a good time for a little escape so she could think about this puzzle.

She stood up. "I'm going to head up the hall. If you want to split a dessert, I'm game. But I'll pass on any coffee." She needed to get away from what looked like hurt, an odd twin emotion to anger in Vince's gaze.

*****

Fell asleep on Randy's couch? What the hell had they been doing there? Did she think he was a complete fool?

He knew Randy's reputation, and the three failed marriages had more to do with his so-called friend being unable to keep things zipped than anything else. What he had implied about his relationship with DK, even with the protestations of never leaving New York, was more than Cassidy could bear. It hurt to think of him and the woman he cared about so much together, even if it had happened before he'd ever known her.

He should come straight out and ask her, see if she had slept with Randy. Or it was probably more like how many times. She'd said it herself, she'd had to barter to get started, and what else would she barter with?

For that matter, he wanted to ask how many men she had slept with. But it really wasn't any of his business, now, was it? If she wanted to ask him, would he confess to the lackadaisical attitude he'd had around the world? He really wasn't proud of it, but it was the way he'd operated.

And he'd been exclusive since he'd met DK.

It just floored him that DK, someone who seemed smart and knowledgeable about the ways of the world, would be taken in by a piece of work like Randy, trading her body for contacts in the art world. But she was so naive, she probably didn't think there was any other way to get known.

Then he contemplated the careful satin and candlelit seduction scene, the fancy box of condoms, the friends with benefits statements. Maybe Red wasn't as innocent as he thought. He wasn't sure what to believe anymore, other than it hurt like hell to think about her in any man's arms other than his.

He was going to signal the waiter for their bill, ready to leave and have this out in private, but before he could even turn to look around, Roxy slid into DK's seat across the table.

"How was your meal?" She smiled sweetly, but Cassidy sensed that she was feeling anything but good-natured towards him.

"It was excellent, one of the best I've ever had, and that includes some of the best around the world." It was true. He'd have no problem writing a raving review about the place.

"Well thank you for that compliment, Mr. Vincent Michael Cassidy, lifestyle snark extraordinaire."

She stopped him short. He had taken considerable pains to hide his full name and his true profession in town. It seemed that he'd failed on that score, at least with Roxy. Looking at the protective expression on her face, he doubted she was worried about what he thought about her cooking.

He looked her in the eyes with all of the sincerity he could channel. "I mean it. It was a terrific meal and I have no problem writing honestly about that. I write the truth. It's what people expect of me." Well, it was the truth, but the delivery could use a little better tone most of the time. Even his compliments could come out sounding like censure.

Roxy waved his comment aside and then put a big smile back on her face.

"I really don't care about your review. I have more than enough terrific reviews to keep the tables full. The honesty you claim to find so important is so often veiled in criticism that people don't know what to think when they read your work. But that's not why I'm here."

She leaned across the table, still smiling, but the intensity of her eyes on his sent a different ferocious message. He felt compelled to lean forward as well.

"DK has the biggest heart of anyone I know. She's innocent and trusting, and she hurts when someone deceives her. It's taken her years to build her self-confidence, years to be proud of her profession and herself. She may have gone into this whole fling with you as a lark," and here Roxy poked a finger at his chest, "but she'll hurt if you use her callously."

Cassidy didn't know what to say. One minute she's the siren on an agent's couch and then the next minute one of her best friends is calling her an innocent.

Roxy leaned back again, her expression one of a pleasant conversation with a patron. "If you hurt her feelings or are anything other than gentle, you will be punished. DK leads with her heart. Let her down easy when you leave. If you don't, I'll know." She leaned forward again, any pretense of a smile gone. "And I'll make sure to spit in your soup if you ever come in this restaurant again." Then, as if adding an afterthought, "and I'll make sure any customer who mentions your name gets equal treatment."

The curse of the chef, he thought. You never know what happens to your food in the kitchen before it comes to you, and it wasn't the first time he'd been blessed with this particular sentiment.

Rising from the table, Roxy said, "It's been a pleasure serving you tonight, Mr. Cassidy. For dessert, can I recommend the flourless chocolate cake? It's heavenly, a light little trifle." And with that, she walked away, patting DK on the shoulder and exchanging a few quick words as she passed.

He didn't know what to think anymore. Was DK the siren or the innocent? She did seem very trusting of people, and yet there were so many signs that she was more worldly, or at least a little less inhibited, than her friend implied.

And so much of it didn't matter, he realized, because his heart was overruling his head. His heart already belonged to DK.

*****

That night, he wanted to hold DK and try to think through everything he'd heard today. She seemed content with that, tired and sleepy, curled up against him. Trusting was what came to mind.

He played with the curls that lay red against his chest. "What's it like when it's long?"

She seemed not to hear his question, then she sighed.

"My hair you mean? It's a mess. Growing up, my mama expected me to keep it in long pigtails or a braid. It's what good girls did back then, at least in my Irish Catholic neighborhood in Chicago. Ma would have me spend hours trying to keep the tangles out of it, but it had a mind of its own. She'd say it was being difficult just to make her life more of a challenge, and she never quite approved of whatever I was doing with it. It was like I made my hair hard to deal with on purpose."

She shifted, snuggling deeper, and Cassidy felt compelled to tighten his arms around her, still stroking her hair. She murmured what sounded like a purr.

"Anyway, I kept it long all through college, because I'd get grief when I went home if I'd cut it. I tried styling it ever which way, but it was still a stubborn mess. It wasn't until after I moved here to Flynn's Crossing and I started welding in earnest that I cut it. I was afraid I'd set myself on fire otherwise." She gave a little laugh at the memory.

Soon her breathing fell into an even pace, her breathing soft. She was sleeping, and Cassidy was left playing with the curls. He thought about the little girl who was always trying to please everyone else, and he wondered how far from her DK had wandered these days.

Chapter 32

"Back again, are ya?" Thomas was sitting at a high table, intent on carving some intricate design into a tall narrow vase of soft clay.

Cassidy called before coming over this time. He wanted to try to convince the old potter to consider looking for broader distribution for his work. He was a master at his craft, and yet in asking around, Cassidy had learned that the only places he sold his pieces were locally through the gallery or through his studio directly.

Camera in hand, Cassidy prowled the shelves looking at the displays once more. He stopped in front of the statue of the naked woman, arms outstretched, long hair streaming down her back, admiring it again. Maybe he could talk the old guy into selling it to him today. Just in case, though, he snapped off a couple of pictures from different angles.

"Ya still wanting that one, eh?" The old man chuckled and continued with his carving.

"Yes, I want to buy it. What would it take to get you to part with it?" Cassidy tried his most sincere and guileless smile. He wasn't sure it would work.

Thomas looked at him for a moment, then cackled his weird laugh and went back to his carving.

"So why do ya want it?"

The question stopped Cassidy in his tracks. Why did he want it? Because he liked it? No, it was more than that. Something drew him to the statue, and he wasn't sure what it was.

"I like it?" He thought that would be a good enough reason, but he realized he was adding his own question to the old man's.

"And there wouldn't be any other reason, eh?" The carving continued as if Cassidy wasn't even in the room.

Shaking his head no, Cassidy continued to walk around the room, but his eyes kept returning to the statue. There was still something familiar in it that he couldn't place.

"Ya see, young man, I'm kinda fond of that statue myself. Kinda fond of the young lady who posed for me. Reminds me of good times." He'd stopped working and was now staring at the statue as well, though he hadn't left his stool. Then he coughed and turned back to the soft clay.

"Tell ya what. I'll sell it to you, but only if you do right by the model herself."

And then Cassidy saw it, realized what had drawn him to the piece in the first place. The model, long hair and all, was DK.

*****

He didn't have time to hide the shock before Thomas saw it and cackled again in glee. It was too late to quibble about the price, not after his recognition about who the girl was appeared all over his face. DK when her hair was still long, back when she was sharing studio space with Thomas. He wanted to take it home with him right away. He would keep it at the rental house, then have it packed up and shipped to New York after Thanksgiving.

She'd posed for him, the potter had said. It was hard again to reconcile this DK with the one he thought he knew, the innocent her friend proclaimed her to be, a timid mouse who would never parade around naked in front of an old man. Or was that all there was to it? Did they have something more? The shiver of revulsion shot through him at the picture this created in his mind.

Was she the shy innocent that she often appeared, or the powerful and carefree woman who could take off her clothes and take a man to bed as casually as she chose her breakfast? He wanted her to be the woman he saw in his own mind, the one who was just coming into her own as an artist and as a self-confident person.

What he certainly didn't want was a female version of himself.

He paid Thomas, a check written so quickly that he barely remembered to note the price. Then wearing bubble wrap and plastic, he'd gently placed the statue in the passenger seat of the convertible, strapping it in for good measure. He was extra careful on the turns into town.

He placed the statue on the table in the dining room of the small rental, empty of his materials and laptop now. Those were all at DK's house, as were most of his things. All he had left here were a few summer clothes he hadn't needed.

Cassidy already told Lisa not to bother sending the cleaning service in since he wasn't there to make a mess. The statue would remain hidden here, more hidden than she had been at Thomas's studio. The time would come soon enough to pack this up too and turn in the keys before he flew away.

*****

DK didn't understand what had changed, but something had shifted in Vince. He was moody at times, other times almost giddy, and always a demanding and passionate lover. These last couple of weeks would fly by. Thanksgiving and its major celebration at her house were just over a week away. Vince's last weekend here would follow like a flash on its heels.

She was almost sorry she had agreed to the use of her house for the big party. She wanted Vince all to herself. But when she'd brought it up, he'd seemed cheerful and even pleased to be sharing the time with all of her friends.

He'd met the girl tribe, and had taken the time to talk with each person individually, which surprised her. The women had each shared that they thought he could be charming, but while there was nothing they could pinpoint precisely, there was something about him that also made them uneasy.

It wasn't Vince they were concerned about, but more how DK would be once he left. She couldn't blame them. She had gone into this with one set of expectations, and now she realized that from her side, this friends with benefits situation with Vince had evolved into something else completely.

The top piece for the Witch Hill sculpture was almost done. A man and woman wrapped together in tender passion, one arm each wrapped around the other and in a set of hands, a shared glass of wine. It had turned out beautifully, the build of the figures just hinting at their inspiration, she and Vince. Her face was shining up into his. She knew that the only reason she could have formed it so well was because of everything she was feeling for the man who would soon be leaving.

She burnished the joints as she tried to think through the changes that had appeared in this last week. First he'd been attentive but almost angry at Roxy's. Then he'd been asking her all of these odd questions about her past – her childhood, her college years, her agent, her time with Thomas, her activities at her house here.

She'd thought that he was only curious, which she took as a good sign. But when she'd tried to learn more about him, he'd kept his answers short and to the point. It was more like talking to a stranger in an airport lounge than a man she was sleeping beside each night, a man who made her soar with burning passion.

He also seemed to be getting too jovial about leaving. Women's names rolled off his lips with more frequency than she thought appropriate. Each one was a little barb to her heart. His questions about what she planned to do after he was gone were becoming annoying too.

"Come on," he said one day when they were sharing lunch, "I'm sure there are some people you haven't been able to see with me here. Isn't there anyone you'd like to be spending time with?" And he'd winked at her.

No, none of it made sense.

And her heart was breaking a little bit more each day. Once he left, she would need a good long cry, and maybe about a month of silence and solitude here with her work. In the past two weeks, she'd realized that the feelings she'd been trying to hide from herself were a whole lot deeper than she wanted to own up to.

She'd fallen in love with Vince.

And he didn't seem to return the sentiment.

*****

He stared at the e-mail on his screen. The editor he worked with at Lifestyle Worldwide was very interested in the series of articles on the region. But at Randy's suggestion, she was sending her comments directly to Cassidy for the changes she'd like to see made.

"...love the concepts and the topics you're covering, but I miss the sophisticated tone that our readers have so come to admire from you, Mr. Cassidy. That biting commentary which reveals all of the dirty little secrets and the things they love to hate is absent. If you can add that in, I'll be happy to provide you with a publication schedule for the final work."

Snarky, they wanted snarky, just as Roxy had accused him of being. He had never realized how much he wrote his travel articles with that tone. Now, he hated it.

When had he started using that superior attitude in his work? Had it been there for years? He suspected that some it came from his own dissatisfaction with those superficial topics, ignoring the deeper stories beneath the surface as demanded by editors. God, he missed the deeper stories.

"Hey, how's work going?" DK stood in the doorway, shedding her coat. Her hair was fluffed up as if she'd run her fingers through it to get rid of her helmet head, and she was distracted by the zipper on one boot. Then she finally stretched to the ceiling and turned to him.

It was that same motion, that stretch, the one that Thomas had captured so artfully in his clay.

He couldn't say anything, the pain of knowing that she had belonged to others and probably would again after he left too hard for his heart to take. He came into this with no expectations other than to have a casual good time, and wasn't it a hoot that now that had come back to haunt him.

She crossed the living room to the corner desk he'd used to set up shop. It was evident that she was interested in whatever was on the screen, curious to see what he had been working on. He put out a hand to close the lid before she could read the cursed e-mail.

A trace of disappointment crossed her face before she turned away. The contrasting calm in her voice sounded forced, or maybe it was his wishful thinking.

"You should probably put the convertible in the barn. The weather is looking pretty icky right now. It looks like it could snow."

He'd been around the Flynn's Crossing weather predictors, both insects and the human kind, long enough now to know that they put little stock in what they saw on

TV and more in the signs they saw around them. He'd miss that. People he knew in New York didn't have that kind of connection to the earth and skies.

He tried to match her light tone. "Snow, huh? That will make the woolly caterpillar watchers very happy." He forced himself to get up and cross the room to the kitchen counter where she was fiddling with a tea bag.

She looked up at him, and the raw emotion in her eyes nearly made him jump. Then she blinked a couple of times and looked down at the cup in her hand, moving to the sink. By the time it was filled with water and in the microwave, that expression was hidden.

"How is your work going?" He fiddled with a curl that stubbornly stuck out over her ear, fascinated by its color.

She'd been somewhat mysterious about whatever was on the main pedestal in the studio, covering it up when she wasn't working on it, shooing him away when she was and he wanted to visit.

"It's, ah, it's going fine. Almost finished for next weekend – I want to install it before you go so that you can see it in its final exhibit spot." She'd been insistent that it was important for him to see it, which made him feel like there must be some kind of meaning in it that she wanted him to see.

It gave him a little hope that perhaps she would be as sorry to see him leave as he would be to go. He'd be leaving a big part of himself here. In fact, he thought that maybe his roots were now set here and ripping them up to head anyplace else would stunt him for life.

He wrapped his arms around her and mentally counted down the days left. Eleven days, and not even full days. Less than eleven rounds of a twenty-four hour clock. He tightened his hold.

"I'm sweaty and grimy, Vince!" She tried to pull away, but he just held on harder.

"Well if you are, you need a shower, and definitely someone to scrub your back." He tried to put some teasing back into his tone. "And I know just the person to do it."

Chapter 33

Rain started coming down as they snuggled on the living room couch and watched an old movie. DK loved the intimacy of it, the sound of rain on the roof, the fire crackling, being lulled into peace in the arms of the man she loved.

Most of all, she treasured the last part. He would be gone too soon, and while his joking about who he would see back home and his probing questions about what her plans were once he was gone had stopped, something was still off. There were times that he stared at her with pain in his eyes.

She wanted to hope that he was feeling a sense of regret that their time was coming to an end. She dreamed that perhaps he had come to have deeper feelings for her than the casual friends with benefits they had agreed to in the first place. Maybe he would be sorry to go.

He had drifted off to sleep, his face peaceful and the lines of time and experience mere tracings of what they were during the day. She dared to hope that maybe his feelings for her were strong enough to keep him here. That, or at least bring him back quickly once whatever he needed to do in New York was completed.

She could feel the even rhythm of his breathing under her head. Lifting gently so she wouldn't wake him, she looked into his face. She didn't need any more time to memorize each feature. She could fill sketchpads with drawings of him with every conceivable emotion racing across those eyes, that mouth. All of the emotions except the one that would tie him to her – love.

His hands shifted and he opened his eyes lazily. "Are you done yet?"

She had to smile. "Done with what?"

"Your inspection. You've been staring at me for so long the movie ended." His hands rubbed her back and one finally made its way into her hair, pulling her in for a kiss.

This she would take, she thought. She would enjoy each precious moment that she had with him until the end. And then she'd hold her head high until he was out of sight.

*****

The covers on the big bed made it a huge cocoon, and Cassidy didn't even want to open an eye to see what time it was. The rain had stopped during the night, and everything was unusually quiet. He never realized how many little sounds he would hear from nature or from the house without being conscious of them. Right now, though, all was very, very still.

DK shifted against him and he forgot about everything as she turned to him, her eyes just opening. Then emerald green glittered and she was watching him, a playful leer on her face as she ran her hands down his body.

"Good morning. Someone's happy to be awake." Her tone teased him and her smile looked wicked as her hand fisted around him.

He pulled her on top and brought her face down for a long kiss. She tasted, as always, of mint and something that was uniquely DK. He wished he could bottle it and take it with him, an essence of her.

Not now, not today, he thought. Right now he just wanted to give and to take, to make more memories so that when he sat alone in his apartment and stared at the statue of her, he would be able to play long movies of their time together in his head.

He rolled her over and reached for the fancy box besides the bed. Flicking it open, he was surprised to find that it was empty. Ah yes, he'd been shopping and picked up more condoms, but they were downstairs where he'd dumped the bag when he got back from town.

"I'll be right back after a brief commercial announcement," he intoned in a pseudo-announcer's dull voice, kissing her nose. "Time for a refill."

She giggled. He was glad he could keep it light.

The floor was particularly cold under his bare feet, and he jogged down the stairs quickly, wishing he'd taken the time to pull on sweatpants at the very least. But it should be a fast trip and then he'd be back burrowed under the blankets and inside DK where he belonged.

It was the light that warned him first. It was a glaring blue, and it was coming from all of the windows. Normally at this hour of the morning, the sun lit up the great room as it rose in the east, and on cloudy days, it was still brighter in that direction than on any other. DK didn't believe in window coverings of any sort, saying that the deer didn't care what she was doing inside, and no one else was close enough to look in.

Cassidy stopped and blinked. It couldn't be. He moved from window to window as if the view might change with his vantage point. But no such luck.

"Ah, DK? You should come down and see this." He couldn't quite believe it himself. "And could you please bring my sweats with you?"

*****

Here she was, hot and ready and wondering what was taking him so long. She heard him call to her from downstairs. Come down now? Whatever it was could wait.

"What is it?" She didn't want to leave the warmth of the bed and the anticipation of their lovemaking.

"You really need to see this for yourself. And I really need those sweats."

What had gotten into him? She listened and didn't hear any rain. In fact, she didn't hear much of anything at all. The extreme stillness was a little disconcerting.

Well, if he needed sweats, she at least needed a robe, and the chill of the air as she climbed out of bed had her looking for a heavy one and big fuzzy slippers too. Fusion picked himself up off his dog bed in the corner and shook mightily. Then he padded down the stairs ahead of her and she heard the dog door in the kitchen rise and snap shut.

The light was... weird, was all she could come up with. It didn't seem to be coming from any one place, so it wasn't moonlight. It was too bright for that. Besides, the full moon was over a week ago.

At the bottom of the stairs, Vince grabbed his sweats out of her hands and quickly pulled them on. He was shivering, and she had to admit that the room was awfully cold. Sometimes when the fire took a long time to die down during the night, it delayed the heating throughout the house from coming on in the morning. But even so, it should have been running already.

Vince had dressed fast and was pulling her towards the front windows behind him. "Look," was all he said, and he pointed outside even as he stared wide-eyed.

It took her a few seconds to comprehend what they were staring at. Everything was white, very white, as in covered with a whole lot of snow white. Evidently the wet stuff hadn't stopped at all but instead had produced a steady and incredibly deep blanket of snow.

"Wow, those woolly caterpillars should definitely be giving the weather forecasts." Vince's tone was almost reverent. "And I'm damn glad I put the convertible in the barn."

He turned to grin at her. "Snow day!" He grabbed her and danced her around the great room, landing them finally on the couch. "We can make popcorn and watch more old movies and cook decadent comfort food, after we go back to bed for a while anyway." He leered at her.

DK laughed, delighted that he was taking this as a gift instead of complaining that it ruined their road trip plans for the day. He picked her up and whirled her around, and they both laughed until they were hysterical. Fusion came bounding back in and stopped short of them, shaking his coat and spraying snow everywhere.

"God, this floor is freezing," Vince said, hopping from one foot to the other. "And the snow on it doesn't help."

DK wiped her eyes and looked around, thinking she should get an old towel to mop up the puddles that would form quickly now that Fusion had tracked in so much snow. "Go find some shoes, or at least some socks," she said as she pushed Vince towards the stairs.

He grumbled, trying to pull her with him.

"I'll be up in a minute. And I don't want your icicle toes greeting me. Find some way to warm up your feet."

Still grumbling, he headed up the stairs. Fusion sat, tail thumping, obviously thinking about breakfast.

"Come on, I'll feed you. And if you track any more snow in, please clean it up yourself, okay?" The big tail wagged harder as the dog followed her into the pantry where his kibble was kept.

DK reached for the switch to turn on the light, intent on filling the dog's bowl and heading up the stairs to the warmth and promise of a morning in bed with Vince. So absorbed in her thoughts was she that it took a few seconds for her to realize nothing was happening when she flicked the switch. She looked up at the fixture in the ceiling.

She was still staring at it, confused, when she heard Vince calling from the top of the stairs. "Ah, Red? Something seems to be wrong up here. The power doesn't seem to be working."

Chapter 34

"Is this what the pioneers had to endure?" Cassidy asked the question even though he knew it was ridiculous. The pioneers had things much worse in their day. At least now they had batteries, sort of.

"Don't you have a generator?" He'd asked the question while DK was busy moving through the house, turning off things that did have batteries to conserve whatever power they still had. She hadn't said anything, just pointed at his laptop and made a cutting motion across her neck.

"No, I don't have a generator big enough to run the house. I have a very small one in the studio for some of the work that I do. But it's not enough to run the whole house, and besides, you need a special electrical panel to do that." She sounded disgusted.

He'd buy her a generator, he thought, a big one along with a panel, whatever the hell that meant. It would be another thing that would remind her about him every time the power went out. He wanted her to remember him, all the time.

She seemed to know what she was doing as she closed things that might leak what little warmth they had left. She called the electrical company to report the outage, mimicking the recorded message as she listened to it, and left an auto-reply message on her cell voicemail about their predicament for any incoming callers to hear before powering it down. He took a page out of her book and did the same.

"I have a car charger that I use in the truck," she informed him, "but I don't want to drain that battery too.

We'll need that to get out if things don't get better." She'd dug an emergency radio out of a kitchen drawer and set it on the counter, tuned to the channel that broadcast the status of the electrical company's work. It sounded like things were a mess everywhere, and there was no way for them to know how widespread the outage was.

"Don't you have a snow blower?" Didn't people in snow country usually have those? He thought they did.

She flashed him a grimace. "It doesn't usually snow like this overnight. And a blower doesn't work very well on a gravel driveway. Plus, the county doesn't plow out this far on our road." Enough said.

Actually, he was liking this adventure. Here he was, stuck in the wilderness, snowed in with a beautiful woman he loved and adored, with wood for the fire and food in the fridge. There was even wine. What more could he want?

There was a story here, he just knew it. Probably a few stories. At least it gave him good material for any tales he came up with about early settlers.

She appointed him fire-keeper and sent him out in the cold to load up on wood from the pile set away from the house. The snow was a lot deeper than he'd realized, looking at it from the windows. It came up well past his knees in most places and it was still coming down.

DK brought up the generator from the studio, and it was a small one. She also brought up a can of gas to run it. "That's all the fuel we have," she informed him, "so we can't run this very often."

Finally, after a fire roared, the snowy puddles left by the dog had been cleaned up, and everything was battened down, DK plopped down on the couch, craning her head around every once in a while to stare out the windows. He settled beside her and pulled her into his arms, content to watch the fire.

"There are so many broken branches out there. The leaves are still on the trees, for heaven's sake. No wonder we don't have any power. There must be lines down everywhere." Her gaze was troubled as she stared out at the falling snowflakes outside.

"It doesn't matter, you know. A day off will do both of us good." He put his chin on her head, enjoying the way the curls tickled him. "We'll sit here for a while, maybe fool around a little bit, take a shower."

DK pushed back and looked up at him. "Ah, Vince? We don't have hot water if we don't have power. We don't have a lot of water either, just what trickles in from the gravity feed on the holding tank. And we'll be cooking on a camp stove, unless you want to roast something on a spit in the fireplace." She eyed him warily. "Do you know how to do that?"

He'd seen it done, but he'd never done it himself. Would he have to hunt something down, kill it, skin it? He shuddered.

"So, no microwave either, I get it. We'll make do with things we can cook on the camp stove."

She was restless in his arms, staring outside again with a solemn expression. "You don't get it. This early in the season and this much wet snow means that the power is probably out all over the county, maybe all over this part of the state. The last time, in 2009, it was out for almost a week. All of northern California was impacted, along with Nevada and Oregon. And unless the snow stops coming down and starts melting, it will be impossible to get out of the driveway in my truck, much less down the road under the trees where the sun doesn't shine. Forget about moving your car."

He thought about this, then considered the fridge and freezer, already loaded up with goodies in preparation for next week's feast.

He pulled her closer, tipping her head back into the crook of his arm. When she would have continued on her rant, he put a finger to her lips to shush her.

"I guess we're stuck here then, my dear, and we'll just have to make the best of it." And he dropped his lips to hers.

Chapter 35

Day 2 of the Great Blizzard, as he had come to think of it, was giving him a whole new appreciation for those early pioneers. They must have gone crazy with the isolation of winter, neighbors living too far away to be in sight and weeks going by before they could travel any distance when the snows were deep. It was amazing anyone survived with a mind clear enough to build a town, much less cross the plains of the country to discover new lands.

He was going a little bit crazy from being so disconnected from the rest of the world. What if a world disaster broke out? How would they even know?

But for the most part, he and DK developed a routine of sorts. They set big pots of snow to melt by the fire, and that was useful for washing up and other chores. A huge pot melted down to only an inch or two of water, but still, they had plenty of time to watch it melt.

The great room became their full time residence, the bed in the loft too cold to tolerate even with a pile of blankets on it for sleeping. They nested instead in front of the fire, and he'd even pulled the mattress down from her loft to make things comfortable. DK laughed at him as Fusion tried to pull the opposite corner to help. In the end, though, she'd agreed that it made things much more pleasant in front of the roaring blaze.

He set the camp stove up right outside the back door on the drifted over patio. The cold temperatures and continuing snowfall guaranteed that he wasn't going to cook a lot, just heat up what they needed and dash back inside. Being a good pioneer, DK had figured out where in the piles of snow they could put some of the food from the fridge that might spoil, since they had to keep opening the door for items. Better it froze outside than spoiled. Their food was safe as long as Fusion and the marauding squirrels stayed out of it.

They talked a lot. Cassidy remembered some games he'd learned around the world, the kinds that didn't rely on electronics, and he collapsed in fits of laughter at her indignant face when he'd bent the rules so that he could get a rise out of her. She added her own laughter – after she retaliated and got even by giving him a face full of snow.

"So tell me more about your family growing up," she asked as they sat cross-legged on the floor in front of the fire, eating fancy grilled cheese sandwiches he'd prepared and canned tomato soup for lunch. "Where did you learn to cook?"

"I learned to cook from Cook."

She was curious. "You had a cook, as in someone who's only purpose was to cook for the family?"

"Well, more to the point, cook for my mother and me. And Mother called her Cook, so that's what I grew up calling her too. Father was gone most of the time, and Mother left me on my own when I became too old for a nanny. I'd hang out in what Mother called the servants' quarters, the backstairs parts of the house."

He hadn't wanted to share that part of himself, the Virginia Cassidy estate one of the things he'd been running away from when he headed to college. He'd enjoyed the influence and the freedom it had given him growing up, but it also burned with loneliness.

DK understood right away. "You didn't have a lot of close friends, I'm guessing, and so the servants became those early friends, didn't they?"

The shock on his face at her instant comprehension must have been obvious.

She laid a hand on his cheek and continued. "You came from money and what's sounded like unfeeling or uncaring parents on those rare occasions when you talk about them. You found your fun wherever you could, and then you got a little wild with it. I understand."

Somehow, he didn't think she could get this, because her own path had been so different. From everything she said about her family, they were hardworking middle class and living hand to mouth most of the time so that their children could succeed. Paying for five kids to go to private Catholic schools couldn't have been cheap or easy. But at least it sounded like they had each other to rely on.

He needed to make his childhood sound less desperate, less like a poor little rich boy who could be the subject of pity. He wanted to be brave or blasé about it. He went for humor.

"Yeah, I was the devil growing up. Cook showed me how to take care of myself in the kitchen because, as she put it, she was sure no girl would have me otherwise except for my money. I got underfoot with the butler and the gardener, stole the car keys from the chauffer who drove Mother around. I even tried to seduce each of the maids when I got into my teens, just to prove that I could."

This memory made him smile. "We went through a lot of maids." He waggled his eyebrows suggestively.

She smiled too, but it didn't reach her eyes. Sadness was in her eyes, and he didn't want her to feel sorry for him. It was time to change the subject.

"What was Chicago like in the winter?" It was easy to get her to tell stories about her hometown.

DK played with the fringe on the edge of the pillow as she framed her answer. "With a big family, there was always a lot going on. When we had a big snow like this one, we'd all head outside, even Ma and Dad. There was a big park close by with a hill, a tiny one compared to what we have around here, and we took turns heading down the slope on pieces of cardboard or plastic bags. Whatever was handy."

She smiled at her own memory, looking a little nostalgic. Cassidy knew her mother continued to pressure DK to come to Chicago for Thanksgiving, and she'd even shared that her mother was insisting he come along too, as her young man. DK had told him, and then had laughed it off with the wave of her hand as if she found the whole thing too unlikely to contemplate.

It stabbed at him, her light attitude about it. Maybe he wanted, just a little bit, to be that young man going home to meet her parents and siblings, subjected to the third degree when it came to their little girl.

He couldn't reconcile it. At times she was the innocent and at others she seemed to be the knowing siren.

Who was she, really?

At another point, she was pensive, locked in some private battle with her thoughts and an outcome that she didn't like. He tried to tease her out of it, playing with her curls until she'd frowned up at him, a trace of melancholy racing across her face before she turned away.

"Hey, what's up? I hate to see you looking sad." It had popped out of his mouth before he had a chance to think.

She kept her head turned away to respond. "Oh, I guess it's the weather and the fact that we can't get out. I wanted to show you more of the county before you go. And I have an installation to finish that I want you to see. It's just over a week away, your leaving, and I wanted it to be done." DK had moved out of the room and away from him at that point.

Something wasn't right, not making sense. She was a caring lover as she wrapped herself around him, holding nothing back. But at times, she was hiding from him, or hiding something from him.

Of course, he wasn't being fully up front with her either, Cassidy acknowledged. On the one brief call to Randy he'd allowed himself since the power went out, he'd mentioned that he was having writer's block.

"Writer's block? You never get that. Why, if anything, you have writer's purge, getting everything out so fast no one can keep up with you. What is it, a woman?" For once, Randy didn't sound like he was joking with him.

"Not sure what's going on. I can't seem to concentrate and get anything down on paper." He aimed for a little levity. "Of course, DK and I are locked up here with no power and nothing to do but lie under the blankets all day. Maybe I'm just worn out."

He waited to hear some ribald comment from Randy, but for once, the agent was acting more like a human being. "So what's really going on? Are you getting stuck on her?"

Stuck? Was that the right way to describe this intense longing to cancel his plane reservation so that they had more time?

He rubbed his eyes and stared again at the unending whiteness of the open field behind the house, the black dog jumping through drifts and barking with obvious enjoyment. "I don't know, man, I just don't know."

Chapter 36

She had to get a grip or she would slip up and blurt out her feelings. She'd wanted to have intense time with Vince, have him to herself, and look what the universe gave her. Snowed in from the blizzard, unable to get down the driveway even in her truck, and no power to top it all off.

DK almost screwed up this morning, snug in their makeshift bed in front of the fire and dozing in the afterglow of another round of passion. He'd been so gentle and loving, though she was sure that wasn't what he was experiencing. He was worldly and sophisticated, and ready, it seemed, to return to the life he had before coming here. She opened her mouth and almost said the words.

"That was amazing, Vince. Every time with you is even more amazing. I can't believe it. Is this what –" and she'd stopped herself just in time. Is this what love feels like? She'd repeated the question silently to herself.

She knew it was. By now, she was pretty sure she had a good handle on the man, and he was amazing. True, he could be, as Roxy had warned her when she waved some of his articles in her face, rude and disrespectful and a generally inhumane human being.

But he could also be loving and kind and considerate. And funny and playful and driving her crazy. She loved all of that about him, and more.

She respected the fact that he hadn't accepted his family's intended future and had made his own way in the world. The lonely little boy who turned into a hellion for the attention broke her heart. The artist in her appreciated the skill he had with words, when he finally allowed her to read something he was currently writing for an academic journal.

And he called to the woman in her at every level when he looked at her with eyes bright with focus and determination and passion.

Yes, she loved all of him, all of the complicated facets that joined to form him. It was nice to dream, to imagine what they could have if Vince loved her as much as she'd found she loved him. It was silly to expect that he felt the same way about her, though. She didn't have his worldly perspective, his confidence that he could tackle any situation, his ease inside his own skin.

And she couldn't compete with the women he'd known around the planet.

Still, the last three days of isolation had been a wonderful little miracle. Time out of time, she thought. When he was gone in a few days, she had this to look back on, to drive the inspiration that would no doubt come through in her work.

The fire was warm on her skin, banked up to a huge blaze so that she could take a sponge bath. Cassidy was supposed to join her, and she anticipated a rollicking conclusion that would leave them both panting. The idea made her heart rate pick up as a smile crossed her face.

No, she needed to guard her tongue. If she told him how she felt, he'd be embarrassed and probably feel sorry for her. That wasn't what a powerful and self-confident woman wanted, right?

*****

At this moment, Cassidy wished he could paint. He wished he could carve in clay or work in metal or anything that could capture the alluring lines and graceful movements of the elf by the fire. Even the camera in his cell phone would have been useful, if it had any battery power left.

As it was, he was only left with his words. They seemed woefully inadequate right now, unable to suggest the gentle curve of muscle and pull of tendon, the dreamy expression on her face or the halo of curls backlit by the fire, the glow of her soft skin. The image, he knew, would be seared into his mind for the rest of his life.

He loved her. The realization, something he'd been hiding from himself and trying so hard to deny, washed over him. It didn't matter if she'd slept with Thomas or Randy or a hundred other men. It only mattered that she was with him now. That was enough.

Her arm raised and he saw the shadow of her breast as she brought the washcloth up to bathe. Her posture was demure and yet it set him on fire, all of his desire pulsing through his body even as wave after wave of love crashed into his heart. They had had each other how many times over the last three days, locked in as they were with the storm? He'd lost count, and now he wanted her again.

Cassidy realized it was more than wanting, though, and much more than the physical satisfaction. He smiled as he thought about her playful teasing when he was in a bad mood, or her frustration with him, hands on hips, when he was being particularly dense. Sometimes he did it on purpose, just so that he could see that temper flare up.

No, it was everything about her, mind and spirit, body and soul, that called to him.

What would she do right now, he wondered, if he told her he'd fallen in love with her? Would she laugh in his face? Would she give him a small smile of knowing pity before turning away? Would she remind him briskly that their agreement was friends with benefits only?

He had to convince her that their pasts didn't matter. He didn't care about hers any longer, and he didn't want her wondering about his. Who they slept with, why they did it, how many times they'd been casual about sex wasn't important.

The past didn't matter as long as they were true to each other in their future, the future they would share together.

God, he really was pathetic, and he could only imagine what his face looked like right now, lovelorn and full of longing to confess it all. He wanted her to know that he understood what she'd had to do to survive when she was starting out. He might never talk to Randy again and he wouldn't let her talk to him either, but that was okay. There were plenty of agents in the world.

She dropped the washcloth back into the bowl by the fire and raised a towel to wrap around her. He missed her nakedness immediately, the natural flush of beauty and innocence. It would be better, he thought, if he let her get dressed, as much to quash his own fire as to put things on an even footing when they had this discussion.

Her dreamy expression was back, even as she reached for her turtleneck and jeans. Cassidy slipped back out of the doorway and headed into the snow to marshal his thoughts and cool his body's fire.

Chapter 37

He'd been acting strangely, DK thought. She was dressed and ready to work on dinner when he'd finally come into the house, his nose red from the cold and steam rising from his jacket as he stood rubbing his hands by the fire. He'd borrow a knit hat and gloves from her, both too small, but at least they filled something of the need for warmth.

Vince had been out there a long time, and she was sorry he hadn't come back to share their little bathing ritual, or drop down to the blankets and indulge in another round of dreamy passion.

Animated throughout dinner, it was like he was competing for her attention in a busy bar. It was almost distracting, and when she tried to ask what had gotten into him, he changed the subject and headed in a new direction.

He'd pulled her chair out for her, making a big display of shaking out the paper napkin and putting it on her lap. The laughter he'd brought her with his imitation of an Italian accent to go with the pasta and sauce had tears rolling down her face.

The gentleness of his kisses and tight embrace as they sat in front of the fire made her want to cry for completely different reasons.

This whole friends with benefits thing was complicated. She'd talked it over with Gabby earlier in the day.

"I'm in way over my head. I'm not cut out for casual affairs, and now this one's backfired on me even more. I'm so in love with the guy I can't think straight and all I want to do is tell him."

"So why don't you?" Gabby's question sounded so simple on the phone.

"Because we had an agreement, the friends with benefits agreement. No commitment, no strings. I agreed to it, he agreed to it. He leaves in a week, Gabby. I don't want to mess it up, not when this is going to have to last me a whole long time in terms of memories, not to mention lust and satisfaction." She'd choked on a laugh at the end, intending to make it funny. The joke, though, was on her.

"Tell him, DK. You don't know what he'll say. Didn't you tell me how gentle and attentive he's been? Maybe you can work something out, keep seeing each other, stay in contact even long distance, until you two get this all figured out. Maybe he has deeper feelings for you too."

Trust Gabby to believe that there was hope in this. She'd lost her true love a couple of years ago, and she still believed that there was hope for everyone, everyone but herself that is.

"What if I tell him and I become a charity case? You know, he continues to sleep with me while he's here, but then once he's gone, I never hear from him again. I couldn't stand to have him leave feeling sorry for me. I want his last thoughts of me to be ones of a powerful woman who blows his mind, not to mention sets his body on fire."

That had made Gabby laugh, and even DK could muster a chuckle. When they'd quieted down again, Gabby shared her last bit of advice.

"Look, you still have a few days. The roads should be passable in another day or so and the weather's supposed to warm up. You wanted to finish the Witch Hill sculpture and show it to him, right? It's filled with how you feel about him, the passion the two of you share. Get it in place, then take him over there and show it to him. Tell him while you're both standing there, when he can see how you feel about him in your creation."

Gabby had a point. DK didn't need to tell him today. In fact, if she showed him, he might spontaneously share his feelings for her. Maybe he was in love with her too and it would all work out.

Or he could feel mortified about her feelings and hop on the next flight to anywhere.

*****

Tonight he'd tell her, Cassidy decided. He'd say that what was in the past was in the past, and they never needed to talk about it again. The future, though, belongs to the two of them exploring what they have together.

One thing led to another, though, and he had a hard time finding the right time to get the words out. He practiced in his mind as he'd paced in the snow, waiting for her to dress after the makeshift bath. He practiced some more when she was inside and he was outside, cooking their simple pasta dinner.

Then he'd babbled like an idiot throughout dinner. He thought that sitting quietly might work out better, but their time by the fire had made him more nervous.

How would she take it? His own self-doubt was wrecking his resolve to forgive and forget. Because after all, she would have to forget all about his dalliances around the globe too. He could assure her, though, that those were now a thing of the past. He didn't want any other woman now that he had DK in his life.

She yawned in his arms, and looking at his watch, he was surprised to find that it was past 10 o'clock. Night had fallen long ago but without the regular schedule of a TV show or the busy activities of an evening when the lights were on, time lost its meaning. He'd been nestled with her in his arms now for more than two hours, shifting only long enough to throw more logs on the fire and pull up the blankets.

It was now or never, because he didn't think he could face another night of waiting.

Cassidy cleared this throat. "Diane, we need to talk."

She went still in his arms. She'd told him more than once that she didn't use her full name anymore. It reminded her of her childhood and left her feeling like she was nine years old and in trouble again. It had slipped out though, something about the seriousness of what he was about to say seeming to need the formality of it.

He turned her so that he could see her face, so that she could look into his eyes and see the sincerity there. He wanted this to come out right. She was staring at him with a guarded expression, one that gave nothing away about what she was thinking, hidden in the brilliant green flames of her eyes.

He started again. "Red, I have some things to tell you, some things to say. I don't want you to respond until I'm done, okay?"

Her eyes had gotten large at his tone and he wished he'd gone about this differently. But hell, how many times in his life had he tried to tell the woman he loved his feelings before? Never. He was paddling in virgin waters here and his boat definitely had a few leaky holes in it.

He straightened and pushed back restlessly at the blankets, suddenly hot and bothered with his own lack of words. Him, a writer, without the right words. It was a fucking sorry-assed excuse and laughable but he was in love, so what could he expect of himself?

He tried again. "This time with you, it's been..." He stopped. What word was right? Awesome? Incredible? Life-changing?

She was watching him warily now, all hint of sleepiness gone. He tried a smile, but he knew it came off as forced. She tried one too, but it was uncertain.

"I didn't expect to..." What hadn't he expected? To find a woman here? He had started out thinking that she would be a pleasant diversion while he was staying here. To fall in love? That was completely unexpected, a fucking unknown.

Would she pat his cheek and give him that slightly sad look that she'd had when she'd felt sorry for the lonely little boy in the stories of his childhood?

Best to blurt things out, kind of like pulling off a bandage. Get the pain over with quickly and see where things stood between them.

What he wouldn't give for some of his usual sarcastic bravado right now.

*****

She'd heard the phrase time stood still used a few times, but she never had a true idea of what it meant. That was, until now.

This was it, she thought. Three days of unending togetherness in their isolated conditions and he was tired of her, of all of it. He was going to say it, going to say that he would be leaving as soon as he could get out. It had been great but it was just a physical thing. Thanks for the wonderful times, but he was moving on again.

She couldn't stand it. Her hard-won self-confidence crashed around her and she wanted to burrow under the blankets so that she couldn't hear however he was going to let her down easy. He would be pitying her as her tears would undoubtedly fall.

It was better to take charge. Better to be the one doing the letting down than to be on the receiving end. His ego could handle it.

Hers clearly couldn't.

She put a big smile on her face and straightened her spine. "Ah, come on, you really don't want to talk, do you?"

Running her hands down her body in what she hoped was a sensual tease, she leaned closer, close enough to read the surprise in his eyes and feel him pull back slightly to watch her. The surprise turned to confusion, and then to hurt suspicion.

The scent of him drew her in, the clean-air woodsy smell that all of the time outdoors today only accentuated. For a moment, she closed her eyes and breathed him in. When she opened them, he was sitting back, his expression hooded and unreadable, waiting.

It was now or never. What would an experienced woman full of her own power do? She'd take what she wanted. And oh, she wanted him.

DK decided on wicked, and put on what she thought was her best come-hither smile. She traced a finger that thankfully wasn't shaking down his cheek and outlined his lips. He didn't move, didn't respond. Playing hard to get, eh? But after the weeks they'd spent together, the many hours locked around each other, she knew how to move him.

This might be the last time, she realized. He might still want to say goodbye once they were spent. With that in her mind, she couldn't help but put all of the love she had for him into the kiss. It seared her, his lips finally moving as if he was unwilling but unable to stop himself.

She leaned in, holding herself above him as he lay back in the nest they'd made for themselves by the fire. His hands stayed fisted by his sides, which was fine with her. She wanted to be in complete control, wanted to let him feel everything in the passion she was bringing him.

DK slanted her mouth and let her tongue dive in deep, dancing with his, teasing and then taking. She opened her eyes to see Vince's were on her. The brown burned with light that seemed to reflect an inner fire. It shook her heart and sent fire racing through her.

Seduce him, that's what she wanted to do. Give him a night that he wouldn't forget when he was thousands of miles away in the arms of another woman. He'd be thinking, ah yes, this is nice, but it isn't as nice as DK.

Sitting back, she slowly raised her sweater, letting it pull her hair back as she shrugged it off. She hadn't bothered with a bra today, and with a faint shiver at the cold, she lifted the turtleneck in a slow movement that she hoped was sensuous.

Vince still hadn't moved, watching her with eyes that were hot but with his famous control in place. Damn the man, she wanted him panting for her, and she couldn't even pull that off. The knowledge hit a nerve and made her angry, ready to ravage him and remind him of all that he was giving up.

Letting her hands roam slowly down her body again, she saw the second his resolve cracked. His eyes changed from molten to something deeper, something almost desperate. It made her heart sing and set her body on fire. She caressed one breast, then the other, and his hands rose slowly to trace the path she had just taken. Her nipples hardened and she felt the wetness pool between her legs.

Such a small thing, a light touch, and yet look what it did to her. She wanted to make him crazy, unable to keep himself from ravaging her. His fingers gently shaped her breasts, his eyes intent on what he was doing. His expression, though, was still unreadable.

DK found herself getting lost in the moment, lost in the sensuous feelings that he always brought her. Her hands followed his for a time, gently touching the fine hairs on the backs and teasing the pulse inside his wrists. Then she let her hands travel lower, unbuttoning and then unzipping her jeans slowly. His gaze fell to her hands and a small sigh escaped him.

He moved slowly, as if he too was feeling the trance that had overtaken her. He covered her hands with his. "Let me," he whispered, so low she almost couldn't hear it. His hands covered hers, dwarfing them, and then he pushed hers aside to slide fingers inside her jeans and begin pushing them down her hips.

It took hours to do this, he was moving so slowly, hours before she was stepping out of the denim and scrap of lace. It gave her time to caress his face, memorizing again each line, each dip and contour. The hollow just below his cheekbone, the whirl of hair just above his ear. It would all remain deep in her memory of him, always.

His hands had stilled on her hips, thumbs tracing her shape as if he too was memorizing her. He wasn't looking at her face, and she missed the connection to the chocolate depths of his dark eyes and the passion she would see rising there. She put a finger under his chin and raised his face to hers. There was sadness in his gaze, and she felt an echo answering in her own measured look. Such sweet memories for both of them to take.

She lowered her lips again, intending to take him slowly until things flared between them. The gentleness in his returning kiss almost undid her, leaving her shaking inside with the softness of it. His hands wound into her hair and he held her face to his, running kisses along her features until she thought tears would come.

It would be better, she knew, if she could pull off the playful mating that they sometimes indulged in, a way to keep her distance so that he couldn't read her heart. But she couldn't do it.

All of what she felt for him, every ounce of love inside her, went into the kiss she placed on his lips. If she couldn't tell him, she could at least show him the depth of her love.

He shuddered, and she felt a surge of incredible power, the knowledge that at least here, she was the confident and capable woman she wanted to be. She took the kiss deeper, and he shook beneath her. Pulling back, she looked into his eyes and saw the turmoil warring within him. The fire burned inside.

Chapter 38

He didn't know what he wanted, to go forward or to hold back. Her kisses were so sweet, he thought. There was no other word for it. He wanted to return the gentleness while he showed her the passion of his feelings for her. The dilemma was if he did, he was afraid that the words would spill out of him, and then there would be no going back.

Cassidy put his hands on her shoulders and shoved her away from him, literally dumping her to the side in his haste to move. He needed to stand, clear his head, make a decision. Now would be the time to say something, if he was going to. Now before another wave of intimacy carried them off into oblivion.

He moved away to stand in front of the blazing fire. The heat was comforting, a reflection of the same searing heat that she caused inside him. Would it be enough to share that passion once again and then walk away? He doubted that he could.

He didn't hear her, intent on his thoughts. She wrapped her arms around him, pressing her naked body against his back, and he could feel her warmth through his layers of clothes. She hugged him, running a single finger down the row of buttons of the flannel shirt. One by one, they popped open until she had spread her hands against the t-shirt below.

He reached back to find her, feeling the silky texture of her skin. Turning in her arms, his hands found the line of her spine and his eyes met hers as he looked down into her face. The fire lit her hair with dancing lights, and the emerald of her eyes glowed. A small smile creased her lips, and he had to have a taste.

Her taste was like the finest wine, the most exquisite flavors of a gourmet meal, as rich as any gooey dessert. Her skin was the softest satin under his hands. The spicy floral scent of aroused woman, his aroused woman, filled his head until he knew he would carry that with him no matter how far he traveled. He sank to his knees in front of her, carrying his kisses down her body as she moaned and shifted, unsteady on her feet.

His hands cupped her buttocks and braced her upright while his lips traced the lines where her legs met her core. His tongue plunged in as she gave a small cry. This release he could give her, he knew, with every ounce of love he felt for her pouring into his intimate flicks. Her shudders quickly turned to quakes and her moans sent him soaring with the satisfaction he was giving her. Her body stiffened and she cried out, music to his ears.

Lifting his eyes, he thought how magnificent she looked as the orgasm washed over her. Her head was thrown back and her mouth was open, her hands gripping his shoulders in an attempt to anchor herself. He supported her as she shook and then as she quieted. Her face, the glory of it, was the most beautiful thing he'd ever seen.

She came back to earth slowly, her face turning down to his as he stayed kneeling in front of her. She sank to the floor as well, and her mouth captured his in a kiss that let him know he had moved her as perhaps he never had before.

"Vince, I…" It wasn't the time for words, and he caught whatever she was going to say next in another searing kiss. Her hands fluttered at the base of his shirt, finding the edge and lifting it. He moved back to shake it over his head and she dropped it to the side. He smiled at the dreamy look on her face as she ran her hands lightly down his chest to the waistband of his jeans.

He couldn't say the words he wanted to share with her, couldn't tell her how he felt, but he could show her with his body. DK worked the button of his jeans free and was moving to the zipper, skimming the skin underneath and making him hiss in a breath. The movement, even after all of their times together, still made him quiver with need. It was so innocent, she was so innocent in these simple touches.

Rising and pulling her with him, he crossed to their nest in front of the fire. He got rid of his remaining clothes quickly and he loved the fact that she settled back on to the mattress, licking her lips at the sight of his jutting erection. She moved to take him in her hands and he knew that he wouldn't last long if she touched him for more than a second. The glaze of fingers set him throbbing, a silky touch that had him quivering for completion. He lay down on top of her, tucking her into position as he settled between her legs.

For once, there would be no barrier between them, nothing but the love he had for her, the love he couldn't confess but could show her. He levered himself inside in one quick stroke, and she sighed and twisted her fingers into his hair. His fingers ran over skin heated with their lovemaking and the fire.

Would he ever find another woman who fulfilled him in every sense the way DK did? He doubted it. He would travel to all of the continents and never again know this feeling of completion, the knowledge that he would never again be this happy driving him to slow the pace. With each stroke, he let her know he loved her, even when he couldn't speak the words.

There was something in her kisses, her care in each taste of him as if she too was savoring what they shared. Her hands were never still, until he ran first one hand and then the other up her arms to grip them. He held himself above her and met her eyes, reluctant to let her go, unwilling to let himself find the completion his body craved, unable to believe that there would ever be anything more for him after her.

His body and hers, though, would not be denied. He felt her rising crest coming to match his, the pace of her body in perfect synchronization with his. They rose and fell together, the meeting of bodies coming faster as they continued to stare into each other's souls. Everything else disappeared, so concentrated was he on her blazing look and the feel of her body beneath him.

Finally, when he could delay it no longer, he felt her hands tighten their grip on his. He never wanted this to end, but there was no avoiding it. His eyes boring into hers, never letting her break their gaze, he felt her clench around him, and his body shifted one last time as he emptied into her with a harsh cry.

Chapter 39

She couldn't bear it, DK thought. Last night was incredible, there was no other word for it. Never had she and Vince been so in tune with each other, their bodies coming together in a wave of intense heated pleasure that surpassed anything that had come before. It was painful to contemplate, the time so soon to come when she wouldn't have him any longer.

Watching him sleep, she thought back over the last few hours. He had been such a gentle and considerate lover. He never looked away, his eyes locked on hers as they both jumped off the edge of that cliff of completion rocking her to the core. Coming down, he stayed with his hands tight in hers until their breathing slowed. Then he'd lowered his head and met her lips in a kiss that shook her even more than the orgasms had.

It was going to be so hard giving him up, letting him get on that plane and return to his life of distant adventures. It would be harder still thinking about him with any other woman, locked in someone else's arms in some foreign city.

Still, she was grateful for this time with him. She had learned so much about herself, and what she had experienced with him would surpass anything she would ever know again.

She would never love another man the way she loved him.

Shifting against him, she didn't want to move, even as the light was coming up and the living room was brightening. The snow was melting and the truck would make it down the driveway. She could tramp down the snow to allow him to get his car out as well.

Today they would have to return to reality.

It was so nice, though, to be tucked tight against his side. Last night, he had rolled and taken her with him, holding on to her and pulling her against him as if he would never let her go. And he hadn't throughout the night, even as his deep breathing told her he was asleep. Even in sleep, he'd held on.

The time had come to move on, though, time for her to tuck away these memories for the future and put a smile on her face. He could never know how deeply she loved him. She didn't want to feel him pulling away or see the pity on his face. Friends with benefits didn't hold on tightly, did they? She gave him a gentle fleeting kiss as she slipped out from under the covers to dress.

*****

The first thing he thought as he woke was that he felt cold despite the covers, empty for some reason. And there was a buzz of noise he couldn't identify. Light pressed insistently against his closed eyelids.

He automatically reached for DK, his hands searching across the makeshift bed as he felt for her creamy skin and sheltering heat. He wanted to pull her against him, curl her underneath him and bury his body inside hers again. All night, he had been content to hold her, but he needed her again right now.

How could he ever move on now? Last night, the passion spent and their eyes still locked, he was afraid that for the rest of his sorry fucking life he was going to be that lonely little rich boy he'd described to her.

No one and nothing was ever going to be as amazing as DK.

His hands reached the edges of their nest of blankets, and he didn't feel her. Reluctantly, he opened his eyes and found that he was alone. He listened for her, trying to tell if she was someplace close by in the house, but as attuned as he now was to her energy, he couldn't sense her anywhere near.

And as he looked up, he realized what the sound was. The ceiling fan was turning above him.

The power had come back on.

Damn the woman, where was she? He called out to her, hoping she would wander back into the living room and back into their bed. Just because they had power didn't mean they couldn't enjoy their special place in front of the fire. She must have banked up the blaze because it was dancing cheerfully when he threw back the covers to search for her.

He wandered through the first floor, then called up the stairs to the second. DK didn't answer, and he'd cursed as he found his clothes in various corners of the room and pulled them on quickly. He couldn't imagine that she'd be out in the studio working at this early hour. There was no note from her that he could find.

Fusion greeted him at the back door, prancing with a very wet ball in the melting snow. The sounds outside surprised him. You wouldn't think that this far away from neighbors in the country, there would be so much noise from all of the electronics in the area coming back on. But there was a deep buzz in the air, and unlike the previous three days, it wasn't the sound of chainsaws.

The studio door stood shut. It creaked its familiar noise as he stuck his head inside and called to DK again. No response. In the dim light, he could see that she had winched whatever she had been working on, that piece for installation that she had insisted he was going to need to see, into the back of her truck. It was covered in a plastic tarp and hidden. He was curious, but it could wait until he found her.

In the light of day, Cassidy was again unclear about his intentions. Last night he wanted to explain everything to DK, tell her that he was in love with her and see if she felt anything in return, anything that might give them time to explore these feelings further. But she'd cut him off.

He couldn't read her, which disconcerted him more than anything else. It was like she dropped a mask in place any time he wanted to discuss feelings. Did she want to protect him, let him down easy? After all, he'd been convinced friends with benefits was the way to go, a nice distraction during his visit. She'd even suggested it.

But it appeared that the joke was on him.

Fusion brought the ball again, and Cassidy looked at him quivering his excitement at the opportunity for a game. "Where is she, boy? Did she tell you where she was going?"

The dog woofed but just nudged the ball again. Cassidy picked it up and threw it a distance towards the big oaks in front of the house.

Another sign of how things had changed. He was not only talking to a dog, he was picking up a slobbery ball and playing with him. There were women all over the world who would be laughing their asses off to see this mushy side of him.

He looked around in the snow for some sign of which way she could have gone. They had been outside enough times over the past few days, walking down the driveway or around the house and studio and into the fields, that it was difficult for him to tell which tracks were new and which had been melting for a while.

It was unlike DK to wander off without at least a note. Hell, she even left him a note when she was working in the studio. Where could she be?

He walked around the house again, staring out at the fields and hillsides surrounding the house. No sign of any movement and no flash of the bright blue color of her winter jacket. The air was warming, pings of water dripped, and birds that were suddenly active twittered. But no noise that might be DK.

In case she had been hiding in her office and unable to hear him for some reason, he checked the studio again. He prowled inside from wall to wall in the old barn, tempted to shuffle through the sheets of drawing paper on her desk but unwilling to spend that time until he found her. He remembered her quick movements to shove something under a large binder when he'd surprised her there yesterday.

He was getting scared now, a frisson of fear riding up his spine. Had she gone for a walk and fallen someplace, hit her head and knocked herself out? But then, the dog wouldn't be ready to play. Fusion was as devoted a creature as Cassidy had ever seen and he would be at DK's side.

And she hadn't driven out. Her truck and his car were both still there, no sign of tire tracks in the driveway. Walking any distance was out of the question, since there really wasn't anywhere to go.

Cell phones! If she'd gone anywhere, she'd have turned it on and taken it with her, a safety precaution she said. He hurried back inside and grabbed his cell, turning it on and waiting impatiently for the thing to boot up. Scrolling through the stored numbers, he hit the send button when he got to hers and waited again, tapping his boot.

And her cell rang on the kitchen counter.

Chapter 40

The snow was melting quickly now. In another day, there would be few signs of the depth of drifts that had blocked them in for the last three days. DK was almost sorry to see it go, since it meant returning to what passed for normal in her life. It would take Vince away from her that much faster.

She heard him on the phone in the kitchen just as she pushed through the front door.

"Well if you hear from her, would you please let me know? I'm getting a little concerned."

Puzzled, she stared at Vince's back as he held her cell phone, a worried expression on his face. He spun around when the door slammed shut and the profound relief on his face was chased away quickly.

"Wait, she's just walked in. Yes, she seems to be fine. Sorry to bother you." He disconnected the call with a savage poke and the phone hit the counter with a slam.

"Where have you been?" He covered the space from kitchen to front door in rapid strides and took her by the shoulders, shaking her and staring down into her face in clear anger.

"Outside. Just across the way. Why, what's wrong?" She was perplexed. He'd been sleeping so heavily when she'd gone out to check the driveway that she didn't think he'd wake up for hours.

"What's wrong is I couldn't find you. I didn't know what happened to you. You shouldn't be wandering around like that." He was shaking her now. "Damn it, Red, you don't have a lick of sense! You leave doors unlocked, don't pay attention to the world around you, and wander off without letting anyone know where you'd gone!"

Shouldn't be wandering around like what? She wanted to shout at him. What did he think she did here, living by herself? She sure didn't check in with someone every time she wanted to open the door.

Her anger was rising to meet his. "Look, I live here, by myself." She emphasized the last words for good measure and stabbed a finger into his hard chest.

He loosened his grip a little.

"If I want to go outside, I go outside. If I want to walk up the driveway, I do it. I don't need to check in with anyone and I certainly don't need to ask you for permission!"

Vince seemed to be stunned suddenly. He dropped his hands but remained standing in front of her, blocking her path. He'd gotten quiet, but that didn't lessen her own anger.

Who the hell did he think he was?

She turned to stomp around him, heading for the kitchen. "Not that I owe you an explanation, but I was standing at the window looking at the driveway and I noticed that there was no smoke coming out of Mrs. Bellechois's chimney. I was worried that something had happened to her, so I got dressed and walked over. She was talkative, which was unusual, but I think the isolation of the storm has even gotten to her. So I chatted with her for a while."

She started cleaning up some of the dishes in the sink, stacking the dishwasher. Her anger, always as quick to fade as it was to flash, was quieting. "The power came back on while I was there, so I helped her get her house in order a bit."

She drew in a deep breath, trying to calm her suddenly raw nerves. Her eyes staying on her task, she continued. "I'm here by myself all the time, remember. I know how to take care of myself, by myself. End of story. Thank you for your concern."

Vince hadn't said anything, and she turned in time to see some fleeting raw emotion dash across his face before he shuttered his eyes in a neutral look. He opened his mouth to say something, then closed it again as he shook his head and headed up the stairs.

"I'm taking a shower."

She watched his retreating back and wondered why he'd suddenly gotten so mad at her. He was leaving, and she needed to get back to her own life and her independence.

*****

The hot shower felt great after the past few days of sponge baths. Cassidy let the water beat on his head, even though he felt like beating his head against the tile wall instead.

He'd over-reacted, he knew it. He should know by now that DK would be fine, was used to living here on her own in the middle of nowhere. He wanted her to depend on him, wanted to be her knight in shining armor, her hero.

But she didn't need a hero and she clearly didn't need him.

The towel felt rough, and he realized he was thinking about the tender soft touch of her fingers on his body instead. It made him tighten and stir and he thought about moving back under cold water to get rid of the sudden heat of his body.

He made himself move to the cooler temperature of the loft bedroom instead and looked out its front window to see DK heading up and down the drive in her big truck, knocking down a path that would allow him to get his convertible out to the main road.

She was ready for him to leave. He'd overstepped that invisible line and now she wanted him to go. Last night had been so special, he thought, a connection between them on a deeper level. But clearly it seemed that was all on his side.

He dressed slowly, trying to gather thoughts that were scattered in too many directions. He wanted to tell her what he was feeling. He thought he should race to the airport and head out of town as quickly as possible. He longed to admit out loud that he loved her. He wanted her to reply that she loved him too. They could spend the rest of their lives together, cocooned and safe against the world.

She'd pulled the blankets and sheets off the mattress in front of the fire, and he heard the washer churning away in another corner of the house. The sound made him sad, like she was trying to wash away memories. She'd also set the comforters back in their appointed places in the living room and cleaned up the kitchen. It was like she wanted to wipe away all evidence of their idyllic time for the past few days.

He could do his frigging part, Cassidy thought glumly, the painful hurt in his heart almost overwhelming him. He picked up the handles on the mattress and dragged it back up the stairs, setting it on the box springs in the bedroom. He stroked a hand over it, remembering times up here too. It wasn't the mattress, though, or even the place.

It was the thoughts of DK, curled against him or rising in passion, moaning as he entered her or laughing as she tickled him. Her face lit in laughter and her green eyes glowing. Years from now, those images would still be fresh in his mind.

His heart ached, each beat painful and aware, and his groin stirred again at the memories. The future stretched in front of him, empty and cold. It would be a very long time, probably never, before the raw hurt would fade.

*****

She parked the truck out of the path of his car. She would take a shower, call the winery and see if she could come by and install that top piece to the sculpture, then stop at the store to pick up food in preparation for the Thanksgiving party later this week. She avoided thinking about whether or not she wanted Vince to accompany her on any of this. He didn't seem to be too pleased with her right now.

His concern had been touching, or at least she'd liked to think so. But he was a temporary part of her life, and insecure or not, she'd been standing on her own two feet long before he showed up on the scene.

And she would have to do it again now.

"Looks like we can get out." He'd come up behind her as she was staring at the driveway. She turned and took in the wet hair and clean clothes, feeling suddenly grubby and itchy, ready herself for a shower.

"Yes, I think I've knocked down what's left of the snow enough for you to be able to get out."

She stared at him, hoping that her look was as neutral as his.

"I, ah, need to go into town and take care of some things." He hesitated.

"I need to get some stuff done too." She went for brisk and business-like, making a big show of jingling her keys and turning her wrist to check her watch.

He moved forward, standing in front of her. His eyes held her gaze for a moment, then he lowered his head and gave her a brief hard kiss. He pulled back, searching her face again. A fleeting disappointment crossed his features, and setting his sunglasses on his face, he folded himself into the car.

He fired it up and backed out of the barn without looking at her, then slowly drove away without so much as a wave in the mirror.

Chapter 41

It had been a busy day. He was looking at the town through different eyes now, he realized. He wanted to belong here, but the woman he wanted to belong to seemed to be ready to return to her regular life. Read, her life before him, without him.

He took his Brew Bank coffee into the art gallery and wandered the displays, seeking out DK's pieces. The older woman who had worked with DK that day of their first date bustled up and asked if she could help him.

"Yes, you can." He put a big winning smile on his face. "I'm looking for pieces by DK McGiven."

The woman smiled at him in return, a rage of interest on her face. "Aren't you that young man who had the date with her a while back?"

Small towns, he thought. "Yes ma'am. I was wondering which of her pieces were here. I wanted to buy something to take home with me, to remember Flynn's Crossing."

She turned and crooked a finger at him over her shoulder. "Back here, I think I have just what you might be looking for."

It was stunning, a miniature tree that he immediately recognized as one of the huge oaks in front of her house. It was bare of leaves, a view that was quickly coming with the late fall weather. The details were exquisite. Branches that were gnarled with old growth twined around each other. It was like real life nature had come to life in the sculptured metal.

And at the base, there was the small form of a dog laying with head down. Fusion in a rare moment of rest.

Cassidy smiled. It reminded him of good times already, times when they'd walked under the oaks, had picnics under the big trees, talked about what those old things must have seen in the course of their lifetimes. It had been fanciful and fun.

"I'll take it."

There was no sound from the older woman, and he turned to see her staring at him.

"Don't you want to know how much it is?" She sounded slightly excited.

"I don't care how much it is." He pulled out his wallet and selected a credit card at random. Handing it to her blindly, he remained where he was, staring at the piece and lost in thought.

"Ah, do you want me to put the total on this, or would you like to make a down payment?" The woman was walking to the counter at the back of the store.

"All of it right now. I want to take it with me." He was sure he could lift it and carry it up the hill to the rental house.

The woman began to chatter behind him, suddenly enlivened by something. She mentioned that he might like to look at some of the work of other artists that they had available, perhaps pick up some art for his walls?

He ignored her, picturing where he would place this work.

When he didn't respond to her comments, she came back to him with a small clipboard in hand and a pen pointed towards him expectantly. He turned away from the little tree to take the charge card and slip from her, grabbing the pen impatiently.

The clipboard felt so small in his big hand, and he looked down at the charge form to find the signature line. Then he looked at the total charge.

No wonder the woman was smiling.

*****

The top piece had gone into place without a hitch, fitting as she'd planned it. A couple of welds had completed the process, and she was standing back and staring up at the completed work when Marguerite came up beside her. She didn't say a word, putting an arm around DK's shoulders and giving her a tight squeeze. When DK was ready to leave, Marguerite asked quietly if she was all right.

She just shrugged and shook her head.

Roxy's store was understandably busy, with only two days to go before Thanksgiving and people still struggling out to replenish supplies after the storm. She moved through in a trance, her mind unable to do much more than repeat the words 'five more days' in a silent litany. When the checker had looked at her strangely, she realized the girl was talking to her and she hadn't even heard. She tried to smile and headed out the door pushing her laden cart to the truck.

Vince's car was not there when she pulled in. He hadn't said when he'd be back, and Fusion bounded out of the house when she'd opened the door. Maybe he'd have called her and left a message on the house line.

Nothing blinked on the machine, and she checked her cell again in case he'd called when she'd been in a dead zone. Nothing again. She was regretting the way that they'd parted this morning, and she wanted to make things right.

She sighed. In fact, she wanted to confess all. His pending departure had made all of her old insecurities come racing back to the surface. She was an independent woman before he'd arrived, and she'd still be one when he left.

But maybe there was some hope for the future. Maybe he'd be back soon. Maybe they could continue to explore whatever this was between them.

She knew it was love on her side, but what was it on his?

Setting the first round of bags on the kitchen counter, she sensed that something was different. The house felt full when Vince was here, and she missed his energy. She walked back through the living room and stood for a moment looking at the place by the fire where they'd spent so much wonderful time the last few days. He'd carried the mattress upstairs. It was cleaned up, furniture back in place and the room straightened.

Turning to walk back outside for the next load of groceries, she stopped, unsure of what she was seeing. The table he'd been using for his makeshift desk was clean, empty of his things and set back in its usual place against a far wall. On it, a single envelope with her name written in tight script was propped up.

And next to the envelope was a key, the one she'd given him to the front door.

Chapter 42

DK saw Tess walking up the steps with a cornucopia centerpiece for the dining table from her perch on a stool in the corner of the kitchen. Roxy was at the stove, Gabby was chopping something at the counter, and Marguerite was moving things around in the fridge. Serena would be arriving any minute as well with her boyfriend Dane who'd been assigned the task of watching the big turkey soon to be set out in the smoker.

It was hard for her to get motivated to do much of anything. For the first few hours after she'd read Vince's note, she hadn't moved. Fusion finally roused her, sitting patiently in front of her for a long time before he licked her face in concern. Then she realized that she'd left the truck standing open and half the groceries still on the back seat.

She hadn't called anyone, hadn't thought to ask for support or help. She put away everything methodically, then sat at this same table staring outside, thinking back on all of the wonderful memories she had from the last few weeks.

They played like a series of movies in her mind. Vince standing behind her with his arms wrapped tight, kissing her neck. Vince arguing with her over some topic that really, in the end, ended up not being important. Vince laughing at Fusion's antics. Vince bowed above her or rising beneath her, his passion joining hers until they were both flying.

She sighed.

DK nibbled on a nail, not caring if her hands were a mess at this point. Someone cleared their throat behind her. She looked up, forgetting there was a roomful of friends here, and found all of them staring at her.

Gabby gave her a small smile. "So what did the note say exactly, sweetie?"

When she'd finally pulled herself out of her pity party the day after finding Vince's note, she'd called Gabby first and given her the basics, a very abbreviated version of what had happened. After assuring her that she would be right over, her best friend's concern about everything that came next was obvious.

"Look, we'll cancel Thanksgiving, just say you're sick or something. It's not far from the truth, right? They'll all understand."

No, DK insisted. The party was still on. No need to cancel it. Having a houseful of people would be just what she needed. She relied on Gabby to tell the other women, which she had. Everyone else would be blessedly in the dark when they arrived later on for the festivities.

Now, though, the girl tribe was waiting for her to say something.

She really didn't know where to start. Her words were halting when she finally could speak. "He, ah, he said he had to head back to New York early, something about a story that was moving along faster than he had expected. How much he enjoyed our time together here, how much he appreciated me taking the time to introduce him to the area, blah, blah, blah." Which was pretty much how she was feeling too.

Marguerite found her voice first. "Did you ever show him the final piece of the sculpture, DK? Did he get to see what you created, what the two of you created together?"

DK shook her head, too saddened by this turn of events to speak.

"Did he say if he'd be back?" Roxy seemed to be stirring the food in the pan more vigorously than necessary.

"No."

"Did he say anything about how he feels about you?" Tess ignored the flowers and decorations cascading over the counter where she'd set them to move behind DK and rub her shoulders. DK leaned back against her friend.

"No. He signed it with a V, that was it."

Gabby became indignant at that. "Not even a 'warmly' or 'hugs' or anything? Not even a 'thanks for the memories'?"

That made DK smile. "No to that too. Of course..." She trailed off.

Gabby took her up on that. "Of course what, sweetie?"

DK cleared her throat and sighed again. "Of course, I never told him how I feel either. It seemed safer that way, you know?"

She turned around for confirmation from the room, and met the solemn stares of the women. "I just couldn't. What if I'd told him and he felt sorry for me? I don't want his pity! That's not how a friends with benefits relationship ends, right? And besides, I'm an empowered and confident woman. I don't need him to validate me."

Angry with herself, she got up to pace the room. Her friends glanced at each other, and one by one, they each went back to their tasks intently.

Tess grabbed DK in passing, gave her a quick hug, and pulled her over to the flowers. "Here," she said gently, "these need tending."

*****

It took him a day and a half to get home, but that suited his mood just fine. It gave him something concrete to be mad at, something other than himself or DK.

Damn, the woman had tied him up in knots. After he'd hauled the metalwork back to the rental house, he'd tracked down Lisa and asked her for a favor. Could she please get someone to come in and package the pottery statue and the metal piece and ship them to his condo in New York right away, as fast as possible and damn the expense? She was more than happy to help, saying she'd do it herself that afternoon.

And he let her know that he would be leaving immediately. He refused the offer of a refund for the final week, saying that it was his call to leave early, giving some vague excuse about work and that he didn't want to leave her in the lurch. He hung up on her as she was still trying to say how much they had enjoyed having him for a guest and encouraging him to call again when he next came to town.

He didn't think he'd ever be back.

No, DK made it pretty clear by her words and her actions that it was time for him to move on. He'd gotten his heart and emotions involved, and that was his problem. She was an independent woman and their time had been great, but hit the road.

At least that's what he thought she meant. Sometimes he wasn't sure, but it hurt too much to examine that feeling and got on with his packing. He drove back to her place, knowing that she was elsewhere working on the installation she insisted needed to be done today.

It was the one she wanted him to see, but he wasn't going to be around for that. No, he was going to get out of town as fast as he could, just to preserve what little self-respect he had left. It was his own damn fault for not maintaining his distance.

Otherwise, he'd be begging that they try to see what could develop between them. He already knew what he felt, and if he could convince her that she felt something too, maybe they could work things out. But that was before she summarily told him she was her own woman and doing her own thing, by herself thank you very much.

He walked around DK's house, remembering scenes from each room. Some made him laugh, others made him hard, and they all made his heart ache with longing. The house was so empty without her presence.

He shoved papers, books and computer into his briefcase and tossed clothes in his duffle without paying any attention to what he was doing. Fusion came to sit next to him, leaning against him as he had a habit of doing. For once, Cassidy didn't mind and dropped down for a good rub of the thick soft coat while he gave the dog orders to take care of DK.

Fusion seemed to understand and set his big head on Cassidy's shoulder for a time. The dog was a comfort.

Finally, with everything packed into the car and a last painful look around, he left the envelope and key on the desk, shut the door on the dog, and drove out to the road, staring in the rear view mirror the whole way.

He had plenty of time to think things over since then. He'd called the airlines to see if he could get a flight east, but since it was the Tuesday before Thanksgiving, they basically laughed at him. They finally found him a standby on Wednesday, and he'd spent his final night in his little Flynn's Crossing bungalow wide awake, remembering DK here too.

Restless and angry, he drove to the airport in the middle of the darkness, way too early for his possible flight, and spent the empty day sitting at one gate or another and finally at the bar. Whiskey was doing little to put a dent in his painful isolation.

They squeezed him on the last flight of the day, a middle seat in the back of the coach section and he didn't even care. He sat up and thought more about the past couple of months, his mood alternating between laughter, passion and intense anger, but he wasn't even sure who he was mad at anymore, himself or DK. Coating it all, though, was intense love.

He'd hoped throughout the days since that perhaps she'd call when she read his note, if for no other reason than to say goodbye, but his phone remained silent.

His ride from the airport to his condo had taken much longer than expected, with the crowds for the annual Macy's Thanksgiving Day parade causing major roadblocks in downtown Manhattan. He'd gone down to the deli on the corner for some basic food and a large bottle of Irish whiskey. He'd been fond of the local El Dorado County wines he'd gotten used to with DK, but wine didn't seem to have enough octane for him right now.

Besides, the whiskey was Irish.

He sipped the amber liquid and appreciated the biting taste as it slid down his throat. The apartment was cold and he kept it dark because that's how he felt. Besides, it better suited the lights he'd decided to shine on the long wall holding his treasures. The living room was no longer sterile and empty.

It had become his DK room.

They'd arrived on Saturday morning, the door buzzer waking him out of an alcohol-induced night tossing and turning.

"Mr. Cassidy? Express delivery. Hey, must be pretty special to want 'em on a Saturday."

The UPS man eyed him carefully, no doubt taking in his bleary-eyed appearance and smelling the lack of a recent shower. His doorman stood behind the guy, more curious than helpful. Thanking them both with a stutter while he kept his gaze on the boxes, he peeled off a bill for each of them.

"Hey, thanks Mr. Cassidy! Happy holidays, sir!" The glee both men displayed probably meant he'd given them each a twenty or more since he didn't look at the bills.

He'd been almost afraid to open the containers. What if the power of them, the feelings, were already gone?

But the power hadn't been. In fact, it was even stronger.

He pulled a tall sofa table against the bare living room wall and set what he'd come to think of as his starring piece in the middle, the statue by Thomas. The light from the recesses in the ceiling caught the flowing lines and innocence perfectly, and the sight of it made his heart pound with an ache unlike any pain he'd ever felt before.

The oak tree occupied the corner of the long space, lit by both the lights above and the lights from the nearby window during the day. It hit the little version of Fusion just so, and it looked like the dog was resting peacefully in the sun.

This morning he had prowled restlessly again, knowing something was missing, and he booted up his computer and downloaded everything in his camera. He flipped through pictures of DK, laughing and serious, at work and when they'd had adventures. He found a dozen that he loved best and he'd printed them out at a local office support store in the largest size they could handle, eleven by fourteen. A framing shop for a stack of off-the-shelf frames to fit them was his next to last stop. The corner store was down to its last bottle of his favorite brand of Irish.

His gallery was now more like a shrine, he realized, and someone who didn't know the back story would undoubtedly think he was stalking someone. The wall was full of enlargements of DK, and he'd moved the rest of the sparse furniture to the side and placed his favorite leather chair in the center of the room facing it. With the two works of art in front and the pictures gracing the wall, all he had to do was sit back and stare to fill himself with the sight of her.

And still, nothing eased the shaft of loneliness piercing his heart.

Chapter 43

It was getting kind of old, DK groused, all of this caring on the part of everyone trying to make sure she was okay. She wouldn't be okay, not for a long time if ever, and they'd better get used to it.

The crowd on Thanksgiving had been good, and while she couldn't exactly appreciate the fun of it, she was grateful for the houseful of friends to distract her. Even busybody Bettie, trying to get her aside and talk to her about 'her young man', and Thomas, who just kept patting her on the back and chuckling, didn't bother her.

Friday, Roxy called to ask if she could come decorate the restaurant for the holidays, begging DK since she had such a great artist's eye and would undoubtedly do a much better job than Roxy and her staff by themselves. When the decorating was done, Roxy had pressed her to stay for dinner at the restaurant, her treat, and wouldn't take no for an answer.

On Saturday, it was Tess's turn to beg for some help on a big order of holiday swags and other decorations that had suddenly come in. Of course, it was clear that this was no last minute deal since her flower coolers were full of the supplies needed and the work space was emptied in preparation. But still, it gave DK something to do.

When Gabby arrived on DK's doorstep at midday Sunday, requesting special help in creating a scrapbook of Jeremy's year to present to his grandparents for Christmas, she had to call a stop to the attention.

"Really, I'm okay, or as okay as I'm going to be for a long time. You don't all need to be setting up a schedule to babysit me." DK tried not to sound snippy and gave what she thought was a brave smile.

Based on the look of sympathy Gabby gave her, it didn't seem to be very effective.

"Look, we're just worried about you, okay? We know you'll handle it because that's what you do. But we want to be here for you too."

"There isn't much anyone can do about it right now. I just have to get past the worst of the hurt."

She fingered the cell phone that she kept with her always, hoping he'd call to check in. She'd scrolled to his number and looked at his picture next to it a thousand times in the past few days, but she'd been strong and hadn't called.

When she was alone, she brooded. She tried to work, in the past always finding that it was a good release for whatever emotions were boiling around inside her, but she couldn't come up with a single idea. She grabbed her pencil and pad to sketch fall's baring branches and followed Fusion outside, only to find herself drawing Vince instead.

Vince with his back to her, set against the big oak tree in front. Vince in a serious mood, talking convincingly on some topic. Vince's face lit by laughter and their shared passion. Vince, his face full of brooding emotion.

She was almost embarrassed with her one-track mind. She couldn't get it off him. But since the only creature there was Fusion and the dog was sticking close by her side, seeming to understand her bleak mood, she considered it acceptable.

Her cell rang on Tuesday afternoon, marking a week since Vince left her, and she started, almost dropping it as she boggled the case out of her pocket to look at the caller id. It wasn't him, some local number instead. She let it got to voicemail and later, listened to the message.

"Hello, ma'am? This is Mike at Excellent Electrics. Listen, I got an order here to put in a generator for you and a panel and all. It's all been paid for by a Mr. Cassidy. Said it was a present for you. Wanted me to call you myself to schedule a time to scope out what you need and install it. Can you give me a call back so that we can get that on the books?"

A generator, a present from Vince. He would pay for a generator for her, but he wouldn't call her after a week to see if she was okay, to see how she was doing. Her feelings warred between hope and anger.

They'd never even said a real goodbye.

She waited until Wednesday to call Tess and ask her opinion about it. "He clearly wanted you to have something useful, I guess. Really, it is a very considerate gift. Maybe he doesn't want you stuck out there nesting with anyone else in the future."

The teasing tone on the phone did a little something to perk up DK's mood. She called the electrician back and scheduled the work.

"You know you should call him and thank him, don't you?" Gabby had chided her when she'd found out about the gift. "It's the polite thing to do."

But she didn't want to be polite.

And then on Thursday, a full week after Thanksgiving, a battered old pick-up drove up and Thomas climbed out from behind the wheel, stretching and coughing and watching DK carefully when she came out the studio door.

"You look thin and peaked," he grumbled, before pulling her into a big bear hug. Setting her back and examining her face closely, he continued, "And you don't seem to be getting much sleep neither. So what's bothering you, girl?"

She was ashamed that she almost burst into tears at his caring, because he was the closest thing she had to father around here. But she set her shoulders back and put a half smile on her face, disengaging from the old man and walking back into the studio's less revealing light.

He didn't say anything more, just followed her inside and headed to her office as if he owned the place. Looking around, he saw the jumble of papers on her desk and started pulling out the drawings one by one.

Thomas harrumphed, and DK wished she'd hidden things better. She hadn't expected anyone to come visiting and certainly not in here. But the old guy had always been different, nosy in a good way, caring in his own gruff manner.

"So that's how it is, is it? You hankering after him something bad." It wasn't even a question, so she didn't bother denying it. He could see it in her drawings.

"Ya know, did I tell you about him and me doing a little business?" Thomas turned to her with a sharp eye that didn't miss much, and when she shook her head, he continued.

"He came to the studio oh, what, two, three times. First time out, he fell in love with the statue, the one I did a-you, remember?"

Of course she remembered. She'd been mortified at first that Thomas had done something so revealing, even if she'd never posed for it, but he'd asked her somewhat indignantly at the time if she thought that the skinny tank tops and short shorts she wore around when she was renting studio space from him hid much at all. He'd used his imagination for what he couldn't see, and as it turned out, his artist's eye was pretty accurate.

"Well, he wanted to buy it, and I told him no. Next time, he insisted again. Offered me a shitload of money for it, more than I'd expect even from a New Yorker." Thomas said the last in distain. "I told him he could buy it if he did right by you. Said he would, and looked pretty serious about it at the time. Said he absolutely had to have it, particularly once he realized it was you."

The old man chuckled at the memory, and DK felt a little something break free inside her and a bubble of hope rise up.

"Yea, first he seemed kind of mad, and I think that he thought you'd posed for me. Yup, that's what I thought. He never asked, and I never told. But he bought it alright."

DK looked into the distance, unseeing, and after a few minutes she realized that Thomas had stopped talking and was watching her, his expression now solemn.

He cleared his throat. "And there's more." He sat down heavily on a nearby welding platform and motioned for her to sit as well. She paced in front of him instead, suddenly nervous at what he had to say.

"Bettie did the totals for the end of the month at the gallery and she called me, all a-twitter, the old biddy. Said that we had a record month, and it was all because of one sale. Your old oak tree piece, the one you were asking a few grand for? He bought that one too."

Her mind reeled at this. The oak tree had taken her weeks to perfect, and she'd been unwilling to discount the value of all of that labor and the piece of her heart that went into it. Everyone at the cooperative gallery thought it was a lot to ask for a piece by a local artist. Still, it brought in customer traffic and people then bought smaller, less expensive work by all of the artists, so no one complained about its presence.

Vince had bought it. She wondered what that meant, or if she was attaching an importance to it that really didn't exist.

Thomas wasn't done yet. "So, I ran into Lisa at the coffee place. She was telling me what happened to them pieces. Seems this Vince Cassidy guy asked her to pack them up real good and ship them to New York City," he sneered the name again, "and wanted them expedited." He stretched out the last syllables, clearly pleased with the word.

Was this all some kind of joke? First, he gives her a thanks-so-much note, much like you'd give a hostess after a dinner party, and leaves the key on the table. Then he buys up her work and Thomas's work with her in it, and wants it all in New York pronto.

"Do you know where he shipped it? I mean, did he send it to a gallery there, or what?" She didn't want to hope.

Thomas got a sly grin on his face. "I don't know, girl, but Lisa can tell ya."

*****

"Come on, Vinnie, you need to get out. Come over to the office, we'll watch them light up the big tree, drink ourselves sick, make fun of everybody. It'll be like old times."

Randy's voice boomed through the phone, but Cassidy wasn't listening. He'd been staring at a picture of DK and imagining her on Randy's couch, under his friend in some semblance of passion, the kind of passion he himself had shared with her. He just couldn't do it.

"Listen, I can't, man. I've got some plans. You know, a woman in every port and all that. A whole bevy of beauties lined up."

There was a pause, a long one, before the voice on the phone began again, quieter now. "Ah, Vinnie? This is ol' Randy you're talking to. I heard what you've been up to. The gallery called me to tell me that one of DK's pieces sold, one of the really high end ones. And they said you bought it, wanted to thank me for turning you on to them."

So that cat was out of the bag too. Cassidy had called around until he'd found the gallery that carried DK's work exclusively in the city. They'd been more than happy to accommodate his desire for an immediate private appointment.

The modern piece was different from others he had seen of hers, filled with energy and freedom. It reminded him of her laugh, and he had to have it. He hadn't even been shocked by the four zeros following the generous number in the price. His credit card company must be ringing their hands in profound seasonal happiness when his account number came up.

"So I like her work, what of it? Into art appreciation, that's all." His words slurred and the heart ache that was his constant companion stabbed him again.

Randy was silent again, and Cassidy felt no need to fill in the silence, looking now at the piece in question gracing the other end of the long wall. It balanced everything out perfectly. Until he needed another DK hit.

"You sure there's nothing else going on? You been back now for over a week and I haven't seen you. You don't want to go out for drinks. You don't even drop by, which you always do. So what gives?"

Cassidy wanted to get him off the phone, the picture in his mind of DK sleeping on the casting couch in Randy's office too vivid for him to ignore.

"Look, I'm busy writing, that's all. And I'm thinking that I'll head overseas, Europe before Christmas, and maybe tool around there for a few months. And right now, I've got a hot one, a real beauty, waiting in the wings, you know?" He tried for a casual and slightly leery tone but wasn't sure he pulled it off.

The phone line fell silent for a minute, then Randy came back on. "Okay, man, if you tell me you're alright, then I'll take it that you're alright." He paused. "Europe, huh? Want me to line up some work for you there?"

"Naw, just want to spend some time on my own, see what I find, maybe find me a few cuties to keep my bed warm during those cold winter nights, that's all. Nothing big." If everyone thought he was out of touch on another continent, he could sit here and stare at his gallery for as long as he wanted, undisturbed.

"You'd tell me if anything was happening, right?" Randy sounded seriously concerned.

"Right Randy, right." Yeah, right, Cassidy thought. And clicking off the line, he went back to his silent contemplation of the wall of photos.

Chapter 44

"He wants me to come to New York and meet a new investor. It's someone who has been very interested in my work and needs to meet me in person."

The girl tribe listened with varying degrees of emotion as DK explained the sudden request from her agent. Marguerite looked delighted, Roxy angry, and Gabby was dreamy-eyed. Tess, too tied up with holiday displays to join them, had weighed in already and said that maybe a trip could wait until after Christmas.

The unspoken part was that maybe later would be better, when it didn't hurt DK so much to be in the same city as Vince.

"So is this unusual, this need to meet with a patron?" Marguerite put the French spin on the word and it almost sounded clandestine, DK thought.

"No, if someone is really interested, like a gallery wants to do a show or someone wants to contract for a major work, it's not unusual. It's just that Randy is insistent that it happens before Christmas. Something about this investor going out of the country or something."

Marguerite frowned. "Randy? Who does he work for?"

"He has his own agency – Randolph Gold. He's been my agent for years."

"But why does it have to be right away, that's the part I don't get." Roxy was angry on her behalf, and looked around at the other women for support. She finally huffed out an exasperated sigh. "Really, do you want to be in the same city that he's in?" She spit out the end of the sentence, and there was no doubt in anyone's mind who she was referring to.

DK faltered on this. "I really don't mind, I don't. Maybe I'll call him up when I'm in town, have a drink with him for old time's sake. You know, just for laughs."

She hadn't told them about the conversation she'd had with Lisa after Thomas's big reveal, because it didn't make any sense and she couldn't afford to get her hopes up. Her heart couldn't break into bits any smaller or there would be nothing left.

Lisa had been straightforward. "He said he had to leave for work, something sudden that came up. He had some art that he'd purchased in his rental, and he wanted me to package it up and send it expedited delivery." The woman had paused on the phone. "He was very certain on that part, no matter what the cost."

"What did you send?" It burned her, but she had to know.

Lisa sounded sincerely sorry when she answered. "I don't know. Both pieces were already bubble-wrapped. He didn't tell me what they were, other than art."

Jumping into the blue flame of her torch would be easier to do than putting a voice to her next question. "Do you know where the packages went? Was it a gallery?"

Her distress must have communicated itself to Lisa, because now the woman was fussing with papers in the background. "No, I'm sorry I don't know what it was, other than an address in New York City. Once I confirmed delivery that following Monday, I sent him the receipts. He gave me his credit card for the delivery costs," she explained. More shuffling. "Maybe I could call UPS and find out more about the address for you?"

DK had declined, thanking a still-apologizing Lisa.

She didn't notice the present silence until Marguerite cleared her throat and for the first time, looked a little uncomfortable. "Do you know who his agent is? Vince's, I mean?"

The question crackled across DK's nerves and brought her focus back to the present. "No, I don't. He knew Randy though, I guess by reputation. We talked about him a couple of times. Talking about him seemed to make Vince angry for some reason, so I didn't bring it up again."

Marguerite played with her fork, and frowned. "I got a call the other day from the agency that represents Vince. It seems that they wanted a picture of your sculpture for his article on the winery. Evidently he didn't take one, or it didn't turn out the way they wanted. Anyway, the photographer came out the other day and shot for quite a while. He seemed to be quite taken with the piece, particularly the top." She paused for effect. "The top that you poured so much of your love for Vince into, my dear."

DK wasn't surprised that they'd wanted a photo. And she wasn't surprised that Marguerite and the others could see the love she had for Vince shining out of that work. After all, he had been her big inspiration.

"That doesn't mean anything. They use photos in the articles all the time. I just hope he's nice to Witch Hill in the write-up." She gave a small smile. "After everything that's happened and all."

Marguerite was staring at her. "DK, the agency that made the appointment, it was the Randolph Gold agency. Your Randy." She paused three long heartbeats. "You and Vince have the same agent."

*****

He was losing track of the day of the week. But it didn't seem to matter. Maybe he did need to get out of the city for a few days. Visiting his mother with her unending pressures was out of the question. An anonymous city, someplace where no one recognized him and he distanced himself from everyone and everything, that's what he needed.

But he didn't want to leave his shrine.

The knocking at the door to his condo surprised him. The doorman called up announcing whoever had arrived. Cassidy didn't want to be disturbed unless it was Red, and since there was no chance in hell of that, he ignored it.

The knocking continued, harder this time, and then he heard the fumbling of a key in lock. He hadn't set the chain or turned the deadbolt, he realized, not that it mattered. Only two people had a key. The cleaning service wouldn't be here this late at night.

That left Randy.

Cassidy swore but stayed where he was, unwilling to be friendly or welcoming. The lock finally disengaged and Randy tumbled into the room, a large portfolio under one arm and a brown paper bag carrying a bottle of something in the other.

When his eyes settled on Cassidy, he shifted from wary to relieved. "I wasn't sure what I'd find going on here, an orgy or bloody gore or what. Seems I didn't need to worry." He looked pointedly at the drops of amber in the glass on the arm of the leather chair and pulled a large bottle of Scotch out of the bag. He wagged it in question, and Cassidy shook his head no.

Randy propped the portfolio against a kitchen stool, then shed his heavy coat and opened the cabinet that held bar glasses with unerring precision. He'd been here so many times that he probably knew the place better than Cassidy himself did.

Cassidy waited for Randy to notice the changes in the room. He figured there was no way to hide it and no way to push him out the door before he saw it. And besides, the whiskey made him slow and he was too tired and too hurt to care.

Randy put two ice cubes in the glass and added a generous splash of Scotch, then turned back to the room with his mouth open to start a sentence. And he stopped in midstride when he took it in.

He glanced back and forth quickly, his eyes darting from the statue to the metalwork to the pictures that covered the wall. Slowly, he closed his mouth. Taking a fast sip that seemed to burn him, he looked around again, more slowly this time. Finally, he turned back to Cassidy and stared at the single chair, the disarray in the rest of the room, and the disheveled mess that was the man.

"So, this is how it is?" He walked in cautiously, kind of like he was approaching a ticking bomb, and came to stand beside the chair and turn again to the display. "I thought you said you were alright."

Cassidy picked up his bottle of whiskey and adding more to his glass. He put up the glass to clink with Randy's, and silently they toasted and both took long pulls as they continued to stare at the shrine.

"You are so fucked up, man."

Cassidy could only agree. "Yeah, man, I am so fucked up."

It was easier to talk about, here staring at the wall and the pictures of DK, than it would have been in Randy's office, on the phone, or even in a public place.

"This," Cassidy gestured somewhat drunkenly, "is the way it fuckin' is." He took another long sip and settled back, closing his eyes and waiting for Randy to say something.

It was very quiet in the room, and other than the occasional tinkle of ice in Randy's glass and the hoots of horns from cabs outside, nothing seemed to disturb the empty silence. He heard Randy walk towards the corner where the tree stood, stop as if he was examining it, then slowly pace the length of the wall, stopping in the center at the statue. He continued on to the opposite end and the modern piece, then back to the center. More ice noise.

Cassidy was profoundly tired. He was tired of hiding what he felt and he was tired of fighting the feelings himself. He was tired of Randy for being a dick and sleeping with what he thought of as his, Cassidy's, woman, even though DK hadn't known him at the time.

Most of all, he was tired of being away from DK, but he figured she wasn't minding that part since she hadn't called, not even to thank him for the generator. She was probably well on her way to someone new by now.

Stab went the now-familiar pain.

"So this is how it is." It was a statement this time. "I was wondering."

Cassidy opened one eye to see Randy stepping back from the clay statue, moving from side to side to take in the different perspectives. It made him ill to see the way his friend was eyeing it.

"That her?"

Cassidy's other eye popped open. "Of course it's her, you know it's her after all."

Randy turned and regarded him strangely. "How would I know? I've only met her a couple a times."

"A couple of times? A couple of times on the couch of fame and you don't remember her? She's one in a million, and I can't fuckin' believe you wouldn't remember her!"

He was sputtering and tried to stand, but the booze made him clumsy. The one time in his life he really wanted to deck someone and he couldn't even swing his fist.

"Just what did you think I did with her, you moron?" Randy was looking mad in turn. "She was an innocent kid, working hard to make ends meet while she was trying to break into the art world. Do you know she was working as a checker in a grocery store when I first met her? She flew out here overnight to meet with the gallery owner at that place where you bought that piece," he gestured with his drink at the modern work. "She slept for a couple a hours on my couch, got up and did an amazing presentation of her portfolio, and then hopped on a plane again so that she could work her next shift."

Randy took another angry sip and continued. "She welded at night at the beginning, not sure what she was using for sleep. Once she hit it big, her big present to herself was quitting that shit day job."

Cassidy wasn't sure he'd heard Randy right. He knew he'd heard DK right, saying she'd slept on that couch more times than she wanted to remember. Was it all something innocent?

No, he was sure he was right. DK was too worldly, too much of a siren to be the innocent Randy described.

He fell back into the chair. "Look, man, I know you slept with her. You don't need to lie to me. I can take it." He took another long swallow and wished the alcohol would put him out of his misery.

Randy regarded him with something that looked like sympathy. "Slept with her? No way. I don't violate innocents, you know that. The chicks I sleep with know the score. Besides, I was busy with wifey number two at that point and I didn't need any other stimulation. No, I never slept with her. In fact, I think of her kind a like a little sister."

He moved away from the wall to stand in front of Cassidy's chair, his gaze now filled with profound pity. "You got it bad, my friend, real damn bad."

Yeah, Cassidy thought, he damn well knew that.

*****

The coffee helped. Randy had poured out both of their drinks and started a pot, doubling the beans to make it strong. The taste made him gag, but Cassidy was happy for the discomfort. At least he could feel something other than heart ache.

Randy kept babbling at him, trying to sober him up to what, as he explained it, was a point where Cassidy could see reason.

Or at least see.

"You have really screwed this up royally. What kind of an asshole were you to her?" The words to that effect went on for two cups of the awful brew.

"Look, she knows what she wants. She just about kicked me out the door without so much as a thank you for the sex part." The third cup of coffee burned going down. His eyes teared up, but it was from the coffee, he was sure of it.

Randy had the portfolio at one end of the dining room table, and Cassidy sat at the other. When he was deemed to be awake enough to run a hundred miles even if he wasn't sturdy enough on his feet for it, Randy made a big production of unzipped the black case.

"You see, the magazine wanted a nice picture of the sculpture to go with your article. The ones you took, they didn't capture the full frame. So we sent a guy out to take some new ones, and ends up, it's a good thing we did. Because evidently the sculpture wasn't finished yet when you saw it."

He knew it! There had been something missing, something that DK wasn't willing to share with him.

Randy continued. "I talked to the French woman, Marguerite, who cursed you quite fluently I might add and in at least three languages that I could tell, and she told me that DK just finished installing the work, like two days before Thanksgiving." He paused expectantly. "Like right when you left." He stood waiting for a reaction.

The piece she wouldn't show him, the one she kept covering in the studio, explaining that he would see it when she installed it. He'd never seen it because he'd left town in a hurry.

"You're going to want to see this, my friend. Maybe there was a reason she didn't complete the piece before you two got together. And if you have the feelings for her that I think you do, you're going to want to do something about this."

Randy shoved the portfolio down the long length of the glass table. Cassidy caught it, but left a hand on its closed cover.

His friend walked to the door, grabbing his coat on the way. "One more thing, Vinnie. I've convinced DK to come for a visit, here to New York. I told her I have a major collector with international connections who's interested in her work." He winked at Cassidy. "Looks like I'm not far from wrong," he added, nodding towards the shrine. "She arrives in three days."

And he closed the door behind him.

Cassidy was uneasy, one part of him elated that DK would be so close in such a short time, and another part of him afraid of the cascade of feelings that unleashed. DK didn't want him. She wanted to be footloose.

Or was that the old him talking? He wasn't sure if he was projecting or acting on any real knowledge.

Setting the coffee mug aside, he pulled the portfolio closer and placed his palms on it. It seemed to vibrate. He was afraid of what he would find here. He was also afraid that he would find – nothing. No future with DK and nothing in his own that he wanted either.

Stab, stab, stab. The pain shared the faster beat of his heart.

There was only one way to find out. He opened the cover slowly as if it would bite him.

And gasp when he saw the first frame.

Chapter 45

The view never failed to intrigue her. Right now, the big tree in Rockefeller Center was lit up and people were skating on the ice rink. Strong winds blew the flags out straight. Maybe it was time to take up a different medium, like photography. Nothing else seemed to be working for her right now.

Randy had assured her that the visit would be worth her while, and when she'd questioned him about Vince, he'd been stubbornly non-committal, sending the discussion in a different direction.

Just as well, she supposed. Vince didn't want anything to do with her, and clearly he'd communicated that to Randy. She didn't want to put Randy in the middle since he'd done so much for her career over the years. She dropped that heated subject. He seemed almost disappointed that she didn't bring it up once more.

She looked at her watch again. Randy said that the big distributor was coming by at 6 pm, a little late for a business meeting, but not that unusual in the big city. She'd flown in yesterday and spent last night pacing her hotel room until she couldn't stand the isolation anymore. She'd taken to the streets early this morning to walk for hours, stopping at a few galleries and a couple of museums on the way. Even that, though, did little to burn off her restless energy.

She was in the same city as the man she loved, and she wanted to call him, find him and tell him. Still undecided on this, she thought back to the advice she'd received from the girl tribe.

"What does it hurt to see him, share some drinks, laugh a little, even if you don't tell him how you feel? It's not like you're forgetting him." Marguerite had been characteristically urbane about the whole thing.

"You can at least tell him what an asshole he is." Roxy still hadn't forgiven him for the hurt and pain he'd caused, even though in DK's mind, half of the ownership for that was hers.

Gabby had stayed dreamy-eyed and romantic to the end. "You should meet him someplace and tell him, face to face, how you feel. I can't believe that this is all one-sided. From everything you've described, he's as stuck on you as you are in love with him. Maybe he just can't say the words easily."

She'd gotten a little teary then. "Back when Doug was courting me, and he was courting me hard, he was telling me how he had deep feelings for me all the time. I just couldn't say the words back. I almost lost him before I was able to tell him I loved him." She'd been insistent. "Don't waste the opportunity, DK, or you might regret it for the rest of your life."

Those words had been ringing in her ears on the long flight east and during the hours since. She had convinced herself that she would call him tonight after this appointment. She would set up a time to meet him and she would tell him. He needed him to hear this from her, face to face. And then if he didn't return the feelings, well, at least she'd know for sure. It would never stop hurting completely, but eventually, she'd find a way to move on.

If that damned investor would arrive so she could get this over with, she could implement her plan.

A hundred what-if's played through her mind. What if he was already seeing someone else? What if he refused to see her? What if he was already out of town, on to the next locale for work?

She was so intent on her scenarios that she almost missed the quiet click closing the office door. The lack of light in the room and the reflections of the view outside made it hard to see the person standing there. But all of her senses went on heated alert.

The one scenario she hadn't planned on stood in the room behind her. What if he was the one she was meeting here tonight?

*****

His heart lurched, stopped, started again at a race. It was just as moving as that time she stood bathing in front of the fire, but for completely different reasons.

He'd convinced himself he'd never see her in the flesh again. He'd been staring at her pictures, caressing her statue, and running the movies of their time together in his mind for the last couple of weeks, but they didn't compare to the woman in front of him. She was even more beautiful, her face in profile against the festive lights outside, and she looked very sad. Clothes hugged a frame that looked more elfin somehow.

He stepped further into the room. She hadn't turned around completely, staring at him over her shoulder with her green eyes unreadable. Then she turned her face back to the window.

He came to stand behind her. She smelled just the same, he realized. He'd wondered if the scent of her was something that was special to the woods and the outdoors of home, but here she was, in his messy dirty city, and her spiciness in the air almost made him beg.

"Diane Kathryn, how are you?" Damn, his voice sounded like he was a teenager at the change of life. He cleared his throat and reached for a more personable even tone. "It's good to see you."

She turned now to face him, her back to the view, and she searched his face. Finally satisfied in some way, she opened her mouth to speak. "You know I hate that name."

*****

After everything they'd been to each other and been through together, he called her that? The one name that would undermine her confidence and make her feel inexperienced again, unsure and uncomfortable. She sensed, though, that he wasn't doing it on purpose.

In fact, she had a feeling he was just as lost as she was.

She took a step past him and found a light switch on the wall, turning on the overheads and flooding the room with brightness. She blinked and squinted, the light harsh after the colorful darkness outside. He was blinking rapidly too, though his eyes never stopped watching her.

He moved towards her, and she took a step to the side and away again. She needed to maintain some physical distance to be able to say what she needed to say. Her heart beat a staccato against her bones and nothing burned now. It was more like she'd seared everything away.

The universe, it seemed, played strange tricks on everyone. She'd been thinking about confronting him, and here he was in front of her. If she could just get the words out.

"I'm sorry, that was rude of me. That's my name, and I should own it." She put a game face on and smiled at him, then waved to the seating area. She took a chair, and after a minute's hesitation, he dropped to the couch to face her, sitting on it as if it was burning him.

He seemed ready to speak, opened his mouth, then closed it again and appeared to think the better of it. Then he started again, only to pause once more.

Good, maybe he was as stymied as she was on where to start. It would be a race to see who found their tongue first. If she wasn't in the middle of this herself, she would almost find this funny.

"Look, I'm sorry. I know the full name bothers you. It's just that it's a beautiful name and you're a beautiful woman. And sometimes, it just needs to be said." He seemed pleased with himself for that.

DK realized he was as uncomfortable as she was with this meeting. But he had to know it was her in the room, because he didn't seem startled by her sudden appearance.

"Did you know you were meeting me?"

Vince nodded.

"Did you ask for the meeting?"

He shook his head in the negative and she felt her stomach drop. So it wasn't him wanting her here in New York after all. Her hopes had rocketed up when she'd seen him and that made the pitch down into despair that much steeper.

He cleared his throat. "No, that was all Randy's doing. He saw some of the, ah, alterations to your work, and he thought we should get together."

She was at a loss about what he was referring to. "Alterations? I don't get it."

He looked down at his hands as if finding them attached to the ends of his arms surprised him, and stared that way for a while. When he finally looked back up at her, there was no mistaking the passion flaming in his eyes.

"DK, is it true? Is what you designed into that missing piece of the Witch Hill sculpture the way you feel about us?" He hesitated on the last word, and she wondered what he was going to say instead.

She'd poured all of her love for him into that piece. The hands entwined in that final flush when they reached their peak together. The love in her face shining into his, their eyes locked. The kiss.

Anyone who knew them well, knew their faces, would know it was them. She'd taken a huge risk with it, but it had been worth it. It would be something she had to remind her of Vince forever.

She felt her face heat at the thought of it. She wasn't sure if it was the memory of the piece or the memory of the real passion and love that ignited her, but something did. Vince was watching her carefully, on the edge of his seat and leaning forward.

If she spoke up now, there would be no turning back, no hiding behind the façade of supposed sophistication and detachment. If she jumped into that flame now, it would be with her heart in her hands.

"Yes, Vince, it's true. I couldn't hide it. I couldn't let you see it right away either." She paused, hoping for the right words. "I didn't want to hold you back if you didn't feel the same way."

His face changed, softening in relief so fast she blinked. The grave face and twisting hands gave way to a smile that gave the room's lighting a run for its money, and he moved forward to kneel in front of her. Taking her face in his hands, he kissed her as if he wanted to brand her.

And she poured all of the pent up emotions of the last two weeks into her kiss in return. She hadn't expected this, hadn't thought that he could care for her. Caring, though, was in every stroke of his fingers on her face, each thread of his hands through her hair.

He finally pulled back, but pulled her with him to the couch to settle her against him, arms wound tight. He tipped a finger under her chin and raised her face to his, his eyes moving over every feature and his fingers tracing her as if reading a long forgotten novel. He smiled, and she knew her smile was just as bright.

"Red, I love you."

It was turning out to be a very worthwhile trip indeed.

Epilogue

The last two weeks had been a whirlwind. It had taken them two hours or more to leave Randy's office, only to find their agent sitting at what he called his guard post at his secretary's desk. "Can't have anyone disturbing you, you know, in case you were using the couch." And he'd winked at them.

At Randy's insistence, they took his town car instead of a cab. They retrieved DK's things from the hotel and headed to the condo. She'd been initially knocked back when she'd seen the shrine Vince had built to her, but if she had any doubts about how he felt, the last of those evaporated at the sight.

They talked a lot too. He tried to make her understand the two sides he didn't understand, the woman who was a siren in his arms but seemed like such an innocent. She forgave him for that, since he'd said the siren part.

He asked about the bright little box for the condoms, and she laughed and explained about Gabby the romantic who still had a practical side.

He'd explained his jealousy and confusion over the comments about Randy's couch, and he'd confessed that he didn't care if she had posed for Thomas, but asked that she never do it again. She had to laugh, and related instead the old man's gruff remarks about how he came up with the pose and the piece. Vince looked relieved.

She'd decided that having him feel a little unsure of her and still love her to no end hadn't been a bad thing. It let her know very clearly how much he loved her unconditionally.

And she returned the feelings. She'd told him how hurt she was by his seeming indifference to her independence.

"I promise never to call you by your full name again, unless I really needed to get your attention."

It made her laugh and realize that the name really didn't matter. She found that she had the passionate self-confidence and independence already all that time.

It was Vince who suggested that he pack up his condo, including the art, and send everything to their home in California. She was delighted when they had dinner with Randy and told him of their plans, even more so when Vince called a real estate agent and listed the place for sale.

"Vinnie, he calls you Vinnie." It was even better that he had an annoying nickname she could use too.

They'd flown from New York home to Flynn's Crossing, where Vince had redeemed himself by telling the girl tribe in person that he loved DK, asking them to forgive him for hurting her and being such an ass. Even Roxy was almost mollified.

Thomas, Sarge and Stuart, Lisa and Dannie and the rest of the town seemed to find out within a couple of hours, and pretty soon they were being congratulated no matter where they were. Bettie stopped them on the street, gave DK a big hug, and warned Vince that he'd better take good care of their girl. He said yes ma'am and promised to be on his best behavior.

And it was Vince who had insisted that they travel to Chicago and surprise her family for Christmas. Her mother had been overjoyed to see her and had been suitably impressed with what she called a responsible young man who would want to meet a young woman's family. Her brothers were all giving Vince a hard time within minutes, the third degree flowing easily, and her sisters agreed that he was quite the catch.

Tomorrow, the day after Christmas, they would fly home to unpack his boxes, due to arrive later in the week, and then they were off on a big adventure. DK couldn't wait for any of it to start, the long ribbon of their life together in Flynn's Crossing unrolling after their time overseas.

He bought her a high end digital camera, and she'd been playing with it almost nonstop since she unwrapped the box on Christmas Eve at her parents' house. It was preparation, he said, for the trip, something she could use to capture all of the images she wanted to bring home.

She gave him an album of the drawings she'd done of him, and he'd been moved to speechlessness, instead pulling her close and putting his face in her hair until her father had an excuse to interrupt them.

They'd go back to the house in the morning and spend a few more hours, but for now, it was the two of them in a hotel room that afforded them a little privacy.

Vince seemed anxious, even overly eager to get back to their room, and given the zoo that was a house filled with children of all ages, ribbing siblings and over-interested parents, she could relate to the feeling.

"Wait, I'll take your coat. Give me a sec with the lights." He sounded nervous.

A big box waited in the middle of the bed.

"What's that?" They'd agreed that on one present a piece for each other. They didn't need anything else since they had each other.

Vince was watching her, his earlier anxiety seeming to nail him to the floor.

"Vince, what is it?"

He cleared his throat. "Open it, why don't you, and see what it is?"

Her curiosity was piqued. The shape and size didn't give anything away. She crossed to the bed and slipped out of her shoes, kneeling in front of the package. The gold foil ripped easily and the plain brown cardboard underneath carried no label.

Vince took off his loafers and sat opposite her, waiting and watching. Heat was coming off him in waves. She ran a finger along the tape and the big box popped open.

His current state of stillness was almost nerve-wracking, and she looked at him with even more curiosity. He started to fidget and leaned towards her. "Go on," he urged. "Open it up."

She pulled back the flaps and inside, nestled in the center of reams of white and purple tissue, was a very small box. A very small, purple box.

She froze, and he grabbed it out and opened it for her, pulling out the sparkling setting with its big diamond and holding it in front of her wide eyes.

"Diane Kathryn McGiven, I love you with all of the fire inside me. Will you do me the honor of becoming my wife?"

She should probably give him a hard time about the full name, but he had her attention, every single bit of it. Her smile grew until her face hurt with it.

Yes, tomorrow she was going to be the center of it all in the family circle, and she wouldn't mind it one bit.

THE END

Excerpt from
NAKED INTOLERANCES

If you enjoyed *Flashes of Fire*, stay tuned for the next book in the Flynn's Crossing series, Naked Intolerances.

And here's an excerpt:

He wrapped her long dark hair around his fingers and pulled her head back to kiss her neck. The waves washed over them, adding warm caresses to hands that were everywhere.

"Ah Gabriella, the love you inspire in me is constant, like the sea, and as relentless as these waves."

She smiled in satisfaction, knowing that neither one of them would be able to stand the teasing much longer. The sand was hot beneath her back, churning cool water tickled her legs, and possessive fingers traced the curves of her body.

His mouth covered hers in a kiss that was searing, one that left no doubt about how much she stirred him. He was insistent, despite their spot at the edge of the rising tide. His body throbbed against hers.

"Gabriella, I want you, now."

She breathed in his scent mingled with flowers on the shore and the tang of saltwater. Her bikini disappeared magically, melting away, and she was naked in the unyielding sun.

He pulled her to her feet and soon they were running across the sand. They tumbled into a hammock strung between the palms and she laughed aloud at the boldness of it, romping around where anyone could see them.

"I desire you more than anything in the world." His eyes burned deeply into hers.

Triumphant, she rose above him to caress his face, his chest, the evidence of his desire for her. The tropical sun on her back was almost as hot as his body beneath her.

His hands were wandering again, setting fire to her skin. "Gabriella, I love you. You are the most beautiful woman in the world. I will be with you always."

He pulled her closer in the most intimate of caresses. She couldn't help the feeling of exaltation, the celebration of so much more to come. For years, this would be hers. She would be this beautiful, joined with this man, with nothing to separate them and a future that was endless.

She moved to his lips, her hair a curtain to hide their faces, eager right now to kiss him and show him how much he meant to her. "Doug", she whispered, "I love…"

"Mom? MOM! Fusion ate a dead bird. Do you think he'll be okay?"

Gabby gasp and reached blindly, trying to find something to pull over her body and cover them both, surprised to find flannel and denim instead of sand and sun. Confused, she raised her hands to push back her curtain of hair to see this intruder and found instead a ponytail that was coming apart. She blinked and realized she was lying on a couch with sun pouring in through the windows.

"Mom, are you okay?" The boy stood in front of her with a concerned scrunch on his face, an expression that she knew mirrored hers.

Jeremy. His name was Jeremy. He was the product of that passion and love, the stuff that dreams were made of, his blue eyes a reflection of his father's.

She put out a hand to reach for the boy, and he came to her hesitantly. Her arms wrapped around him and he squirmed.

"Mom? Fusion ate a bird. Is that okay?" He wasn't happy being held like this, but she needed it.

Gabby sighed and loosened her grip. "I'm sure he'll be fine. We'll watch him and make sure, okay?" She pushed back the dark hair flopping across his forehead and thought that she'd better make sure he had a haircut soon. The blue eyes looking back at her reminded her again of everything they had lost.

Oh Doug, she thought, you'll always be with me. But you are gone. The love of my life. How will I stand it?

About the Author

I love to hear from readers, so feel free to contact me through my website, www.yvonnekohano.com, or directly on Facebook as Yvonne Kohano, on Twitter @yvonnekohano, and at yvonne@yvonnekohano.com. Please leave an honest review of this novel at Amazon, Goodreads, or your favorite book discovery site of choice.

A HOLT Medallion Award of Merit recipient in Romantic Suspense, Yvonne enjoys channeling her characters' voices and passions as they overcome real world problems and discover love. Her Flynn's Crossing contemporary romantic suspense series is set in a fictional northern California foothills town not unlike the one where she used to live. Of course, the beauty and wonders of the Sierra Nevada Mountains and the surrounding counties play costarring roles in her work.

The first six books in the Flynn's Crossing series follow the developing love interests of the girl tribe, a group of successful women who work through real world conflicts and challenges to find acceptance and love - with some suspenseful happenings thrown in! In the next six books, single guys in the wolf pack find their true loves, but not without their own issues to conquer. Periodically, Yvonne will be adding seasonal novellas to the series, featuring the first person voice of a character from one of her previous books experiencing an event that we can all relate to.